THE INVADERS . . .

SO THE white men are back! And trying once again to build themselves a town, without so much as asking anyone's permission. I wonder how long they will stay this time. It sounds as if these have no more sense than the ones who came before.

They certainly pick the strangest places to settle. Last time it was that island, where anyone could have told them the weather is bad and the land is no good for corn. Now they have invaded Powhatan's country, and from what you say, they seem to have angered him already. Of course that has never been hard to do.

Oh, yes, we hear about these matters up in the hills. Not many of us actually visit the coastal country—I don't suppose there are ten people in this town, counting myself, who have even seen the sea—but you know how these stories travel. We have heard all about your neighbor Powhatan, and you eastern people are welcome to him. Was there ever a chief so hungry for power? Not in my memory, and I have lived a long time.

But we were speaking of the white men. As you say, they are a strange people indeed. For all their amazing weapons and other possessions, they seem to be ignorant of the simplest things. I think a half-grown boy would know more about how to survive. Or how to behave toward other people in their own country.

And yet they are not the fools they appear. Not all of them, at least. The only one I ever knew was a remarkably wise man in many ways.

Do not make that gesture at me. I tell you that there was a white man who lived right here in our town, for more than ten winters, and I came to know him well.

ARE WE HAVING FUN YET?
AMERICAN INDIAN FANTASY STORIES

WILLIAM SANDERS

WILDSIDE PRESS

ARE WE HAVING FUN YET?

Published by:
Wildside Press
P.O. Box 301
Holicong, PA 18928-0301
www.wildsidepress.com

First Wildside Press edition: July 2002

CONTENTS

INTRODUCTION

I CAME late to the short story.

Most writers—in the SF genre, anyway—begin in the short form and work their way up to the novel; and this is as it should be. In fact one of the few bits of advice I hand out to beginners and hopefuls (along with "Don't do it, kid! You'll break your mother's heart!" or, that failing, "Learn how to get on food stamps in your state") is: "Forget the novel for now. Begin with the story. When you've mastered that, when you can write a clean short story that really works, then you can write anything."

And I go on to point out that the short story still represents the cutting edge of speculative fiction in this country; traditionally and historically so, of course, but now more than ever. Because the magazine and anthology editors are still willing and able to take chances, to publish work that pushes and occasionally even ruptures the envelope—they can afford to do so; they don't have the entire success or failure of a single issue or antho riding on a single piece—while the big book publishers have become increasingly cautious, their lists dominated by media tie-ins or mass-produced series fantasy, and very little chance for anyone but the biggest names to do really creative work....

But it's a case of do as I say, not as I did, because I had something like a dozen published books behind me before I ever even attempted the short form.

I'm not sure why. I had always enjoyed and admired the story, first in so-called mainstream literature (I can still re-read Ernest Hemingway's best short stories with pleasure, and no small awe) and later in speculative fiction. In fact one of the books that first interested me in the possibilities of SF was a collection of short stories: Harlan Ellison's justly famous *Dangerous Visions*.

Yet somehow—barring a couple of supremely forgettable things published in martial-arts magazines back in the seventies—I never tried my own hand. I think I didn't write short stories because I assumed I couldn't, and I assumed I couldn't because I never had. Thus demonstrating once again that seamless logic for which the literary mind is known.

Then one night in the fall of 1993 Roger Zelazny called me up and asked me to do a story for an anthology he was working on.

I said, "Hell, I don't know, Roger, you know me, I'm a novelist, I wouldn't have a clue how to write a short story-"

"Well, try it anyway," Roger said. "You might find out you're good at it."

What could I say? I didn't really think this was going to work; but when somebody like Roger Zelazny calls you up and invites you to write something, you can't just say huh-uh and hang up. I figured I had to at least give it a shot. Besides, I needed the money . . . which Roger knew, and to this day I think he was just trying to help me out.

Be that as it may, I sat down at the typewriter and scratched my head a couple of times and a few hours later I had written "Elvis Bearpaw's Luck."

It looked okay to me, but I was still greatly relieved when Roger phoned, a week or so later, to tell me how much he'd liked it. Then he said, "You know, there's a guy doing an anthology of Native American fantasy stories, you could probably do something for him—I've got his phone number here—"

Another phone conversation, some more head-scratching, and "Going After Old Man Alabama" was done. That one practically wrote itself. Hm, I thought, is that all there is to it? Talk about easy money.

And yet I didn't write another story for two years.

There were a lot of reasons; my life had become unmanageable, through a series of personal and family catastrophes, an account of which would not be edifying. Mainly, though, I still didn't take myself seriously as a short-story writer. The two stories had been flukes, as I saw it; something done for laughs and a bit of extra cash. I didn't expect I'd ever try it again.

Then Roger died.

After I got past the shock and the initial depression—and how quick and easy that sounds now, but it wasn't at the time—I did some thinking. Roger had believed in me; at times he had been almost the only one. What was the most fitting thing I could do to honor his memory? The answer was obvious: I would quit sitting around drinking and brooding, and I would write a story. It would be the best story I had ever written. It would be the best story I could write.

The story turned out to be "The Undiscovered." After that I didn't look back.

*   *   *

The stories in this collection all have to do with American Indian (or "Native American") themes. There are a few things I should perhaps explain up front.

I do not speak Cherokee fluently; I know only bits and scraps. Nor am I in any sense expert in the traditions of the People. I know only what a few elders have been kind enough to teach me. If I have made mistakes in these stories, and I am sure I have, I hope their spirits will forgive me.

(There are also, frankly, certain deliberate errors I have introduced. For me to give an accurate account of, for example, a tobacco-remaking ritual would be sacrilegious. There are things I am sworn not to talk about. Since these are works of fiction, rather than anthropological papers, I have felt free to substitute harmless bits of invention. So sue me.)

I have not been consistent, from story to story, in my attempts to render the sounds of the Cherokee language phonetically. In the earlier stories I wrote the words down as they sounded to me. Later, I adopted the system of transliteration in general use.

I considered going through the texts and regularizing the spellings, but decided to let them stand as originally published. After all, it hardly matters; some of the sounds in question have no English equivalent and cannot be accurately reproduced with the Roman alphabet. (In particular the nasal grunting vowel which I first wrote as "uh" and later, following the officially approved system, as "v".) Nor is there any way to indicate the tones and glottal stops that make Cherokee pronunciation so difficult for those not brought up in the language.

Enough. Let's get on to the stories.

THE UNDISCOVERED

SO THE white men are back! And trying once again to build themselves a town, without so much as asking anyone's permission. I wonder how long they will stay this time. It sounds as if these have no more sense than the ones who came before.

They certainly pick the strangest places to settle. Last time it was that island, where anyone could have told them the weather is bad and the land is no good for corn. Now they have invaded Powhatan's country, and from what you say, they seem to have angered him already. Of course that has never been hard to do.

Oh, yes, we hear about these matters up in the hills. Not many of us actually visit the coastal country—I don't suppose there are ten people in this town, counting myself, who have even seen the sea—but you know how these stories travel. We have heard all about your neighbor Powhatan, and you eastern people are welcome to him. Was there ever a chief so hungry for power? Not in my memory, and I have lived a long time.

But we were speaking of the white men. As you say, they are a strange people indeed. For all their amazing weapons and other possessions, they seem to be ignorant of the simplest things. I think a half-grown boy would know more about how to survive. Or how to behave toward other people in their own country.

And yet they are not the fools they appear. Not all of them, at least. The only one I ever knew was a remarkably wise man in many ways.

Do not make that gesture at me. I tell you that there was a white man who lived right here in our town, for more than ten winters, and I came to know him well.

I remember the day they brought him in. I was sitting in front of my house, working on a fish spear, when I heard the shouting from the direction of the town gate. Bigkiller and his party, I guessed, returning from their raid on the Tuscaroras. People were running toward the gate, pouring out of the houses, everyone eager for a look.

I stayed where I was. I could tell by the sound that the raid had been successful—no women were screaming, so none of our people had been killed or seriously hurt—and I didn't feel like spending the rest of the day listening to Bigkiller bragging about his latest exploits.

But a young boy came up and said, "They need you, Uncle. Prisoners."

So I put my spear aside and got up and followed him, wondering once again why no one around this place could be bothered to learn to speak Tuscarora. After all, it is not so different from our tongue, not nearly as hard as Catawba or Maskogi or Shawano. Or your own language, which as you see I still speak poorly.

The captives were standing just inside the gate, guarded by a couple of Bigkiller's clan brothers, who were holding war clubs and looking fierce, as well as pleased with themselves. There was a big crowd of people by now and I had to push my way through before I could see the prisoners. There were a couple of scared-looking Tuscarora women—one young and pretty, the other almost my age and ugly as an alligator—and a small boy with his fist stuck in his mouth. Not much, I thought, to show for all this noise and fuss.

Then I saw the white man.

Do you know, it didn't occur to me at first that that was what he was. After all, white men were very rare creatures in those days, even more so than now. Hardly anyone had actually seen one, and quite a few people refused to believe they existed at all.

Besides, he wasn't really white—not the kind of fish-belly white that I'd always imagined, when people talked about white men—at least where it showed. His face was a strange reddish color, like a boiled crawfish, with little bits of skin peeling from his nose. His arms and legs, where they stuck out from under the single buckskin garment he wore, were so dirty and covered with bruises that it was hard to tell what color the skin was. Of course that was true of all of the captives; Bigkiller and his warriors had not been gentle.

His hair was dark brown rather than black, which I thought was unusual for a Tuscarora, though you do see Leni Lenapes and a few Shawanos with lighter hair. It was pretty thin above his forehead, and the scalp beneath showed through, a nasty bright pink. I looked at that and at the red peeling skin of his face, and thought: well done, Bigkiller, you've brought home a sick man. Some lowland skin disease, and what a job it's going to be purifying everything after he dies. . .

That was when he turned and looked at me with those blue eyes. Yes, blue. I don't blame you; I didn't believe that story either, until I saw for myself. The white men have eyes the color of a sunny sky. I tell you, it is a weird thing to see when you're not ready for it.

Bigkiller came through the crowd, looking at me and laughing. "Look what we caught, Uncle," he said, and pointed with his spear. "A white man!"

"I knew that," I said, a little crossly. I hated it when he called me "Uncle." I hated it when anyone did it, except children—I was not yet that old—but I hated it worse when it came from Bigkiller. Even if he was my nephew.

"He was with the Tuscaroras," one of the warriors, Muskrat by name, told me. "These two women had him carrying firewood—"

"Never mind that." Bigkiller gave Muskrat a bad look. No need to tell the whole town that this brave raid deep into Tuscarora country had amounted to nothing more than the ambush and kidnapping of a small wood-gathering party.

To me Bigkiller said, "Well, Uncle, you're the one who knows all tongues. Can you talk with this whiteskin?"

I stepped closer and studied the stranger, who looked back at me with those impossible eyes. He seemed unafraid, but who could read expressions on such an unnatural face?

"Who are you and where do you come from?" I asked in Tuscarora.

He smiled and shook his head, not speaking. The woman beside him, the older one, spoke up suddenly. "He doesn't know our language," she said. "Only a few words, and then you have to talk slow and loud, and kick him a little."

"Nobody in our town could talk with him," the younger woman added. "Our chief speaks a little of your language, and one family has a Catawba slave, and he couldn't understand them either."

By now the crowd was getting noisy, everyone pushing and jostling, trying to get a look at the white man. Everyone was talking, too, saying the silliest things. Old Otter, the elder medicine man, wanted to cut the white man to see what color his blood was. An old woman asked Muskrat to strip him naked and find out if he was white all over, though I guessed she was really more interested in learning what his male parts looked like.

The young Tuscarora woman said, "Are they going to kill him?"

"I don't know," I told her. "Maybe."

"They shouldn't," she said. "He's a good slave. He's a hard worker, and he can really sing and dance."

I translated this, and to my surprise Muskrat said, "It is true that he is stronger than he looks. He put up a good fight, with no weapon but a stick of firewood. Why do you think I'm holding this club left-handed?" He held up his right arm, which was swollen and dark below the elbow. "He almost broke my arm."

"He did show spirit," Bigkiller agreed. "He could have run away, but he stayed and fought to protect the women. That was well done for a slave."

I looked at the white man again. He didn't look all that impressive, being no more than medium size and pretty thin, but I could see there were real muscles under that strange skin.

"He can do tricks, too," the young Tuscarora woman added. "He walks on his hands, and—"

The older woman grunted loudly. "He's bad luck, that's what he is. We've had nothing but trouble since he came. Look at us now."

I passed all this along to Bigkiller. "I don't know," he said. "I was going to kill him, but maybe I should keep him as a slave. After all, what other war chief among the People has a white slave?"

A woman's voice said, "What's going on here?"

I didn't turn around. I didn't have to. There was no one in our town who would not have known that voice. Suddenly everyone got very quiet.

My sister Tsigeyu came through the crowd, everyone moving quickly out of her way, and stopped in front of the white man. She looked him up and down and he looked back at her, still smiling, as if pleased to meet her. That showed real courage. Naturally he had no way of knowing that she was the Clan Mother of the Wolf Clan—which, if you don't know, means she was by far the most powerful person in our town—but just the sight of her would have made most people uneasy. Tsigeyu was a big woman, not fat but big like a big man, with a face like a limestone cliff. And eyes that went right through you and made your bones go cold. She died a couple of years ago, but at the time I am telling about she was still in the prime of life, and such gray hairs as she had she wore like eagle feathers.

She said, "For me? Why, thank you, Bigkiller."

Bigkiller opened his mouth and shut it. Tsigeyu was the only living creature he feared. He had more reason than most, since she was his mother.

Muskrat muttered something about having the right to kill the prisoner for having injured him.

Tsigeyu looked at Muskrat. Muskrat got a few fingers shorter, or that was how it looked. But after a moment she said, "It is true you are the nearest thing to a wounded warrior among this brave little war party." She gestured at the young Tuscarora woman. "So I think you should get to keep this girl, here."

Muskrat looked a good deal happier.

"The rest of you can decide among yourselves who gets the other woman, and the boy." Tsigeyu turned to me. "My brother, I want you to take charge of this white man for now. Try to teach him to speak properly. You can do it if anyone can."

KNOWE ALL ENGLISH
AND OTHER CHRISTIAN MEN:

That I an Englishman and Subjeckt of Her Maiestie Queene *Elizabeth*, did by Misadventure come to this country of *Virginnia* in the Yeere of Our Lord 1591: and after greate Hardshipp arriued amongst these *Indians*. Who haue done me no Harme, but rather shew'd me most exelent Kindnesse, sans the which I were like to haue dyed in this Wildernesse. Wherefore, good Frend, I coniure you, that you offer these poore Sauages no Offence, nor do them Iniurie: but rather vse them generously and iustly, as they haue me.

Look at this. Did you ever see the like? He made these marks himself on this deerskin, using a sharpened turkey feather and some black paint that he cooked up from burned wood and oak galls. And he told me to keep it safe, and that if other white men came this way I should show it to them, and it would tell them his story.

Yes, I suppose it must be like a wampum belt, in a way. Or those little pictures and secret marks that the wise elders of the

Leni Lenapes use to record their tribe's history. So clearly he was some sort of *didahnvwisgi*, a medicine man, even though he did not look old enough to have received such an important teaching.

He was always making these little marks, scratching away on whatever he could get—skins, mostly, or mulberry bark. People thought he was crazy, and I let them, because if they had known the truth not even Tsigeyu could have saved him from being killed for a witch.

But all that came later, during the winter, after he had begun to learn our language and I his. On that first day I was only interested in getting him away from that crowd before there was more trouble. I could see that Otter was working himself up to make one of his speeches, and if nothing else that meant there was a danger of being talked to death.

Inside my house I gave the stranger a gourd of water. When he had eased his thirst I pointed to myself. "Mouse," I said, very slowly and carefully. *"Tsis-de-tsi."*

He was quick. *"Tsisdetsi,"* he repeated. He got the tones wrong, but it was close enough for a beginning.

I held my hands up under my chin like paws, and pulled my upper lip back to show my front teeth, and crossed my eyes. I waggled one hand behind me to represent a long tail. *"Tsisdetsi",* I said again.

He laughed out loud. *"Tsisdetsi,"* he said. *"Mus!"*

He raised his hand and stroked his face for a moment, as if thinking of something. Then without warning he turned and grabbed my best war spear off the wall. My bowels went loose, but he made no move to attack me. Instead he began shaking the weapon above his head with one hand, slapping himself on the chest with the other. *"Tsagspa,"* he cried. *"Tsagspa."*

Crazy as a dog on a hot day, I thought at first. They must have hit him too hard. Then I realized what was happening, and felt almost dizzy. It is no small honor when any man tells you his secret war name—but a stranger, and a prisoner!

"Digatsisdi atelvhvsgo'i," I said, when I could finally speak. "Shakes Spear!"

I am him that was call'd *William Shakspere*, of *Stratford-vpon-Auon*, late of *London*: a Player, of Lord *Strange* his Company, and thereby hangs a Tale.

*   *   *

Look there, where I am pointing. That is his name! He showed me that, and he even offered to teach me how to make the marks for my own. Naturally I refused—think what an enemy could do with something like that!

When I pointed this out, he laughed and said I might be right. For, he said, many a man of his sort had had bad luck with other people making use of his name.

It hapt that our Company was in *Portsmouth*, hauing beene there engaug'd: but then were forbid to play, the Mayor and Corporation of that towne being of the *Puritann* perswasion. For which cause we were left altogether bankrupt: so that some of our Players did pawne their Cloathing for monny to return Home.

Perhaps someone had cursed him, since he sometimes said that he had never meant to leave his own country. It was the fault of the Puritans, he said. He did not explain what this meant, but once he mentioned that his wife and her family were Puritans. So obviously this is simply the name of his wife's clan. Poor fellow, no wonder he left home. The same thing happened to an uncle of mine. When your wife's clan decides to get rid of you, you don't have a chance.

But I, being made foolish by strong Drinke, did conceive to hyde my selfe on a Ship bownd for *London*. Which did seeme a good Idea at the Time: but when I enquyr'd of some sea-faring men, they shewed me (in rogue Jest, or else mayhap I misconstrew'd their Reply, for I was in sooth most outragiosly drunk) the *Moonlight* which lay at the Docke. And so by night I stole aboord, and hid my selfe vnder a Boate: wherevpon the Wine did rush to my heade, and I fell asleepe, and wak'd not till the Morrow: to finde the Ship at sea and vnder Sayle, and the morning Sun at her backe.

Naturally it was a long time before we could understand each other well enough to discuss such things. Not as long as you might think, though. To begin with, I discovered that in fact he had picked up quite a bit of Tuscarora—pretending, like any smart captive, to understand less than he did. Besides that, he was a fast learner. You know that languages are my special medicine—I have heard them say that Mouse can talk to a stone, and get it to talk back—but Spearshaker was gifted too. By the time of the first snow, we could get along fairly well, in a mixture of his language and mine. And when words failed, he could express almost any idea, even tell a story, just by the movements of his hands and body and the expression of his face. That in itself was worth seeing.

> When I was discouer'd the Master was most wroth, and commanded that I be put to the hardest Labours, and giuen onely the poorest leauings for food. So it went hard for me on that Voyage: but the Saylors learn'd that I could sing diuers Songs, and new Ballads from *London*, and then I was vsed better. Anon the Captaine, Mr. Edward *Spicer*, ask'd whether I had any skill in Armes. To which I reply'd, that a Player must needs be a Master of Fence, and of all other Artes martiall, forasmuch as we are wont to play Battles, Duelles, Murthers &c. And the Captaine said, that soone I should haue Opportunity to proue my selfe against true Aduersaries and not in play, for we sayl'd for the *Spanish Maine*.

All this time, you understand, there was a great deal of talk concerning the white man. Most of the people came to like him, for he was a friendly fellow and a willing worker. And the Tuscarora girl was certainly right about his singing and dancing. Even Bigkiller had to laugh when Spearshaker went leaping and capering around the fire, and when he walked on his hands and clapped his feet together several women wet themselves—or so I heard. His songs were strange to the ear, but enjoyable. I remember one we all liked:

> "Wid-a-he
> An-a-ho
> An-a-he-na-ni-no!"

But not everyone was happy about his presence among us. Many of the young men were angry that the women liked him so well, and now and then took him aside to prove it. And old Otter told everyone who would listen that once, long ago, a great band of white men had come up from the south, from the Timucua country, and destroyed the finest towns of the Maskogis, taking many away for slaves and killing the others. And this was true, because when the People moved south they found much of that country empty and ruined.

Spearshaker said that those people were of another tribe, with which his own nation was at war. But not everyone believed him, and Otter kept insisting that white men were simply too dangerous to have around. I began to fear for Spearshaker's life.

At length we came vnto the *Indies*, being there joyn'd by the *Hopewell* and other Ships whose names I knowe not. And we attack'd the Spanish Convoy, and took the Galleon *Buen Jesus*, a rich Pryze: and so it came to pass that Will *Shakspeare*, Actor, did for his greate folly turn Pyrat vpon the salt Sea.

Then, early next spring, the Catawbas came.

This was no mere raid. They came in force and they hit us fast and hard, killing or capturing many of the people working in the fields before they could reach the town palisade. They rushed out of the woods and swarmed over the palisade like ants; and before we knew it we were fighting for our lives in front of our own houses.

That was when Spearshaker astonished us all. Without hesitating, he grabbed a long pole from the meat-drying racks and went after the nearest Catawba with it, jabbing him hard in the guts with the end, exactly as you would use a spear, and then clubbing him over the head. Then he picked up the Catawba's bow and began shooting.

My friend, I have lived long and seen much, but I never was more surprised than that morning. This pale, helpless creature, who could not chip an arrowhead or build a proper fire or even take five steps off a trail without getting lost—he cut those Catawbas down like rotten cornstalks! He shot one man off the palisade, right over there, from clear down by the council house. I do not think he wasted a single shot. And when he was out of arrows, he picked up a war club from a fallen warrior and joined the rest of us in fighting off the remaining attackers.

Afterward, he seemed not to think he had done anything remarkable. He said that all the men of his land know stick-fighting and archery, which they learn as boys. "I could have done better," he said, "with a long bow, and some proper arrows, from my own country." And he looked sad, as he always did when he spoke of his home.

From that day there was no more talk against Spearshaker. Not long after, Tsigeyu announced that she was adopting him. Since this also made him Bigkiller's brother, he was safe from anyone in our town. It also made me his uncle, but he was kind enough never to call me *edutsi*. We were friends.

Next we turn'd north for *Virginnia*, Capt. *Spicer* hauing a Commission from Sir Walter *Ralegh* to calle vpon the English that dwelt at *Roanoke*, to discouer their condition. The Gales were cruel all along that Coast, and we were oft in grave Peril: but after much trauail we reached *Hatarask*, where the Captaine sent a party in small Boates, to search out the passage betweene the Islands. And whilst we were thus employ'd, a sudden greate Wind arose and scattered the Boates, many being o'erturned and the Mariners drown'd. But the Boate I was in was carry'd many Leagues westward, beyond sight of our Fellowes: so we were cast vpon the Shore of the Maine, and sought shelter in the Mouthe of a Riuer. Anon, going ashore, we were attack'd by Sauages: and all the men were slaine, save onely my selfe.

Poor fellow, he was still a long way from home, and small chance of ever seeing his own people again. At least he was better off than he had been with the Tuscaroras. Let alone those people on the coast, if they had caught him. Remember the whites who tried to build a town on that island north of Wococon, and how Powhatan had them all killed?

Yet hauing alone escap'd, and making my way for some dayes along the Riuer, I was surprized by *Indians* of another Nation: who did giue me hard vsage, as a Slaue, for well-nigh a Yeere. Vntil I was taken from them by these mine present sauage Hostes: amongst which, for my Sinnes, I am like to liue out my mortall dayes.

*   *   *

I used to have a big pile of these talking skins of his. Not that I ever expected to have a chance to show them to anyone who could understand them—I can't believe the white men will ever come up into the hill country; they seem to have all they can do just to survive on the coast—but I kept them to remember

Spearshaker by.

But the bugs and the mice got into them, and the bark sheets went moldy in the wet season, and now I have only this little bundle. And, as you see, some of these are no more than bits and pieces. Like this worm-eaten scrap:

> as concerning these *Indians* (for so men call them: but if this be the Lande of *India* I am an Hebrewe *Iewe*) they are in their owne Tongue clept *Anni-yawia*. Which is, being interpreted, the True or Principall People. By other Tribes they are named *Chelokee*: but the meaning of this word my frend Mouse knoweth not, neyther whence deriued. They

I think one reason he spent so much time on his talking marks was that he was afraid he might forget his own language. I have seen this happen, with captives. That Tuscarora woman who was with him still lives here, and by now she can barely speak ten words of Tuscarora. Though Muskrat will tell you that she speaks our language entirely too well—but that is another story.

Spearshaker did teach me quite a lot of his own language—a very difficult one, unlike any I ever encountered—and I tried to speak it with him from time to time, but it can't have been the same as talking with a man of his own kind. What does it sound like? Ah, I remember so little now. Let me see. . . "*Holt dai tong, dow hor-son neib!*" That means, "Shut up, you fool!"

He told me many stories about his native land and its marvels. Some I knew to be true, having heard of them from the coast folk: the great floating houses that spread their wings like birds to catch the wind, and the magic weapons that make thunder and lightning. Others were harder to believe, such as his tales about the woman chief of his tribe. Not a clan mother, but a real war chief, like Bigkiller or even Powhatan, and so powerful that any man—even an elder or a leading warrior—can lose his life merely for speaking against her.

He also claimed that the town he came from was so big that it held more people than all of the People's towns put together. That is of course a lie, but you can't blame a man for bragging on his own tribe.

But nothing, I think, was as strange as the *plei*.

Forgive me for using a word you do not know. But as far as I know there is no word in your language for what I am talking about. Nor in ours, and this is because the thing it means has never existed among our peoples. I think the Creator must have given this idea only to the whites, perhaps to compensate them for their poor sense of direction and that skin that burns in the sun.

It all began one evening, at the beginning of his second winter with us, when I came in from a council meeting and found him sitting by the fire, scratching away on a big sheet of mulberry bark. Just to be polite I said, *"Gado hadvhne?* What are you doing?"

Without looking up he said in his own language, *"Raiting a plei."*

Now I knew what the first part meant; *rai-ting* is what the whites call it when they make those talking marks. But I had never heard the last word before, and I asked what it meant.

Spearshaker laid his turkey feather aside and sat up and looked at me. "Ah, Mouse," he said, "how can I make you understand? This will be hard even for you."

I sat down on the other side of the fire. "Try," I said.

O what a fond and Moone-struck fool am I! Hath the aire of *Virginnia* addl'd my braine? Or did an Enemy smite me on the heade, and I knewe it not? For here in this wilde country, where e'en the Artes of letters are altogether unknowne, I haue begun the writing of a Play. And sure it is I shall neuer see it acted, neyther shall any other man: wherefore 'tis Lunacy indeede. Yet me thinkes if I do it not, I am the more certain to go mad: for I find my selfe growing more like vnto these *Indians*, and I feare I may forget what manner of man I was. Therefore the Play's the thing, whereby Ile saue my Minde by intentionall folly: forsooth, there's Method in my Madnesse.

Well, he was right. He talked far into the night, and the more he talked the less I understood. I asked more questions than a rattlesnake has scales, and the answers only left me more confused. It was a long time before I began to see it.

Didn't you, as a child, pretend you were a warrior or a chief or maybe a medicine man, and make up stories and adventures for yourself? And your sisters had dolls that they gave names to, and talked to, and so on?

Or. . . let me try this another way. Don't your people have dances, like our Bear Dance, in which a man imitates some sort of animal? And don't your warriors sometimes dance around the fire acting out their own deeds, showing how they killed men or sneaked up on an enemy town—and maybe making it a little better than it really happened? Yes, it is the same with us.

Now this *plei* thing is a little like those dances, and a little like the pretending of children. A group of people dress up in fancy clothes and pretend to be other people, and pretend to do various things, and in this way they tell a story.

Yes, grown men. Yes, right up in front of everybody.

But understand, this isn't a dance. Well, there is some singing and dancing, but mostly they just talk. And gesture, and make faces, and now and then pretend to kill each other. They do a lot of that last. I guess it is something like a war dance at that.

You'd be surprised what can be done in this way. A man like Spearshaker, who really knows how—*ak-ta* is what they are called—can make you see almost anything. He could imitate a man's expression and voice and way of moving—or a woman's— so well you'd swear he had turned into that person. He could make you think he was Bigkiller, standing right there in front of you, grunting and growling and waving his war club. He could do Blackfox's funny walk, or Locust wiggling his eyebrows, or Tsigeyu crossing her arms and staring at somebody she didn't like. He could even be Muskrat and his Tuscarora woman arguing, changing back and forth and doing both voices, till I laughed so hard my ribs hurt.

Now understand this. These *akta* people don't just make up their words and actions as they go along, as children or dancers do. No, the whole story is already known to them, and each *akta* has words that must be said, and things that must be done, at exactly the right times. You may be sure this takes a good memory. They have as much to remember as the Master of the Green Corn Dance.

And so, to help them, one man puts the whole thing down in those little marks. Obviously this is a very important job, and Spearshaker said that it was only in recent times, two or three winters before leaving his native land, that he himself had been accounted worthy of this honor. Well, I had known he was a *didahnvwisgi*, but I hadn't realized he was of such high rank.

> I first purpos'd to compose some pretty conceited Comedy, like vnto my *Loue's Labour's Lost*: but alas, me seemes my Wit hath dry'd vp from Misfortune. Then I bethought my selfe of the Play of the Prince of *Denmark*, by Thomas *Kyd*: which I had been employ'd in reuising for our Company not long ere we departed *London*, and had oft said to Richard *Burbage*, that I trow I could write a Better. And so I haue commenced, and praye God I may compleat, my owne Tragedie of Prince *Hamlet*.

I asked what sort of stories his people told in this curious manner. That is something that always interests me—you can learn a lot about any tribe from their stories. Like the ones the Maskogis tell about Rabbit, or our own tale about the Thunder Boys, or—you know.

I don't know what I was thinking. By then I should have known that white people do *everything* differently from everyone else in the world.

First he started to tell me about a dream somebody had on a summer night. That sounded good, but then it turned out to be about the Little People! Naturally I stopped him fast, and I told him that we do not talk about. . . *them*. I felt sorry for the poor man who dreamed about them, but there was no helping him now.

Then Spearshaker told me a couple of stories about famous chiefs of his own tribe. I couldn't really follow this very well, partly because I knew so little about white laws and customs, but also because a lot of their chiefs seemed to have the same name. I never did understand whether there were two different chiefs named *Ritsad*, or just one with a very strange nature.

The oddest thing, though, was that none of these stories seemed to have any *point*. They didn't tell you why the moon changes its face, or how the People were created, or where the mountains came from, or where the raccoon got his tail, or anything. They were just. . . *stories*. Like old women's gossip.

Maybe I missed something.

> ~~To liue, or not to liue, there lyes the~~
> ~~To liue, or dye? Shall I~~

~~To dye, or~~
~~To be, or what? It~~

He certainly worked hard at his task. More often than not, I could hear him grinding his teeth and muttering to himself as he sat hunched over his marks. And now and then he would jump up and throw the sheet to the ground and run outside in the snow and the night wind, and I would hear him shouting in his own language. At least I took it to be his language, though the words were not among those I knew. Part of his medicine, no doubt, so I said nothing.

God's Teethe! Haue I beene so long in this Wilder- nesse, that I haue forgot all Skill? I that could bombast out a lyne of blank Uerse as readily as a Fishe doth swimm, now fumble for Wordes like a Drunkard who cannot finde his owne Cod- peece with both Handes.

I'm telling you, it was a *long* winter.

For who would thus endure the Paines of time:
To-morrow and to-morrow and to-morrow,
That waite in patient and most grim Array,
Each arm'd with Speares and Arrowes of Misfortune,
Like *Indians* ambuscaded in the Forest?
But that the dread of something after Death,
That vndiscouered country, from whose Shores
No Traueller returnes, puzzels the Will,
And makes vs rather beare that which we knowe
Than wantonly embarke for the Vnknowne.

One evening, soon after the snows began to melt, I noticed that Spearshaker was not at his usual nightly work. He was just sitting there staring into the fire, not even looking at his skins and bark sheets, which were stacked beside him. The turkey feathers and black paint were nowhere in sight.

I said, "Is something wrong?" and then I understood. "Finished?"

He let out a long sigh. "Yes," he said. *"Mo ful ai,"* he added, which was something he often said, though I never quite got what it meant.

It was easy to see he was feeling bad. So I said; "Tell me the story."

He didn't want to, but finally he told it to me. He got pretty worked up as he went along, sometimes jumping up to act out an exciting part, till I thought he was going to wreck my house. Now and then he picked up a skin or mulberry-bark sheet and spoke the words, so I could hear the sound. I had thought I was learning his language pretty well, but I couldn't understand one word in ten.

But the story itself was clear enough. There were parts I didn't follow but on the whole it was the best he'd ever told me. At the end I said, "Good story."

He tilted his head to one side, like a bird. "Truly?"

"Doyu," I said. I meant it, too.

He sighed again and picked up his pile of *raiting*. "I am a fool," he said.

I saw that he was about to throw the whole thing into the fire, so I went over and took it from him. "This is a good thing," I told him. "Be proud."

"Why?" He shrugged his shoulders. "Who will ever see it? Only the bugs and the worms. And the mice," he added, giving me his little smile.

I stood there, trying to think of something to make him feel better. Ninekiller's oldest daughter had been making eyes at Spearshaker lately and I wondered if I should go get her. Then I looked down at what I was holding in my hands and it came to me.

"My friend," I said, "I've got an idea. Why don't we put on your *plei* right here?"

And now is Lunacy compownded vpon Lunacy, *Bedlam* pyled on *Bedlam*: for I am embark'd on an Enterprize, the like of which this Globe hath neuer seene. Yet Ile undertake this Foolery, and flynch not: mayhap it will please these People, who are become my onely Frends. They shall haue of Will his best will.

It sounded simple when I heard myself say it. Doing it was another matter. First, there were people to be spoken with.

We *Aniyvwiya* like to keep everything loose and easy. Our chiefs have far less authority than yours, and even the power of the clan mothers has its limits. Our laws are few, and everyone knows what they are, so things tend to go along without much trouble.

But there were no rules for what we wanted to do, because it had never been done before. Besides, we were going to need the help of many people. So it seemed better to go carefully—but I admit I had no idea that our little proposal would create such a stir. In the end there was a regular meeting at the council house to talk it over.

Naturally it was Otter who made the biggest fuss. "This is white men's medicine," he shouted. "Do you want the People to become as weak and useless as the whites?"

"If it will make all our warriors shoot as straight as Spearshaker," Bigkiller told him, "then it might be worth it."

Otter waved his skinny old arms. He was so angry by now that his face was whiter than Spearshaker's. "Then answer this," he said. "How is it that this dance—"

"It's not a dance," I said. Usually I would not interrupt an elder in council, but if you waited for Otter to finish you might be there all night.

"Whatever you call it," he said, "it's close enough to a dance to be Bird Clan business, right? And you, Mouse, are Wolf Clan—as is your white friend, by adoption. So you have no right to do this thing."

Old Dotsuya spoke up. She was the Bird Clan Mother, and the oldest person present. Maybe the oldest in town, now I think of it.

"The Bird Clan has no objection," she said. "Mouse and Spearshaker have our permission to put on their *plei*. Which I, for one, would like to see. Nothing ever happens around this town."

Tsigeyu spoke next. *"Howa,"* she said. "I agree. This sounds interesting."

Of course Otter wasn't willing to let it go so easily; he made quite a speech, going all the way back to the origins of the People and predicting every kind of calamity if this sacrilege was permitted. It didn't do him much good, though. No one liked Otter, who had gotten both meaner and longer-winded with age, and who had never been a very good *didahnvwisgi* anyway. Besides, half the people in the council house were asleep long before he was done.

After the council gave its approval there was no trouble getting people to help. Rather we had more help than we needed. For days there was a crowd hanging around my house, wanting to be part of the *plei*. Bigkiller said if he could get that many people to join a war party, he could take care of the Catawbas for good.

And everyone wanted to be an *akta*. We were going to have to turn some people away, and we would have to be careful how we did it, or there would be trouble. I asked Spearshaker how many *aktas* we needed. "How many men, that is," I added, as he began counting on his fingers. "The women are a different problem."

He stopped counting and stared at me as if I were wearing owl feathers. Then he told me something so shocking you will hardly believe it. In his country, the women in a *plei* are actually *men wearing women's clothes!*

I told him quick enough that the People don't go in for that sort of thing—whatever they may get up to in certain other tribes—and he'd better not even talk about it around here. Do you know, he got so upset that it took me the rest of the day to talk him out of calling the whole thing off. . .

Women! Mercifull *Jesu*! Women, on a Stage, acting in a Play! I shall feele like an Whore-Master!

Men or women, it was hard to know which people to choose. None of them had ever done anything like this before, so there was no way to know whether they would be any good or not. Spearshaker asked me questions about each person, in white language so no one would be offended: Is he quick to learn? Does he dance or sing well? Can he work with other people, and do as he is told? And he had them stand on one side of the stickball field, while he stood on the other, and made them speak their names and clans, to learn how well their voices carried.

I had thought age would come into it, since the *plei* included both older and younger people. But it turned out that Spearshaker knew an art of painting a man's face, and putting white in his hair, till he might be mistaken for his own grandfather.

No doubt he could have done the same with women, but that wasn't necessary. There were only two women's parts in this story, and we gave the younger woman's part to Ninekiller's daughter Cricket—who would have hung upside-down in a tree like a possum if it would please Spearshaker—and the older to a cousin of mine, about my age, who had lost her husband to the Shawanos and wanted something to do.

For those who could not be *aktas*, there was plenty of other work. A big platform had to be built, with space cleared around it, and log benches for the people who would watch. There were torches to be prepared, since we would be doing it at night, and special clothes to be made, as well as things like fake spears so no one would get hurt. Locust and Blackfox were particularly good workers; Spearshaker said it was as if they had been born for this. They even told him that if he still wanted to follow the custom of his own tribe, with men dressed as women, they would be willing to take those parts. Well, I always had wondered about those two.

But Spearshaker was working harder than anyone else. Besides being in charge of all the other preparations, he had to remake his whole *plei* to suit our needs. No doubt he had made a fine *plei* for white men, but for us, as it was, it would never do.

Many a Play haue I reuis'd and amended: cut short or long at the Company's desyre, or alter'd this or that Speeche to please a Player: e'en carued the very Guttes out of a scene on command of the Office of the Reuels, for some imagin'd Sedition or vnseemely Speeche. But now must I out-do all I euer did before, in the making of my *Hamlet* into a thing comprehensible to the *Anni-yawia*. Scarce is there a line which doth not haue to be rewrit: yea, and much ta'en out intire: as, the Play within the Play, which *Mouse* saith, that none here will vnderstande. And the Scene must be moued from *Denmark* to *Virginnia*, and *Elsinore Castle* transformed into an *Indian* towne. For marry, it were Alchemy enow that I should transmute vnletter'd Sauages into tragick Actors: but to make royal *Danskers* of swart-fac'd Indians were beyond all Reason. (Speak'st thou now of Reason, Will Shakespere? Is't not ouer-late for that?)

You should have seen us teaching the *aktas* their parts. First

Spearshaker would look at the marks and say the words in his language. Then he would explain to me any parts I hadn't understood—which was most of it, usually—and then I would translate the whole thing for the *akta* in our language. Or as close as I could get; there are some things you cannot really interpret. By now Spearshaker was fluent enough to help me.

Then the *akta* would try to say the words back to us, almost always getting it all wrong and having to start again. And later on all the people in the *plei* had to get together and speak their parts in order, and do all the things they would do in the *plei,* and that was like a bad dream. Not only did they forget their words; they bumped into each other and stepped on each other's feet, and got carried away in the fight parts and nearly killed each other. And Spearshaker would jump up and down and pull his hair—which had already begun to fall out, for some reason—and sometimes weep, and when he had settled down we would try again.

Verily, my lot is harder than that of the *Iewes* of *Moses.* For Scripture saith, that *Pharo* did command that they make Brickes without Strawe, wherefore their trauail was greate: but now I must make my Brickes, euen without Mudd.

Let me tell you the story of Spearshaker's *plei.*

Once there was a great war chief who was killed by his own brother. Not in a fight, but secretly, by poison. The brother took over as chief, and also took his dead brother's woman, who didn't object.

But the dead man had a son, a young warrior named Amaledi. One night the dead chief appeared to Amaledi and told him the whole story. And, of course, demanded that he do something about it.

Poor Amaledi was in a bad fix. Obviously he mustn't go against his mother's wishes, and kill her new man without her permission. On the other hand, no one wants to anger a ghost—and this one was plenty angry already.

So Amaledi couldn't decide what to do. To make things worse, the bad brother had guessed that Amaledi knew something. He and this really nasty, windy old man named Quolonisi—sounds like Otter—began trying to get rid of Amaledi.

To protect himself Amaledi became a Crazy, doing and saying everything backward, or in ways that made no sense. This made his medicine strong enough to protect him from his uncle and Quolonisi, at least for a time.

Quolonisi had a daughter, Tsigalili, who wanted Amaledi for her man. But she didn't want to live with a Crazy—who does?—and she kept coming around and crying and begging him to quit. At the same time his mother was giving him a hard time for being disrespectful toward her new man. And all the while the ghost kept showing up and yelling at Amaledi for taking so long. It got so bad Amaledi thought about killing himself, but then he realized that he would go to the spirit world, where his father would *never* leave him alone.

So Amaledi thought of a plan. There was a big dance one night to honor the new chief, and some visiting singers from another town were going to take part. Amaledi took their lead singer aside and got him to change the song, telling him the new words had been given to him in a dream. And that night, with the dancers going around the fire and the women shaking the turtle shells and the whole town watching, the visiting leader sang:

"Now he pours it,
Now he is pouring the poison,
See, there are two brothers,
See, now there is one."

That was when it all blew up like a hot rock in a fire. The bad chief jumped up and ran away from the dance grounds, afraid he had just been witched. Amaledi had a big argument with his mother and told her what he thought of the way she was acting. Then he killed Quolonisi. He said it was an accident but I think he was just tired of listening to the old fool.

Tsigalili couldn't stand any more. She jumped into a waterfall and killed herself. There was a fine funeral.

Now Amaledi was determined to kill his uncle. The uncle was just as determined to kill Amaledi, but he was too big a coward to do it himself. So he got Quolonisi's son Panther to call Amaledi out for a fight.

Panther was a good fighter and he was hot to kill Amaledi, because of his father and his sister. But the chief wasn't taking any chances. He put some poison on Panther's spear. He also had a gourd of water, with poison in it, in case nothing else worked.

So Amaledi and Panther painted their faces red and took their spears and faced each other, right in front of the chief's house. Amaledi was just as good as Panther, but finally he got nicked on the arm. Before the poison could act, they got into some hand-to-hand wrestling, and the spears got mixed up. Now Panther took a couple of hits. Yes, with the poisoned spear.

Meanwhile Amaledi's mother got thirsty and went over and took a drink, before anyone could stop her, from the poisoned gourd. Pretty soon she fell down. Amaledi and Panther stopped fighting and rushed over, but she was already dead.

By now they were both feeling the poison themselves. Panther fell down and died. So did Amaledi, but before he went down he got his uncle with the poisoned spear. So in the end everyone died.

You do?

Well, I suppose you had to be there.

And so 'tis afoote: to-morrow night we are to perform. Thank God *Burbage* cannot be there to witnesse it: for it were a Question which should come first, that he dye of Laughter, or I of Shame.

It was a warm and pleasant night. Everyone was there, even Otter. By the time it was dark all the seats were full and many people were standing, or sitting on the ground.

The platform had only been finished a few days before—with Bigkiller complaining about the waste of timber and labor, that could have gone into strengthening the town's defenses—and it looked very fine. Locust and Blackfox had hung some reed mats on poles to represent the walls of houses, and also to give us a place to wait out of sight before going on. To keep the crowd from getting restless, Spearshaker had asked Dotsuya to have some Bird Clan men sing and dance while we were lighting the torches and making other last preparations.

Then it was time to begin.

What? Oh, no, I was not an *akta.* By now I knew the words to the whole *plei,* from having translated and repeated them so many times. So I stood behind a reed screen and called out the words, in a voice too low for the crowd to hear, when anyone forgot what came next.

Spearshaker, yes. He was the ghost. He had put some paint on his face that made it even whiter, and he did something with his voice that made the hair stand up on your neck.

But in fact everyone did very well, much better than I had expected. The only bad moment came when Amaledi—that was Tsigeyu's son Hummingbird—shouted, "*Na! Dili, dili!*"—"There! A skunk, a skunk!"—and slammed his war club into the wall of the "chief's house," forgetting it was really just a reed mat. And Beartrack, who was being Quolonisi, took such a blow to the head that he was out for the rest of the *plei*. But it didn't matter, since he had no more words to speak, and he made a very good dead man for Amaledi to drag out.

And the people loved it, all of it. How they laughed and laughed! I never heard so many laugh so hard for so long. At the end, when Amaledi fell dead between his mother and Panther and the platform was covered with corpses, there was so much howling and hooting you would have taken it for a hurricane. I looked out through the mats and saw Tsigeyu and Bigkiller holding on to each other to keep from falling off the bench. Warriors were wiping tears from their eyes and women were clutching themselves between the legs and old Dotsuya was lying on the ground kicking her feet like a baby.

I turned to Spearshaker, who was standing beside me. "See," I said. "And you were afraid they wouldn't understand it!"

After that everything got confused for a while. Locust and Blackfox rushed up and dragged Spearshaker away, and the next time I saw him he was down in front of the platform with Tsigeyu embracing him and Bigkiller slapping him on the back. I couldn't see his face, which was hidden by Tsigeyu's very large front.

By then people were making a fuss over all of us. Even me. A Paint Clan woman, not bad-looking for her age, took me away, for some attention. She was limber and had a lot of energy, so it was late by the time I finally got home.

Spearshaker was there, sitting by the fire. He didn't look up when I came in. His face was so pale I thought at first he was still wearing his ghost paint.

I said, "*Gusdi nusdi?* Is something wrong?"

"They laughed," he said. He didn't sound happy about it.

"They laughed," I agreed. "They laughed as they have never

laughed before, every one of them. Except for Otter, and no one has *ever* seen him laugh."

I sat down beside him. "You did something fine tonight, Spearshaker. You made the People happy. They have a hard life, and you made them laugh."

He made a snorting sound. "Yes. They laughed to see us making fools of ourselves. Perhaps that is good."

"No, no." I saw it now. "Is that what you think? That they laughed because we did the *plei* so badly?"

I put my hand on his shoulder and turned him to face me. "My friend, no one there tonight ever saw a *plei* before, except for you. How would they know if it was bad? It was certainly the best *plei* they ever saw."

He blinked slowly, like a turtle. I saw his eyes were red. "Believe me, Spearshaker," I told him, "they were laughing because it was such a funny story. And that was your doing."

His expression was very strange indeed. "They thought it comical?"

"Well, who wouldn't? All those crazy people up there, killing each other—and themselves—and then that part at the end, where *everyone* gets killed!" I had to stop and laugh, myself, remembering. "I tell you," I said when I had my breath back, "even though I knew the whole thing by memory, I nearly lost control of myself a few times there."

I got up. "Come, Spearshaker. You need to go to sleep. You have been working too hard."

But he only put his head down in his hands and made some odd sounds in his throat, and muttered some words I did not know. And so I left him there and went to bed.

If I live until the mountains fall, I will never understand white men.

If I liue vntil our *Saviour's* returne, I shall neuer vnderstande *Indians*. Warre they count as Sport, and bloody Murther an occasion of Merriment: 'tis because they hold Life itselfe but lightly, and think Death no greate matter neyther: and so that which we call Tragick, they take for Comedie. And though I be damned for't, I cannot sweare that they haue not the Right of it.

Whatever happened that night, it changed something in

Spearshaker. He lived with us for many more years, but never again did he make a *plei* for us.

That was sad, for we had all enjoyed the Amaledi story so much, and were hoping for more. And many people tried to get Spearshaker to change his mind—Tsigeyu actually begged him; I think it was the only time in her life she ever begged anyone for anything—but it did no good. He would not even talk about it.

And at last we realized that his medicine had gone, and we left him in peace. It is a terrible thing for a *didahnvwisgi* when his power leaves him. Perhaps his ancestors' spirits were somehow offended by our *plei*. I hope not, since it was my idea.

That summer Ninekiller's daughter Cricket became Spearshaker's wife. I gave them my house, and moved in with the Paint Clan woman. I visited my friend often, and we talked of many things, but of one thing we never spoke.

Cricket told me he still made his talking marks, from time to time. If he ever tried to make another *plei,* though, he never told anyone.

I believe it was five winters ago—it was not more—when Cricket came in one day and found him dead. It was a strange thing, for he had not been sick, and was still a fairly young man. As far as anyone knew there was nothing wrong with him, except that his hair had fallen out.

I think his spirit simply decided to go back to his native land.

Cricket grieved for a long time. She still has not taken another husband. Did you happen to see a small boy with pale skin and brown hair, as you came through our town? That is their son Wili.

Look what Cricket gave me. This is the turkey feather that was in Spearshaker's hand when she found him that day. And this is the piece of mulberry bark that was lying beside him. I will always wonder what it says.

> We are such stuff as Dreames are made on: and our little Life
> Is rounded in a sle

AUTHOR'S NOTE:

This is the one everybody made a fuss about. It was nominated for the Hugo, Nebula, and Sturgeon Awards; it won the

Sidewise Award for Alternate History, and was chosen for a couple of "Best" anthologies.

It had its origins in a couple of casual conversations with local friends. One day some of my homies and I were talking about how white people find Indian names amusing, yet plenty of white names are just as funny if you think about what they mean. And I observed that one of the most famous white men of all had a perfectly good Indian name: Shakes Spear.

It was just an idle remark, but it must have stuck in my head. Some time later—it might have been the following year—I got into a conversation with one of my buddies about *Hamlet*; it turned out that both of us had seen it performed in various languages. I mentioned a particularly good one I had seen, done by the Ghana national theater in traditional African costume; and so, inevitably, we started kicking around the idea of a Cherokee production.

But then my friend said, "No. It's not gonna work. We just don't hang around talking to ghosts." He laughed. "Shortest play in history—you see the ghost, then you see the skins running down the road, curtain."

Somewhere in the lower depths of my brain, though, the two conversations must have hooked up; and though it took a long time for the results to surface, "The Undiscovered" is what happened.

A few additional background notes:

1. Elizabethan spelling was fabulously irregular; the same person might spell the same word in various ways on a single page. Shakespeare's own spelling is known only from the Quarto and Folio printing of the plays, and the published poetry; and no one knows how close the published texts are to Shakespeare's original in wording, let alone spelling. All we have in his own hand is his signature, and this indicates that he spelled his own name differently almost every time he wrote it.

I have followed the spelling of the Folio for the most part, but felt free to use my own judgment and even whim, since that was what the original speller did.

I have, however, regularized spelling and punctuation to some extent, and modernized spelling and usage in some instances, so that the text would be readable. I assume the readers of this story are reasonably well-educated, but it seems unfair to expect them to be Elizabethan scholars.

2. Cherokee pronunciation is difficult to render in Roman letters. It hardly matters, since we do not know how sixteenth-century Cherokees pronounced the language. The sounds have changed considerably in the century and a half since the forced march to Oklahoma; what they were like four hundred years ago is highly conjectural. So is the location of the various tribes of Virginia and the Carolinas during this period; and, of course, so is their culture. (The Cherokee may not then have been the war-like tribe they later became—though, given the national penchant for names incorporating the verb "to kill", this is unlikely.) The Catawbas were a very old and hated enemy.

3. Edward Spicer's voyage to America to learn the fate of the Roanoke Colony—or rather his detour to Virginia after a successful privateering operation—did happen, including the bad weather and the loss of a couple of boats, though there is no record that any boat reached the mainland. The disappearance of the Roanoke colonists is a famous event. It is only conjecture—thought based on considerable evidence, and accepted by many historians—that Powhatan had the colonists murdered, after they had taken sanctuary with a minor coastal tribe. Disney fantasies to the contrary, Powhatan was not a nice man.

4. I have accepted, for the sake of the story, the view of many scholars that Shakespeare first got the concept of *Hamlet* in the process of revising Thomas Kyd's play on the same subject. Thus he might well have had the general idea in his head as early as 1591—assuming as most do, that by this time he was employed with a regular theatrical company—even though the historic *Hamlet* is generally agreed to have been written considerably later.

5. As to those who argue that William Shakespeare was not actually the author of *Hamlet*, but that the plays were written by Francis Bacon or the Earl of Southampton or Elvis Presley, one can only reply: *Hah!* And again, *Hah!*

WORDS AND MUSIC

JIMMY HOMINY was fifty-four years old and had been a *didahnvwisgi*—what the whites called a shaman or medicine man; a lot of Cherokees said *adanvsgi*, wizard, and some said plainly *'sgili*, witch, though not to his face—for most of his adult life. He had also done a hitch in Nam, played guitar for Buck Owens on two national tours, and been married to a Kiowa woman, so all in all he figured he'd been around and not much could surprise him. But when the preacher from Limestone showed up at Jimmy's trailer out of Stick Ross Mountain Road and said his church house was being witched, Jimmy's chin dropped so far it nearly hit his chest.

"*Doyu?*" he said, rubbing a big callused hand over a face the color and texture of an old saddle. "Somebody's witching a church?"

"So they say," the preacher said. "You hadn't heard?"

"Hey," Jimmy Hominy said, "I stay clear of that end of the county. You go listening to those Indians down around Limestone, you're liable to hear anything."

He grinned at the preacher. "But then that's your job, right? Got to love all God's children. Even the ones he probably wishes he'd drowned, like the Sparrowhawk brothers. Better you than me, *chooch.*"

The preacher didn't return the grin. He was a bony-faced man somewhere in his forties, with a big nose and dark brown eyes. His thin straight black hair was combed forward in a failed effort to hide a hairline in full retreat, the inheritance of a white grandfather. He had on a really bad black suit.

His name was Eli Blackbird, but Jimmy Hominy usually thought of him simply as the preacher, because he was the only preacher Jimmy knew personally. Oh, every now and then some local Bible wrangler would come calling with the missionary light in his eyes—it would be a big coup to talk a notorious character like Jimmy Hominy into taking the Jesus road—but they didn't stay long enough to get acquainted.

But this one never got on Jimmy's case about following the old ways, or accused him of worshipping the Devil, and Jimmy had finally decided he was all right. Now here he was sitting at

Jimmy's kitchen table with a story about the Sparrowhawk boys witching his church, and Jimmy didn't know what to think.

The preacher let out a long sigh and began fumbling in the pockets of his suit jacket. "I admit the Sparrowhawks aren't easy to love—"

He pulled out a black briar pipe and a plastic pouch and began cramming tobacco into the bowl, spilling a little blizzard of Prince Albert flakes in the process. Jimmy didn't say anything about it . The place was already in a mess anyway. Had been for a couple of years, ever since his wife died.

Jimmy said, "Yeah, Luther and Bobby Sparrowhawk been nothing but bullies and sneak thieves since they were kids. And yet their mama was a real fine lady."

The preacher nodded. "Oh, yes. Old Annie Sparrowhawk." He was fishing around in his pockets again. Jimmy pushed a box of wooden matches across the table. "Thanks. . . as a matter of fact, that's where the trouble began. Annie left that property to the church when she died, and her sons have been trying to get it back ever since."

He struck a match and applied it to his pipe. "Which," he said, puffing, "they can't do. Annie paid a lawyer to draw up a will, legal and airtight."

"What do they want with it? That rocky old land around Limestone's not worth anything. So damn poor the whites never even bothered to steal it."

"It is now," the preacher told him through a cloud of bluish smoke. "Word is some developer from Tulsa has plans for the area."

Jimmy thought about it. While he thought he held out his hand. "Uh, you think you could spare—"

The preacher handed over the tobacco pouch. Jimmy got his own pipe from his shirt pocket and loaded it and lit up. The preacher didn't notice that Jimmy didn't bother to use a match. Or if he did notice he pretended not to.

"Surprised they don't just burn you out," Jimmy said at last.

"They've made threats. But they're both on probation for assault as it is. Any rough stuff, they go to the pen. The sheriff already warned them."

"So now they're trying to witch you out. Wonder who they got to do it."

The preacher looked disappointed. He must have been hoping Jimmy would know who was doing the witching, or could find out. Probably thought people like Jimmy stayed in touch some way, like those white kids Jimmy's grandson was always talking with on his computer.

Jimmy said, "Could be they're trying to do it themselves. That's crazy, but then they're crazy."

"It's possible," the preacher agreed. "They do have a reputation for dabbling in, uh, the occult. And yet they both got religion last year. Bobby married a white girl from one of those holy-roller churches and now he and Luther are in there at every revival, shouting and speaking in tongues, even handling snakes."

"The snakes got my sympathy," Jimmy said sincerely.

He knew what the preacher was getting at. The boondocks holiness outfits were even stricter than other Indian churches when it came to "heathen" ways; some would kick you out just for going to stomp dances, let alone anything heavy.

But there was nothing so unusual about Cherokees trying to work both sides of that particular street. Almost all the people who came to Jimmy seeking cures for illness or protection against witchcraft or interpretations of dreams—he didn't do love charms—were solid members of Bible churches that officially condemned such things as the Devil's work. It was just something people didn't talk about.

Jimmy said, "I didn't think you preachers believed in these superstitions."

This time the preacher did grin. "That's the white half of me. The Indian half—" He spread his hands. "It doesn't really matter what I think. If the people believe the place is being witched, they'll stay away. You know that. Last Sunday we had half the usual turnout."

"So you thought if they heard you were bringing in your own *didahnvwisgi*—" Jimmy had to laugh. "Boy," he said, "now I've heard everything. The church asking a medicine man for help."

If the preacher minded being redassed he didn't let it show. He said, "Actually, I came to invite you to an all-night gospel singing. We're having one this Friday night."

Jimmy quit laughing. The preacher had hit one of his weak spots. He might be a long way outside the church, but he dearly loved Cherokee gospel music. Both his parents had been noted singers on the Oklahoma gospel scene; his older brother Clyde had sung with them, before running off to become a honky-tonk musician. Some of Jimmy's earliest memories were of all-night singings, and falling asleep in the back of the family pickup to the sound of gospel music coming through the trees.

He said, "Real old-fashioned Indian gospel? Not that fancy new crap, sounds like they're planning to go to Heaven in an elevator?"

The preacher nodded. "Should be a lot of good singers there."

"I thought you said people were staying away."

"They won't if they know you're going to be there."

Jimmy didn't know what to say to that.

"And," the preacher added, "the women are baking pies."

Jimmy groaned softly. Pie was his other weakness. "You got me," he said. "What time do you want me there?"

The preacher stood up. "Come by the house about seven." He was obviously trying hard not to look too pleased with himself. "We may as well go together."

"Howa," Jimmy agreed, getting up too. "You can tell them I'll be there."

Friday evening at almost exactly seven Jimmy Hominy stopped his old Mercury in front of Eli Blackbird's house near the tiny crossroads community of Limestone. The preacher came to the door as Jimmy stepped up on the porch. *"'Siyo, Jimi."*

"'Siyo, chooch." Jimmy nodded in the direction of the Mercury. "Let's take my car." He didn't want to ride in the preacher's little Japanese car, which was cramped and uncomfortable for a man his size and had screwy door latches besides.

"Sure." The preacher followed Jimmy out to the road and bent to open the Mercury's door. The dome light came on and he stopped, staring at the oversized guitar case lying in the back seat. "Bringing that thing?" he said. "Going to play, are you?"

"Could be," Jimmy said, going around to his side. "You never know."

The church was a small low concrete block building with no steeple or other identifying features except a four-by-eight plywood sign that read LIMESTONE INDEPENDENT INDIAN CHURCH. The words were repeated underneath in the curling black letters of the Cherokee alphabet.

Right now the building was dark except for a single bulb burning above the front door. The big grassy clearing beside the church, however, was lit by several floodlights rigged on poles or in the trees. A flatbed truck had been parked at the edge of the woods to serve as a stage, and two men were crouched on its bed doing something to a set of amplifiers, while a tall kid in a Seminole jacket fooled with the tuning knobs of an electric bass. Teenage boys were setting out rows of folding chairs. Other people stood or moved about the area, mostly near the long wooden tables where women served food on paper plates.

"I thought we'd have the singing outdoors," the preacher remarked as they got out of the Mercury. The dusty parking area was already half full of pickup trucks and heavy old cars. "Looks like a nice night for it."

It did. The sky was clear and full of fat white stars; a light warm breeze was coming through the woods, bringing various pleasant smells. It also carried the scent of blackberry pie from the tables. Jimmy's nose began to twitch.

"Well," the preacher said, "I better get up there." He gestured in the direction of the flatbed truck, where one of the men was now adjusting a floor-stand microphone. A brief horrible squeal came from the speakers. "Almost time."

When the preacher was gone Jimmy stood still for a moment, getting the feel of the scene. So far he couldn't detect anything wrong; at least the hair on his arms wasn't standing up, or his fingers tingling, or any of the other warning signs. If this place had been witched, it had been done very badly.

Or else, of course, it had been done very well.

He began to walk, staying in the shadows and avoiding people, making himself ignore the pie smell. As he neared the darkened church he started to pick up a certain vague sourness, like a single out-of-tune string. More curious than worried—whatever it was, it didn't feel dangerous—he moved closer.

He found it easily, under the front steps of the church: a little buckskin bundle, tied with rawhide. Dry things crunched and crackled as he rolled it in his hand. He didn't untie it; he knew pretty much what it contained. He walked back to his car and tossed the little bundle onto the front seat. Later, maybe, he would tie the bundle to a rock and drop it into a moving stream, and then whoever had made it would come down with severe chills for a week or so.

If this was the worst the Sparrowhawks could do, the preacher was worrying about nothing. Still, he was here now and he might as well do the job right.

He dug in his pockets and got out his short-stemmed pipe and the little bag of prepared tobacco, while up on the improvised stage Eli Blackbird commenced speaking into the microphone, welcoming the people who were now starting to drift over and take seats. The men behind him quit messing with the amps and began opening cases and getting out guitars.

Jimmy packed the tobacco carefully into the pipe, making sure not to spill a single flake. He did not sing or speak over the tobacco; there was no need. He had doctored the tobacco that morning, down by the banks of the little creek that ran behind his place, holding it up to the rising sun and stirring it with his forefinger, singing the appropriate *igawesdi* words, four times over. Now the tobacco was programmed, needing only to be burned to release its power.

He lit the tobacco and began walking, puffing. The preacher was now leading the crowd in "Amazing Grace":

> "U-ne-hla-nv-hi U-we-ji
> I-ga-gu-yv-he-i—"

Blowing smoke, Jimmy Hominy circled the church grounds counterclockwise, taking in the building and the singing area and even the two outhouses. The preacher began a prayer in Cherokee: *"Agidoda, galvladi ehi, galvquodiyu gesesdi dejado'a'i—"* He was still at it when Jimmy started around for the second time.

He circled the grounds four times, following carefully in his own tracks. He was aware of people looking at him—mostly sideways or behind his back—but nobody spoke to him, and the few people in his path suddenly found reasons to go stand somewhere else when they saw him coming.

At the end he knocked the ash out of the pipe and stood leaning on the Mercury's fender, listening to the music. The first group of the evening, the Gospel Travelers from Adair County, were hammering down hard on "I Will Not Live Always":

> "U-tli-na-qua-du-li-hv ga-lv-la-di jo-sv-i,
> Ga-lo-ne-dv Ji-sa, u-wo-du-hi-yu,
> Da-ni-no-gi-sdi-sgv-i."

—with skinny little Grover Fourkiller singing bass like a son of a bitch and Louise Soap hitting the highs clean as an Arkansas mockingbird.

Jimmy decided it was time to check out that blackberry pie.

It had been a good season for blackberries and two different women had just set out fresh pies as Jimmy came up to the table. Naturally he had to have a piece of each, so as not to hurt anybody's feelings. He was finishing the second piece when a voice behind him said, *"Siyo, Jimi. Jiyosihas'?"*

Jimmy jumped and turned around. Idabel Grasshopper stood there, holding a big steaming pot. She said, "Want to try some of my chili, big boy?"

Jimmy had never considered that Idabel Grasshopper might show up. A lifelong member of Hogshooter Indian Baptist Church, she was a long way from home. But maybe she'd heard he was coming. Damn that preacher.

He said, "I think maybe your chili's too hot for me."

Idabel Grasshopper giggled and Jimmy made a note to kick himself in the ass, next time he felt limber enough, for encouraging her. As far back as he could remember, her two big goals in life had been to get Jimmy Hominy into the church and into her bed—preferably, but not necessarily, in that order. Change of life hadn't helped; in the last few years she'd just gotten holier and hornier. She'd also picked up about forty pounds and a Don Ameche mustache.

"And here you are at a gospel singing," she said. "Praise the Lord!"

"I just came to listen to the music," Jimmy mumbled. Damn that preacher.

"The music," she said severely, "doesn't mean a thing without the spirit. Now in Philippians two-ten it says—"

But Jimmy was no longer even pretending to listen. Over the top of her Brillo-pad perm, he had spotted the Sparrowhawk brothers coming across the parking area.

He hadn't seen either of them in years but they hadn't improved any in the ugly department. Luther, the older brother, seemed to have a few more facial scars, but otherwise there wasn't much difference between them; just a couple of lumpy, over-

43

grown Indians, nearly as big as Jimmy, with hooky noses and eyes set way too close together.

All of a sudden, right at the edge of the grass, they stopped so hard they practically bounced.

Jimmy Hominy watched, ignoring Idabel, as they looked at each other and then tried again to cross the medicine line he had laid down. It was like watching a pair of big stupid birds flying into a plate-glass window.

Finally, looking pissed off, they turned and stomped back across the parking lot and got into a big pickup truck. A minute later they blasted out of the church grounds, throwing gravel. The crash of bad gear changes drifted back on the breeze as their lights disappeared up the road.

The preacher was standing over by the edge of the trees, smoking his pipe. "Did you see that?" he said as Jimmy came up. "Whatever you did, thanks—"

"Never mind that," Jimmy told him. "I'm going to kill you. That hooting sound you hear is the owl calling your name."

The preacher laughed softly. "Idabel's still after you?"

"'Big boy,'" Jimmy said, shuddering. "Nobody's called me that since Saigon."

Up on stage the Kingfisher Family were getting down with "Orphan Child:"

> *"Ja-ga-wi-yu-hi hna-quu ta-ti-hnu-ga di-je-na-sv*
> *Ju-no-ye-ni-quu de-hi-ni-yv-se-sdi ni-go-hi-lv."*

"Come on," the preacher said. "Let's get some coffee. Going to be a long night."

The night did take its time passing. Singers took their turns on stage, alone or by duets and trios and quartets, and most were at least reasonably good. Even the ones that weren't came off sounding fairly decent, thanks to the backup. Homer Ninekiller and Dwight Badwater had been playing at gospel singings for twenty or thirty years, Homer with his old Les Paul Gibson electric and Dwight with his even older Martin D-28 Dreadnought flattop, and they were good enough to fill in the holes for the most raggedy-assed group. The kid on bass wasn't in their class but he was okay, keeping up a steady boom-boom and not trying to show off.

The audience applauded and occasionally shouted *amen or praise the Lord* and now and then wandered off to the tables for pie and coffee. Little kids ran here and there chasing lightning bugs or just grab-assing around, till at last the night got too long for them and they fell asleep in their mothers' laps or in the back seats of cars.

Jimmy got himself a folding chair and found a place under a big oak tree where he could keep an eye on everything. He still wasn't convinced it was over with the Sparrowhawks. It had been too easy and those two were known for their blind-mule stubbornness. But the hours rolled by and there was no further sign of them. When Jimmy's watch showed midnight he felt sure this would be the time something would happen, but nothing did.

The preacher appeared out of the shadows. "Having a good time, Jimmy? I am, now I don't have to worry about the Sparrowhawks."

Jimmy grunted. It was now well after twelve by his watch and he was starting to think nothing was going to happen after all, but he still wasn't ready to admit it.

On stage the musicians were into an instrumental break while the next singing group was called. Homer Ninekiller was doing amazing things to "He Will Set Your Fields On Fire" and Dwight Badwater and the kid in the Seminole jacket were loping right along with him. *"Asv,"* the preacher said as they finished.

"Picked that one and sent it home naked," Jimmy agreed. "Who's on next?"

"The Disciples."

"Shit."

"Please," the preacher said reprovingly. "This *is* the Lord's service."

"Sorry," Jimmy said. "But I bet that's pretty much the Lord's opinion too."

The Disciples consisted of a loudmouthed preacher named Mason Littlebird, his incredibly fat wife, and their big-knockered teenage daughter. None of them could sing worth a damn and Mason Littlebird had a habit of preaching windy sermons, "witnessing" he called it, between songs. Watching Mavis Littlebird clambering up the ladder to the stage—the truck was already tilted over on its shocks from her mother's weight—Jimmy decided this was a good time to take care of some increasingly urgent business.

"See you," he told the preacher. "Got to visit the BIA office."

There was somebody already inside the outhouse when Jimmy got there. He shrugged and stepped off into the trees. Fine Indian he'd be if he couldn't even take a pee in the woods.

He gave a post-oak a good soaking down, hearing Mason Littlebird's voice blaring through the trees: "And I used to be a sinner, a-men, I drank and gambled, praise the Lord, yes and I sinned with women, thank you Jesus—" Zipping up, he walked back out of the woods and managed to get himself a foam cup of black coffee without being spotted by Idabel Grasshopper, who was gazing toward the stage with a look of holy joy. Maybe, Jimmy thought hopefully, she's getting the hots for Mason instead of me. Amen, praise the Lord, *and* thank you Jesus if she does.

He was finishing his coffee when it all began to happen.

The Disciples were into a long depressing song about sinners going to Hell—the words in English, of course, none of them spoke Cherokee even though Mason claimed to be a full-blood—when all at once there was a Godawful racket from the speakers and then silence except for the voices of the Disciples, trailing off uncertainly as they turned to stare.

Homer Ninekiller and the bass player bent over the silent amplifiers. From the look on their faces Jimmy guessed the breakdown was a major one. He could smell the kind of smoke you got when electric things died.

He felt no serious concern. This sort of thing was always happening at these affairs; the cheap amplifier systems, that were all most Indians could afford, broke down all the time. And, as far as he was concerned, this time was as good as any. Anything that shut the Littlebirds up was okay with him.

Dwight Badwater, though, was speaking to the Disciples, who were still staring at the dead speakers. After a minute they turned back around, while Dwight went into a flatpicking introduction, and began again to sing. Their voices were thin and weak without amplification, but they tried, while Dwight Badwater's big flattop boomed behind them. There was a burst of applause.

Then, with a sickening cracking sound, the bridge tore clear off Dwight Badwater's guitar. It happened too fast to see; one second Dwight was sitting there playing big mellow acoustic chords and the next he was grabbing his right wrist, bloody where the lashing strings had cut it, and looking down in disbelief at the splintered top of that beautiful old Martin.

Jimmy Hominy felt as if he'd been kicked in the stomach. Yet something made him turn his head, just at that moment, and when he did he forgot all about old friends and ruined guitars.

Half a dozen men in white suits were coming across the parking area. Behind them, two more men were getting out of a big white van that practically glowed in the dim light. It was too far and too dark to make out faces or details, except for the man in the lead, but that was okay because he was the only one Jimmy was really looking at.

Not that he was anything special to look at; he was just an average-sized man—maybe a little on the short and slender side—in a fancy white suit. But Jimmy Hominy took one look at him, checked his watch again, and shook his head in disgust. "Son of a bitch," he muttered. "Forgot about Daylight Saving Time."

The stranger crossed the parking ground with a quick sure step that was almost a swagger. When he came to the edge of the grassy area he stopped. The others coming up behind him stopped too.

He stood for a moment studying the ground at his feet. Then his head came up and turned, slowly, until he was looking straight in Jimmy Hominy's direction; and he smiled, a wide flash of very white teeth, and stepped forward again. Along the ground on either side of him was a bright blue flash, too fast and too small to see unless you were looking for it, where the medicine line had been.

Jimmy Hominy felt something with cold feet walking up his backbone. As far as he knew there was only one person in all Creation who could do that. Well, okay, two, but he was fairly certain this wasn't the other one.

The other suits followed their leader through the break in the medicine circle, walking single file, none of them looking down or around. Behind them, shuffling along with hunched shoulders, came Luther and Bobby Sparrowhawk.

Jimmy started to move, to head the strangers off—to tell the truth he didn't know what the hell he meant to do—but Idabel Grasshopper came up beside him and grabbed his arm. "There you are," she said in the way of somebody finding a missing possession. "Look, who's that? Don't they look handsome."

The strangers were standing beside the stage now, while the leader spoke to Eli Blackbird, who nodded and then climbed up on the truck, raising his hands for attention. "Good news," the preacher shouted over the growing noise of the crowd. "We've got a new group here, and they've brought their own equipment. Soon as they get set up, we'll go on with the singing."

The white suits were already trooping back to their van. With amazing speed and efficiency they began carrying things from the van—speakers, amplifiers, cased instruments—and setting them up on stage. Meanwhile the Sparrowhawk brothers took seats on the front row and sat there side by side like a couple of mean toads, staring straight ahead and not speaking to anybody.

"See, Jimmy?" Idabel Grasshopper sighed. "Just when everything was going wrong, the Lord sent us help. That's how it is, if you have faith—"

By the time Jimmy got loose the strangers were all set up and standing ready on stage. The preacher stepped up to one of the shiny new microphones they had brought. "All right." His voice boomed out through the big speakers and rumbled off through the woods. "Let's all give a big welcome to—" He checked a piece of paper in his hand. "Brother Seth Abadon, and a group called Maranatha!"

The crowd applauded and amen'd. The preacher got off the stage, the strangers took a step forward—all together and on the same foot, like a half-time drill team—and the music began:

> *"Oh people, get ready,*
> *Oh people, get ready,*
> *Oh people, get ready,*
> *He's coming to take you away."*

Jimmy Hominy had worked his way up to the front now, and he put his hand to his back pocket, to the little pouch of extra-special tobacco he had brought along in case things got rough. But then, remembering how the stranger had broken that power circle without so much as a song or a word, he changed his mind. That tobacco was strong enough to knock seven witches on their asses at a range of seven miles, on the far side of seven mountains, with one good puff; but he had a feeling that using it against this well-dressed joker would be like trying to stop a buf-

48

falo with a blowgun.

So he let his hand fall empty to his side, and went over and stood under the big tree again, where he could study the men in the white suits. He'd never seen anything like them.

And yet there was nothing weird or shocking in their appearance. In fact the peculiar thing about them was that there wasn't anything peculiar about any of them. Even the most ordinary-looking people had various little details—a crooked nose, a big chin, a mole—that marked them as who they were; even white people, who did tend to look pretty much alike to Jimmy Hominy, had their own faces if you really looked. But these gents, except for their leader, might have come off some kind of assembly line. They were so exactly the same size and build that they could have swapped their snazzy Western-cut white suits around at random and all ended up with just as neat a fit; and Jimmy wouldn't have been a bit surprised to find out they were able to switch arms and legs and heads as well.

That was speaking of the five regular members of Maranatha. The leader—Seth Abadon, if that was his name; Jimmy figured he was also known by many other names—was something else. And that was screwy, too, because he didn't look all that different from the others, in any way you could put your finger on. He was a little shorter and more lightly built, and his suit fit him just a little better, but that was all. . . but he stood out on that stage like a timber wolf in a pack of stray mutts. Something in the way he stood, in the way he held his head; whatever it was, nobody in the world would have needed more than a single glance to know which of the strangers was The Man.

At Jimmy's side the preacher said, "Isn't it great? A real professional group showing up at a little country singing like this, we really lucked out tonight."

Jimmy snorted. "What's a bunch of *yonegs* doing here?"

"You think they're white?" The preacher sounded surprised. "They look Indian to me."

Actually you couldn't tell. The strangers' faces seemed to shift somehow in the yellowish light; it was like looking through a car windshield in a rainstorm, or trying to read with a pair of those cheap glasses off the rack at Family Dollar Store. They wouldn't come into focus; they looked sort of Indian, and then they looked sort of white, and now and then Jimmy caught flickering glimpses of other things he didn't even want to identify.

"Anyway," the preacher said, "who cares? Just listen to that music!"

Jimmy was listening; it wasn't exactly something you could ignore. Whoever these people were, they had brought some serious equipment: gleaming high-tech-looking amplifiers with lots of knobs and switches and colored lights, black studio-grade microphones, and great big speakers like the ones at the rock concert Jimmy had once attended with his grandson. One, standing right behind Brother Seth Abadon up by the truck cab, was easily the biggest speaker Jimmy had ever seen; the damn thing looked to be bigger than his trailer's front door.

The music surged and rolled from the speakers, not blasting nosebleed-loud like at the rock concert, but in a soft pulsing flood that soaked right through your skin and blended with your breathing and your heartbeat. There was no rejecting it; it got to you, like it or not, and Jimmy kept catching himself tapping a foot or nodding his head with the rhythm. Though why this was so he couldn't understand; it certainly wasn't the words of the song, which were simple-headed to the point of childishness:

> "People, have you heard the call,
> Going out to one and all?
> Listen and you'll know it's true—
> He is coming after you."

—they sang, in intricate high-rising harmonies, so tight it was impossible to tell who was singing which part. They had fine voices, too, clear and strong and dead true, never the faintest sourness or roughness to mar that amazing flow. If anything they were too perfect; the effect was that of drinking distilled water—so pure there was no flavor, nothing really there.

But the singing was only a part, and maybe the lesser part, of Maranatha's sound. The vocals rode along atop an elaborate structure of complex chords and driving runs laid down by the instruments: two rhythm guitars, bass, keyboard—the kind that hung around the player's neck rather than standing on legs—a sort of tambourine, and Brother Seth Abadon himself on lead guitar. None of the instruments were of any familiar make; the shapes, in fact, were a little disturbing if you looked closely.

The rhythm guitars chonged and whopped, the bass thudded, the keyboard wheeped and tootled, the tambourine jingle-jangled, and Brother Seth's white solid-body guitar threaded in and out with graceful ease; and over it all sang the voices of Maranatha:

> *"Oh brother, get ready,*
> *Oh sister, get ready,*
> *Oh children, get ready,*
> *He's come to take you away."*

"Who's taking who where?" Jimmy wondered under his breath. To the preacher he said, "Where are these guys from, anyway?"

There was no answer. Jimmy turned and saw that the preacher was staring wide-eyed and slack-faced in the direction of the stage. His head was nodding, his shoulders moved rhythmically, and he shifted his weight from foot to foot in time with the music. He didn't respond when Jimmy spoke his name; he didn't even appear to notice when Jimmy jabbed an elbow into his short ribs.

"The hell," Jimmy said, out loud and not caring who heard him.

Doing some staring of his own, he looked out over the crowd. Sure enough, all the faces he could see were looking toward the stage with the same glazed-and-dazed expression, and a lot of people had begun to sway from side to side in their seats or where they stood. More were standing now, he noticed, than had been before. As he watched, others rose slowly to their feet.

The music swelled and rose, and there was something new, a hungry triumphant note such as you might hear in the voices of a dog pack about to tree a coon. Jimmy turned back around and saw Brother Seth Abadon was looking at him.

—*Who are you?*

The words sounded in Jimmy's mind, not his ears. On stage, Brother Seth's mouth had not stopped singing, or smiling, but Jimmy had no doubt who had spoken. He wasn't particularly startled; he had known several old medicine men who could do that trick of talking to you inside your head.

He said, "I'm that tall Indian you always hear about things being ass-high to. Who wants to know?"

Still singing and smiling, still playing his white guitar, Brother Seth tipped his head to one side. —*Interesting*, said the voice in Jimmy's head. *I didn't expect to find one of your kind here.*

Down front, where he had been standing ever since the amplifier breakdown, Mason Littlebird took an unsteady step toward the stage.

—*This is not your place*, the voice said. *This does not concern you. Go away.*

"Up yours," Jimmy said, and folded his arms.

Brother Seth shrugged. —*Then stay out of the way. I won't answer for your safety.*

The white guitar's neck swung down past horizontal as Brother Seth began a long riff, up through the scale and slipping in and out of the minors. Dense chords crashed from the speakers as the others followed, modulating to a higher key.

Jimmy saw that something strange was happening to the front of the huge speaker that stood behind Brother Seth. The black rectangular surface no longer looked solid; it looked more like a hole, an opening into some place of absolute darkness.

> *"Come to take you away, come to take you away,*
> *Come along, come along, he's come to take you away—"*

Jimmy felt a rush of dizziness, and something tugging him forward. He shut his eyes and clutched at the little leather bag, no bigger than his thumb, that hung around his neck. Almost immediately he felt the four things inside begin to move against his palm, and a moment later the dizzy feeling fell away. He opened his eyes and looked up at the smiling face of Brother Seth Abadon.

"All right, you son of a bitch," Jimmy Hominy said. *"All right."*

Both the Mercury's rear doors were jammed shut and he had to crawl in and reach over the back of the front seat to get the oversized guitar case out of the back. He dragged it out of the car and laid it carefully on the fender and undid the snaps and lifted the lid, saying certain words in a language older than Cherokee.

Inside the case was a guitar that was like no other guitar in the world.

For one thing, there was the sheer outrageous size of it. Back in the Fifties, when Jimmy's brother Clyde had first begun to play roadhouse gigs with it, people said that that crazy Indian Clyde Hominy had built himself a guitar as big as a doghouse bass. That was a little bit of an exaggeration, but it was at least as big as one of those Mexican walking basses, that mariachi players call *guitarron*.

For another thing, the body wasn't wood, but steel. In fact it looked a little like a giant version of the old steel-bodied National, that the black bluesmen used to favor so highly. And then there was that neck, wide as Route 66, and that extra string. . . .

But those were merely the things anybody could see at a glance. What made the big guitar truly unique was known to no living man but Jimmy Hominy: the steel of its body had been cut *from the car Hank Williams was riding in when he died.*

Oh, there was a car somewhere in Tennessee that was supposed to be the Hank Williams death car, but it was a fake. Clyde Hominy had been home from Korea only a couple of months when they broadcast the news that Hank was dead, and he had taken off immediately eastward, hopping freights and riding boxcars in the freezing January nights, till he got to Oak Hill, West Virginia. He had stolen the big white Cadillac right out of the county impound yard, where it was waiting for the legalities to be settled, and had driven it all the way back to Oklahoma without once being stopped or spotted, protected by the special medicine given him by a great-uncle who had in his day been the top horse thief in the Indian Territory.

He had hidden the car in the woods, unsure what to do with it, until one night Hank had appeared to him in a dream and told him. Then he had boosted a welding rig from a bridge construction site, and cut and welded the huge box and its resonator from the heavy steel of the Cadillac's doors and fenders, carving the neck from wood from a lightning-struck walnut tree that stood in a hundred-year-old Indian graveyard near Lost City; and when he was done he had run the remains of the car off a cliff above the deepest hole in the Arkansas River, and had taken the guitar and hit the road.

Nobody but Clyde had ever been allowed to play it—that hadn't been hard to enforce, since few men even cared to try and lift it—until that night in '58 when Clyde, gunned down on a Tulsa street by a drunken and Indian-hating white cop, had passed the guitar and its secret on to his little brother as he lay dying in the hospital.

Jimmy stood for a minute looking down at the guitar, running his fingers over a roughly welded seam; Clyde had been after sound, not looks. Then he picked the guitar up, slung the buffalo-hide strap over his neck and shoulder, fitted the slide—not the usual glass bottleneck, but a four-inch section of twelve-gauge barrel cut from a sawed-off shotgun that had once belonged to Pretty Boy Floyd, and never mind *that* story—to his finger, stuck his pipe between his teeth and lit it, and headed back toward the stage.

When he got there he saw right away that there was no time left to screw around. Half the people were on their feet now and all of them were swaying in unison from side to side, their faces absolutely blank and their eyes huge. Mason Littlebird was at the foot of the metal ladder that went up to the stage, and a long line of men and women had formed behind him—Jimmy saw Idabel Grasshopper in there, and Eli Blackbird, and the Sparrowhawk brothers—all moving with the same strange slow step, as if wading in knee-deep water. The music had grown higher and the beat stronger, and the blackness within the enormous speaker was now lit by a faint red glow.

Jimmy shoved Mason Littlebird aside and went up the ladder fast, no hands. As his feet hit the truck bed he slammed a horny thumb across the strings of Clyde's guitar, making an ugly dissonant crash. He slashed out a wailing slide chord like a jail full of busted whores, walked down through the basses with first and second finger, and screamed back up on the high strings with the slide clear on top of the box. It was as crude and violent as an attack with a broken bottle.

And as effective. The wild riff cut through Maranatha's slick sound—it shouldn't have been able to do that, not even this guitar, not against amplified instruments, but a lot of impossible things were going down tonight—and disrupted the seamless harmony, wrenched the progression just the least bit off track, tangled itself around the pretty melody and turned it into something slightly but definitely nasty. Down front, Mason Littlebird paused with one foot on the ladder, and the people behind him stopped their slow-motion march. The rest of the audience continued their rhythmic swaying, but the motion had become a little uneven.

Brother Seth kept playing. He kept smiling, too, as he

turned to look at Jimmy Hominy, but it wasn't the same smile as before.

—*So? You challenge me?*

"You got it," Jimmy said without taking the pipe from his mouth.

—*You have no idea what you're doing. Look!*

The nearest microphone turned suddenly into a giant rattlesnake, standing on its tail. It rushed at Jimmy, striking at his face, yellow venom dripping from long curving fangs.

And Jimmy laughed, thinking maybe this was going to work after all. Brother Seth Abadon might be—well, who he was—but obviously he didn't know everything. He didn't even know what half the Indians present could have told him: that *inada* was Jimmy Hominy's personal power animal and spirit guide. Jimmy said a couple of words and the rattlesnake slithered up his arm and wrapped itself companionably around his neck and went to sleep. He blew a long stream of smoke that condensed itself into a great monster of a rattlesnake, twice the size of the first, that reared up in front of Brother Seth.

"Mine's longer than yours," Jimmy pointed out.

Brother Seth looked from one rattlesnake to the other. —*Interesting.* He made a gesture with his little finger and both snakes vanished. *Very well, then—*

He nodded to the other suits. Immediately Maranatha began laying down a quick-stepping two-four rhythm: no tune, just a steady repetition of a single major chord by rhythm guitars and keyboard, while the bass looped again and again through the same three-notes-and-rest phrase. It was a monotonous but compelling sound, holding the ear like the drone of a bagpipe.

Jimmy glanced out over the crowd and saw that the swaying had stopped. Everything, in fact, had stopped; people sat or stood in place, even those in obviously uncomfortable or off-balance positions—half out of their seats, or about to step off on one foot—and nobody, nothing, moved. They could have been a collection of window dummies.

—*Forget them.* The voice had an impatient edge. *They will keep, for as long as this takes.*

Without warning Brother Seth took off on a long spectacular guitar solo, picking out shower after shower of high brilliant notes, then dropping down to the bass strings to turn the showers into thunderstorms, and back up to the little frets for a display of lightning. It was a fantastic performance; and when it seemed the elaborate structure couldn't carry any more, Brother Seth spun a dazzling ribbon of sixteenth notes to wrap it all up like a Christmas package.

Whereupon Jimmy Hominy proceeded to play the whole thing back to him, note for note, but adding all sorts of extra little ornamental figures and grace notes. At the end, just for prickishness, he tacked on the opening bars of the theme from *Gilligan's Island*.

"Not bad," he said. "Know any more like that? I could sure use the practice."

And that was how it went for a long time, while the stars wheeled overhead and a small-hours ground mist crept out of the woods and wetted the grass. Brother Seth would build something marvelous, only to have Jimmy Hominy knock it to pieces and then kick the pieces off the stage. Very soon there was no smile at all on Brother Seth's face and what there was instead was not a good thing to see.

He played a moaning dirgelike blues, so mournful and lonesome and crying-about-your-mama sad that several owls in the trees nearby committed suicide by diving headfirst into the ground. Jimmy shut that down by interrupting with mocking puppy whines and hound-dog howls that he made with the slide. Brother Seth switched to a weird hypnotic modal number, like those ragas from India you heard in the Sixties. Jimmy picked up the basic line and turned it into a toe-tapping stinky-finger rag, ending up with a deliberately corny *dew-dew-dewdy-yew-dew* straight off *Hee Haw*.

All this time the audience remained frozen where they were, as they were, with never a twitch or blink. Jimmy wondered if they were all right, and whether they could see or hear what was going on. But he didn't wonder much, because the battle with Brother Seth was taking everything he had and it was starting to look as if even that might not be enough.

The sound from the speakers changed suddenly to a vicious shriek, hard-edged and merciless as a straight razor, as Brother Seth began a series of string-bending riffs evil enough to make the nastiest heavy-metal player sound like Lawrence Welk. Things without shapes appeared in the air and hung there gibbering at Jimmy Hominy. Flames broke out around him and the guitar in his hand started to smoke. The strings burned his fingers.

Well, he hadn't really expected a fair fight from Brother Seth Abadon. He took care of the immediate problems by puffing at his pipe—it was still burning, hadn't gone out all this while even though he hadn't had a chance to reload it; there were only two other men alive who knew that trick—and calling up a little rain to cool things down. He noticed Brother Seth didn't get wet.

But making rain took energy he didn't have to spare. The truth was, Jimmy Hominy was getting tired. His arms and shoulders ached, his hands were cramping, and his back hurt from the weight of the heavy guitar. Worse, his head was going numb; he was running out of ideas. He could still keep in there awhile longer, but he felt very doubtful about the final outcome.

At his side, a voice he hadn't heard in over forty years said, "In trouble, *chooch?*"

Clyde was standing there, grinning at him, a wispy, shadowy Clyde—Jimmy could see right through him—even more wasted-looking than when he was alive. Jimmy said, *"Din'dahnvtli!* What, uh, how—"

"No time." Clyde's voice was thin and scratchy, barely audible through the racket Brother Seth was making. "Here."

Clyde's hand came out and touched the guitar's tuning knobs. Jimmy couldn't see how such an insubstantial figure could hope to move material objects, but Clyde still had power over that guitar. *Whang boing chong*, he retuned the top three strings to a strange straight sixth, like nothing Jimmy had ever heard before. "Try it now."

It took Jimmy only a few seconds to get the hang of the new tuning and an idea of its possibilities. By then Clyde was looking even more washed-out.

"So that's what you do with that seventh string," Jimmy said. "I never did know."

"I'd of told you," Clyde said, "but I was sort of leaky at the time. Listen, you got to quit counterpunching and go after him. Way you're going at this, he's wearing you down. Before long you'll start to lose it." Clyde shook his head. "You don't want to know what happens then, *chooch*. Get him now, while you still got a chance."

He started to drift away. His feet didn't quite touch the stage. Jimmy said, "Don't go, Clyde. Stay with me."

"Can't, *chooch*. I'm already gonna catch hell for this." He glanced at Brother Seth, who was watching him with a bad expression. "And I do mean catch hell . . . ."

He drifted over to the enormous black speaker. There he stopped and looked back. "Oh, yeah. He can't play augmented chords. They make him crazy."

"How do you know so much about him?"

"Shit, *chooch*." Clyde's laugh had been spooky enough in life and it hadn't been improved by death. "Who do you think taught him to play?"

He stepped into the black rectangle and vanished. Just like that.

—*Your brother. I should have known.* Brother Seth was looking at Jimmy in a new way. *You know, I could use a man like you. You'd be worth an infinite number of*— He flicked a contemptuous look down at the Sparrowhawk brothers, still rigid like everybody else. *I would make it worth your while.*

"Full benefit package?" Jimmy said dryly.

—*Among other things, you could talk with your brother whenever you wished.*

"Yeah," Jimmy said, "but if I went to work for you he wouldn't talk to me."

More words sounded inside his head, but Jimmy Hominy was no longer listening. He was playing guitar.

He had no name for what he was playing. He had never played anything like it before, even in his imagination; and he knew as he played that he would never be able to do it again. It was a thing only of that moment, as one-time and singular as a snowflake or a murder.

It began with a few bars of almost aimless riffing up and down the frets, exploring the new tuning, staking out scales. It burst suddenly into a chopped-and-lowered version of "Blackberry Rag"—that was for Clyde, it had been his signature tune—and then slid sideways into a wailing "Third Stone From the Sun." That turned somehow into a peyote-ceremony song learned from a brother-in-law who was in the Native American Church; while he was visiting six-tone country, Jimmy threw in part of a tune the locals used to sing in Vietnam. He came back nearer home with a sobbing ay-ay-ay-ay *ranchera* heard one night on the radio, floating up from Mexico, and then stepped off into a quick "Billy In The Low Ground", using the slide to make the big guitar sound like a dobro. That gave way to something that sounded vaguely Cajun and could have been, Jimmy having briefly driven a truck out of Bossier City, but might have been French Canadian since he had also spent a long-ago summer playing at a club in Montreal and trying to get into a certain Mohawk waitress's pants.

Needless to say, he put in lots of augmented chords.

There was Django and Blind Lemon and Charlie in there, and Les and Merle and Jimi and some of every other crazy bastard who ever picked up a guitar. And, of course, there was plenty of Clyde Hominy. Now and then Jimmy had the feeling it was the guitar that was playing him.

But there was much more going on than a mere blending of odds and ends. Out of the wild mixture something else was growing, stretching itself and gradually taking over; call it music or medicine or magic, there was now a new thing which had never been before.

And Brother Seth Abadon, who had been trying to get in with an occasional frustrated lick of his own, suddenly gestured Maranatha to silence, and unslung his own guitar and let it dangle by the neck from his left hand, and stood there listening, unmoving as the audience, while Jimmy finished. Because— Jimmy understood it somehow, looking at him—for all his abilities and powers and attributes, creation just wasn't a part of what he was about. His talents lay in the other direction.

At the end, when Jimmy had wound up with a fast finger-picking run, Brother Seth smiled once again. —*Well. You seem to have made your point.*

He nodded toward the still-frozen crowd. —*Not, of course, that it matters. This pathetic handful of aboriginal relics? Less than a trifle, in the great game.*

The smile widened. —*And I'll get most of them anyway, in the end.*

"You went to a lot of trouble," Jimmy said, "for a trifle."

Brother Seth shrugged. —*I thought this would be amusing. As it has been, though in unexpected ways, thanks to you. One does require one's diversions.*

"You got some damn mean ways of getting your laughs."

—*I?* Brother Seth's eyebrows rose. *What about my worthy opponent, whom these fools adore? He grows bored and moun-*

tains fall, seas rise, stars explode. Whole worlds and their inhab-
itants vanish, usually in painful ways. And you think me *cruel?*

"Wouldn't surprise me that's so," Jimmy said. "But then I never took much stock in either of you."

—Interesting. Brother Seth seemed to use that word a lot. *You refuse to serve me. Yet neither do you serve my adversary.*

"Guess I'm just not servant material."

—Ah, yes. Brother Seth shook his head. For just a second he looked tired. *I said much the same, a very long time ago . . .*

He fell silent, looking off past Jimmy at nothing in particular. Jimmy realized the sky in the east was getting light.

—Still. Brother Seth waved a hand at the crowd. *I had a deal.*

"Not with me you didn't. Not with them, either."

—And yet one hates to leave empty-handed.

"Take what's yours," Jimmy said. "No problem."

Brother Seth crooked a finger. Down in front of the stage the Sparrowhawk brothers began moving, walking stiffly and clum-sily—actually it wasn't all that different from their usual gait—back to the rear of the truck. They climbed the metal ladder and crossed the stage, not looking at anything or anybody. As Jimmy watched, Luther Sparrowhawk stepped into the front of the huge black speaker and was gone. A moment later Bobby Sparrow-hawk followed.

—And so much for that.

Brother Seth snapped his fingers and Maranatha began packing away their instruments and clearing their equipment off the stage, moving with the same brisk efficiency as before. In hardly any time they had loaded everything back into the white van and were climbing aboard. The white van pulled out of the parking area, making no sound whatever, and disappeared down the road in the direction of Fort Gibson.

At that exact moment the bright disk of the sun cracked the eastern horizon. Immediately the crowd in front of the stage be-gan to move and mill about, heads turning this way and that, arms stretching. There was a low murmuring and a few voices raised in vague surprise, nothing more. A baby started crying.

Jimmy got off the stage before anybody could notice him up there. As he reached the ground Idabel Grasshopper came up and clutched his arm. "Jimmy! Where'd you get to?" She looked up at the empty stage. "What happened to those nice men? I was just enjoying their music so much—"

Suddenly, on the front row, old Nettie Blackfox—nobody knew how old, over ninety for sure, and blind as a rock for the last twenty—stood up and began to sing:

> *"Ga-do de-jv-ya-dv-hne-li Ji-sa?*
> *O-ga-je-li ja-gv-wi-yu-hi—"*

Others joined in, rising to their feet if they weren't already standing, raising their voices in the old hymn that had come all the way from the eastern homeland, that the people had sung on the Trail of Tears while a third of the Cherokees in the world died:

> *"O-ga-hli-ga-hli yv-ha-quu-ye-no*
> *Jo-gi-la-wi-sdv-ne-di-yi."*

Jimmy found himself singing too, coming in on bass, while Idabel's voice beside him went for the highs; one thing you had to give Idabel, she could sure as hell sing:

> *"O-ga-je-li-ga . . . (o-ga-je-li-ga)*
> *ja-gv-wi-yu-hi . . .(ja-gv-wi-yu-hi)*
> *Ja-je-li-ga-no . . .(ja-je-li-ga-no)*
> *ja-gv-wi-yu-hi . . . (ja-gv-wi-yu-hi)"*

—while the sun continued to climb above the trees and somewhere a redbird began warming up for a song of his own.

After the singing ended Eli Blackbird climbed up onto the truck long enough for a quick closing prayer, saying the words almost mechanically, occasionally pausing and. shaking his head. After the amen he climbed slowly back down and made his way through the crowd to the parking lot, where Jimmy Hominy was already standing beside the Mercury, putting the big seven-string guitar back in its case.

"Boy," the preacher said, "I think I must have dozed off there for a while. I didn't even notice when our guests left. Wish I'd thanked them for coming."

He watched as Jimmy snapped the case shut. "I hate to admit it," he added, "but I missed your part, too. Sorry." He looked

Jimmy up and down. "From the look of you, you've been playing to beat the Devil."

Jimmy closed his eyes. "Don't say that, *chooch,*" he said softly. "Don't say that. . . ."

AUTHOR'S NOTE:

I grew up around gospel music; my parents were gospel singers—in fact that's how they met: Mama was playing piano for Dad's quartet. Neither of them would approve of this story.

Indian gospel singing, particularly as practiced in eastern Oklahoma, is a wild and exotic little subculture, though in recent years the traditions have gotten badly corrupted through the influence of white-dominated churches and the continuing loss of the language among later generations. (Though there are plenty of Cherokees who don't speak the language but know most of the old songs phonetically by rote memory.) In the broader gospel-music world, Indian singers have long been held in high esteem; Cherokee and Choctaw basses are particularly respected by white quartet singers, who will tell you—if there are no tiresome pious types in earshot—that "those Indians sing bass like they've got three balls apiece!"

The steel guitar made from auto-body parts was inspired by such an instrument that a white man in Arkansas constructed back when I was young.

The Gospel Travelers and the Kingfisher Family are actual and well-known Cherokee gospel groups. Or rather were; I think they've retired by now. They weren't at the singing this story is based on; I just threw them in for the hell of it. I hope they will not mind my including them in this story. The Disciples are imaginary; unfortunately the sort of thing they represent is all too real and all too common nowadays.

Everything in the first part of the story actually happened; I was there, at the preacher's invitation. There was some concern that the angry brothers might try more direct physical tactics. That was the only time in my life I ever wore a gun to church.

The other stuff may have happened too, for all I know. I had to leave early.

TENBEARS AND THE *BRUJA*

HE CAME riding across the flats in the late afternoon on a very dusty bay horse, heading for the little town or maybe village that hunkered at the foot of the big red mesa. There was no good reason for a town to be there but then there was no good reason for him to be where he was either.

He was a tall lean no-ass Indian in his middle thirties. He wore a black hat with a drooping eagle feather in back, and blue denim shirt and jeans bleached nearly white by the sun. His hair was done in braids that hung halfway down his chest. There was nothing particularly unusual about his appearance unless you counted the medium-sized rattlesnake curled familiarly about his left leg below the knee.

His name was Luke Tenbears. He had been in the desert for six days and he was starting to feel every minute of it. Right now even a pissant town like this one looked good to him.

It definitely wasn't much of a place. Riding slowly down the single street, the clop-clop of the bay's hooves echoing off the adobe house fronts on either side, he decided it just barely qualified as anywhere at all. The biggest structure in sight was a dilapidated old church with a Spanish-style bell tower, facing on a tiny plaza. On the other side of the plaza was a long low adobe building that he took to be something official, since the entrance was flanked by a wind-tattered Stars and Stripes and an even raggedier New Mexico state flag. That answered one question, anyway; he had been wondering if he might have wandered across the line into Mexico without knowing it.

An old Ford automobile sat parked in front of the long building. One of the front wheels was missing and the axle was supported by a stack of adobe blocks. Beside it, perched on its stand, was a shiny black Henderson motorcycle. Both the car and the motorcycle bore the white-lettered word POLICIA. There were no other motor vehicles in sight, but a pretty healthy-looking burro was loitering about near the church.

None of this interested Luke nearly as much as the fountain in the middle of the plaza. He got down, wincing as saddle-stiff muscles raised objections to the sudden movement, and led the bay over to the fountain. Taking off his hat, holding the eagle feather carefully out of the way, he got a hatful of water and held it out. The bay buried its muzzle in the hat crown and drained the water in a single grateful slurp. While Luke was getting the horse a refill a voice behind him said, "Hey, *Indio*."

He waited till the bay was drinking again before he turned around. A fat man with a drooping black mustache stood staring at him. "Yeah, you," the fat man said. Actually it came out more like *joo*; the accent was really intense.

Luke noticed the fat man wore a sagging cartridge belt—though with only a few cartridges in the loops—and a big holstered revolver. Pinned to the sweaty front of his khaki shirt was a large gold badge.

Walking slowly past Luke, he patted the bay's flank. "Nice horse," he said. "What's his name?"

"Doesn't have one," Luke told him, refilling the hat once again. This time he poured the contents over his head.

"No?" The fat man snorted. "Where you steal him?"

Luke wiped water from his eyes and didn't reply. After a moment the fat man said, "What you doing here, *Indio*? Looking for something else to steal?"

"Just passing through." Luke glanced up and down the street. "There anywhere in this town a man could get some eats? Couple of beers, maybe a bath?"

"Not if the man is an *Indio*." The fat man's lip curled. "If indeed an *Indio* can be called a—*chinga!*" His eyes went wide as dinner plates and he leaped backward a good three feet. "You got a rattlesnake on your leg!"

"Sure do," Luke agreed. "Not much gets by you, does it?"

The fat man was grabbing at his holstered pistol, while the snake's tail began a soft whirring buzz. Luke said, "Don't do that."

He didn't raise his voice when he said it, or make any particular moves, and he wasn't wearing a gun of his own; but the fat man stopped still as the statue of St. Bartholomew in front of the church behind him. After a second the chubby fingers fell away from the gun. "You better get out of here," the fat man said, his voice uneven. "Go on, now. No more trouble."

Luke stood and looked at him, thinking of several possible things to do next. While he was thinking a woman's voice called, "*Hola, Indio!* You hungry?"

She stood in the middle of the street on the far side of the plaza: long thick black hair, dark strong face, well-filled white blouse, big black skirt whipping in the dry breeze, bare feet set wide apart in the dust. Hands on hips and very damn splendid hips too from the look of them.

So far not all that remarkable, any number of women to answer that description in any number of towns like this on both sides of the border; but this one was taller than the local average, easily five and a half feet by Luke's slightly dazed estimate, and nothing willowy about her either. He was so busy thinking what a big fine woman she was that she had to call out again before he realized she was talking to him.

"Come on, *Indio*," she said, and gave the fat man a look that would have sliced the balls off a grizzly bear. "Never mind El Jefe. I'll take care of you."

The fat man sputtered, started to speak, and then suddenly turned and gave Luke a big grin. "Oh, yes," he said almost cheerfully. "You go with her, *Indio*. She'll take care of you all right." His grin got wider and his voice higher. "*Es una bruja, Indio.* You know what means *bruja*? Witch!"

He broke into a wet nasty laugh that stopped in a choking gobble when the woman made a curious little gesture at him. Luke put the wet hat on his head. "Right with you," he said to the woman, and reached for the bay's reins. "Okay if I bring my horse?"

"Sure," she said. "And your snake too. Just don't bring that pig beside you."

As they walked together down the street the woman said, "My name's Margarita. You want to tell me yours?" She gave him a quick flash of eye-hurting white teeth. "Or maybe you don't give out your name?"

"Luke Tenbears," he told her. "*Diez osos*," he added in translation.

"I know what it means." She tilted her head to one side. "What kind of Indian? Navajo?"

"Comanche."

"Huh. Long way from home." She glanced down. "Nice snake. Where'd you get him?"

The rattlesnake raised its flat spearpoint head and looked up at her. "I've got a name, you know," it said in a dry reedy voice.

"His name's Dwight," Luke told the woman.

Her eyebrows went way up. "*Dios!* A horse that doesn't have a name and a snake that does."

"Also," the rattlesnake said, lisping slightly, "I really really *hate* it when people talk about me right in front of me. As if I'm some complete *idiot* who can't understand. I mean, it's so *rude*."

"Dwight hasn't eaten for a spell," Luke explained. "He gets kind of snippy when he's hungry."

"Quit *apologizing* for me," Dwight said, and lapsed into sullen silence.

"Here," Margarita said. "This is my house."

She lived in a small brush-roofed adobe house, about like any other house in the little town. When Luke had unsaddled and fed the bay, she said, "Come inside," and led him into the cool dimly-lit space of the single room. To Dwight she said, "There's a big rat under the woodpile out back."

"Muchas gracias, señorita," Dwight murmured formally, and uncoiled himself from around Luke's leg and disappeared out the door, rattling softly to himself.

"So," Margarita said to Luke, "want to wash up first?"

"A bath would be fine," Luke said. "But I hate to put you to the trouble—"

"Forget it," she said, and bent to drag a big old iron tub out into the middle of the floor. "It's worth it just to piss El Jefe off. Now sit down and get comfortable, because this is going to take some time."

She was right about that; it was a hell of a job hauling water in from the nearby well and heating it on the little stove until the tub was full. Luke offered to help but she wouldn't permit it. "It's nothing," she said. "I do this all the time." Watching her, Luke realized that she was fantastically strong. Be damn, he thought, I may be in love. Or trouble. Or both. Assuming there's a difference.

He expected she would leave the room when he started to undress, but she leaned her back against the wall and folded her arms and looked straight at him. "Go ahead," she said. "I want to watch you."

He hesitated and then turned his back, while she laughed deep in her belly. When he took off his shirt he heard her suck in her breath. *"Ay,"* she said softly, and a moment later he felt her fingertips on his back, tracing the big deep scars. "What did this to you?"

"Shrapnel," he said. "You know, shell fragments."

"Ah. You were in the big war, in France? In the army?"

"Marines. Place called Belleau Wood."

He took off his boots and peeled down his jeans and padded over to the tub, feeling her watching him. As he climbed in she walked around to stand at the foot of the tub. "I embarrass you," she said, grinning. "Will this help?"

With a series of quick moves she shucked off the white blouse and then the big skirt. She wore nothing underneath. Her body looked hard and taut, her belly absolutely flat, but her breasts were big and high. Luke felt a shock run from the base of his spine clear to the top of his head.

"Hey," she said calmly, "we were going to end up naked together anyway. We both knew that, soon as we laid eyes on each other. Why be silly about it?"

She giggled, then, like a dirty little girl. "You like to look at my titties, huh?" Suddenly her big brown nipples vanished, to be replaced by a pair of long-lashed brown eyes that gazed warmly at Luke. "All right if they look back?"

Luke sat there in the tub for a second or two, trading stares with Margarita's knockers. Then he lifted his hands and made a series of quick passes in the air, and sang a short high-pitched phrase without recognizable words, up in the back of his throat.

Almost immediately his penis broke water like the bow of a surfacing U-boat. As Margarita clapped her hands and made admiring sounds, it continued to grow, on and on past the limits of normal erection and then those of possibility, two feet and now a yard and soon clear to the low ceiling, where it looped itself twice around a rafter and came shooting back down to circle the room, still lengthening itself, snaking here and there about the furniture and at last wrapping itself around Margarita half a dozen times, to end with the big red-brown knob right in front of her face, tapping her gently on the nose.

"Damn, I'm good," Luke said.

Margarita was laughing delightedly. "Damn, you sure are," she said, as Luke clicked his tongue twice and everything returned to more or less normal. "You some kind of medicine man?"

"My grandfather was," Luke explained. "He taught me a few things." Before they decided he was a witch and killed him, he added in his mind but didn't say.

"Boy." She shook her head, making her long black hair flare out like a crow's wings. "Come on, let's get you cleaned up and I'll fix something to eat. I got a feeling we're both going to need our strength."

When he was done with his bath she dried him with a big rough towel, reaching down at the end to give him a quick friendly tweak. But as he reached for her something else got his attention, maybe a sound from outside, and he stopped and said, "Wait," and went to the door, wrapping the towel around his waist.

A couple of ratty-looking men in straw hats were leading his horse away. One had a shotgun slung across his back and the other wore a holstered pistol. Luke said, "Hey," and then he saw El Jefe standing across the road, giving him a bad-toothed grin.

"Sorry, *Indio*," the fat man called. "I think maybe this is a stolen horse. I got to impound him until you can prove where you got him." He put a hand on the butt of his revolver. "You got any problem with that?" he asked hopefully. "Want to maybe do something about it?"

When Luke didn't reply he laughed. "No? All right, go back to *la bruja.*" He made a complicated obscene gesture with his free hand. "She'll give you a ride!"

As darkness gathered outside, Margarita cooked and served a near-black *mole con puerco* with stacks of warm corn tortillas and all sorts of fascinating little side items. "Holy shit," Luke said reverently, tasting. "Now this is some real magic, all right."

Some time later, over a jug of authentically great mescal, she said, "I'm glad you came. I was going crazy. Man, I hate this town."

She looked out the door. "They hate me back, of course. *Bruja*, they say, and then spit. I get blamed for every cross-eyed baby that's born and every spell of bad weather. Nobody ever talks to me but El Jefe, and he only wants to fuck me. Well, and the priest mumbles at me in Latin when I go by. I'm not sure he doesn't want to fuck me too."

"Why don't you leave?" Luke asked, picking up the jug. "Go somewhere else. Santa Fe, maybe. Even California."

She snorted. "How? Walk away from here, across the desert? You been out there, man, you know what it's like. Even the coyotes carry canteens and box lunches. And nobody around here is going to give me a ride, that's for sure."

She gave him a sudden look. "Come to think of it, you're stuck here too, now El Jefe's got your horse. What you going to do about that?"

Luke shrugged. "Steal another one, I guess. That one wasn't much good anyway."

"Take me with you when you go," she begged. "Please."

Luke considered it, nodded. "Sure." He slugged at the mescal and set the jug carefully on the table before turning to her. "Hey," he said, "we can worry about all that later. Right now—"

He held out his arms and she came to him, snuggling fiercely against his chest. "Oh, yes," she said breathlessly, and that was when the roof caught fire.

There was no warning smell of smoke, no preliminary flickers and crackles; there was just a big loud rush of flame overhead, all at once, and blazing bits of brush starting to fall as Luke and Margarita jumped to their feet. This, Luke realized without even having to think about it, wasn't the work of some stray spark; a fire like this had to have been set on purpose. And now he could hear, over the fast-growing roar of the flames, voices from outside. He couldn't make out the words but he had a pretty good idea they weren't friendly.

He grabbed up his boots and hat—luckily he'd put on his jeans and shirt for dinner—and reached for Margarita, who was slapping out a bit of burning roof that was trying to set fire to her skirt. But as they started out the door a gun went off and something small and nasty went *wheeow* off the adobe next to the entrance. "Shit!" Luke said, ducking back out of the doorway, yanking Margarita with him, hearing her cursing in Spanish. "Now what the hell—"

"Hey, *Indio!*" came El Jefe's unmistakable voice from outside. "Come on out! We let you go, okay? We just want *la bruja!*"

Luke was already reaching down the front of his shirt, pulling out the little buckskin bag that hung around his neck on a sweat-black thong. "Hang on a minute," he said to Margarita.

"A minute?" She glanced around with fear-wide eyes. "I don't think we *got* a minute, man—"

She was right about that; the little house was already full of smoke, so dense and pungent it was almost impossible to breathe, while overhead the blazing roof was clearly about to collapse as the flames ate through the cottonwood rafters. But Luke got the little bag open and shook some dark fine powder into the palm of his hand. "Here we go," he said, dipping a fingertip in the stuff. "Hold still."

Quickly he drew his finger across her forehead, leaving a single narrow line, and then put a dot on each cheek. His finger dipped again and he made the same marks on his own face, chanting softly as he did so in a language that was neither Spanish nor Comanche but much older than either. "All right," he said, and stepped toward the doorway. "Come on."

Margarita shivered. "Why not?" she said, and shrugged. "Better to get shot than burn up."

"No, it's okay." He took her hand and led her through the door. Nobody shot at them. "See?"

The house was surrounded by a lot of rough-looking people, mostly men but a few women too. Quite a few of them held guns or machetes, and several others carried torches. The burning house lit the scene almost as bright as day. El Jefe stood in front of the house, his pistol in his hand. Beside him was a tall, lean, long-faced man in a dark robe, holding a large wooden cross that he waved in the direction of the house. His lips were moving but Luke couldn't hear any words for the roar and crackle of the fire.

Luke began walking in the general direction of El Jefe and the priest. After a moment's hesitation Margarita fell in beside him. "Crazy," she muttered.

"Hey, *Indio,*" El Jefe shouted again. He was looking past Luke and Margarita, still looking at the flaming house. "Last chance. Why you want to burn with her?"

By now Luke was close enough to hear the priest mumbling rapidly in what he took to be Latin. His eyes were truly weird in the firelight, and his lips were loose and wet. He too was watching the house, ignoring Luke and Margarita even though they were now right in front of him.

"My God," Margarita said. "They can't see us?"

"Or hear us," Luke told her as they walked past El Jefe and the priest, close enough to brush elbows. "Comanche horse-stealing charm. Been in my family for seven generations. Not much of it left," he added. "I been saving it for an emergency."

They walked through the line of villagers, still undetected, and on up the empty street. Dwight slithered out from between a couple of darkened houses and wrapped himself around Luke's leg. "What a *ghastly* little town," he remarked. "I *told* you we should have gone to Taos."

The plaza was deserted and there were no lights showing in the long building; evidently all of El Jefe's men were down at the burning. Luke noticed the motorcycle still standing there, its chromework picking up the light from the rising moon. "That El Jefe's bike?" he asked.

Margarita nodded. "He got the town to pay for it, said it was for police work. But it's just his toy. You should see the fat fool trying to ride—" She stopped and turned to look at Luke. "Oh," she said. "Yes. I love it."

The Henderson rocked gently forward as Luke pushed at the handlebars. The stand folded up with a soft clunk as the tires took the weight and Luke began pushing the motorcycle across the moonlit plaza. Charm or no charm, he wasn't quite ready to actually fire the damn thing up right in front of the police station.

At the edge of town he stopped and bent to study the bike's layout. "You know what you're doing?" Margarita asked skeptically.

"Learned to ride one in the Corps," he said, fiddling with the gas cock and the choke, adjusting the spark advance. "Only that was a Harley and this is a Henderson—"

It took a good many kicks and he was starting to wish his grandfather had given him a medicine for starting balky engines, but then there came a sudden coughing roar and the Henderson began to vibrate under his hands. He dropped his ass onto the saddle with a sigh of relief and Margarita climbed on behind him. "Get a good grip," he advised her. "This is about to get seriously bumpy."

The desert floor shone white in the Henderson's headlight as Luke gunned the heavy bike across the flat. Now and then there was a clump of cactus or brush to be dodged, and a couple of times the tires hit soft patches of sand and he almost lost it, but somehow he kept the motorcycle more or less upright and more or less on course. Behind him he could hear Margarita alternately laughing and cursing, her arms gripping his body tightly, her face pressed against his back.

Out in the empty land, beyond sight of the lights of the town—there was a faint reddish glow, if you knew where to look, that had to be the light from the burning house—he slid the Henderson to a sand-flying stop. "Here?" he asked.

"Yes," Margarita said, "please," so he held the bike steady while she got off and then he laid it carefully down, no use even trying to get the stand to hold in this soft sandy ground, and turned to see that she was already taking off her clothes. The moon was big and high and her skin shone in its light like Navajo silver.

"I imagine *you* two want to be *alone,*" Dwight observed, uncoiling from around Luke's leg. "Think I'll go see if I can find a nice gopher. I never *did* catch that tiresome rat."

"Hurry," Margarita said, stepping out of her skirt. "Holy Mary, that big hot thing jumping and shaking between my legs, I never felt anything like it in my life. I'm so wet, hurry please."

She began rubbing her bush with both hands, moaning excitedly, while Luke clawed at his own clothes. When he was naked she stretched out on the sand, beckoning to him. "Come on," she urged, raising her bottom and rolling her hips. "Get on top of me."

"No." Luke dropped to his knees beside her. "This way."

He flipped her over and she said, "Oh, yes, like animals, that's good," and arranged herself on hands and knees as he knelt behind her. Holding his almost painful erection in one hand, twisting the other in her hair and pulling her head back, he mounted her. As his penis slid into her she made a low guttural sound and then, *"Empuje!"* and her hips slammed back to meet his thrust. "Like animals," she said again. "Yes, wait, let me try something—"

Just like that, she was a mountain lioness, twisting and squalling beneath him, her tail curving and jerking to one side, while he dug at the ground with his hind paws and his own tail thrashed in time with the violent jabs of his short barbed penis. The scent of her maddened him and he raised his own voice in a long yowling wail and bit at her furry pelt—

—and with a wrenching *snap* they were a wild mare and her stallion, lunging and bucking, whinnying their shared brainless ecstasy. His big square teeth nipped her neck; his long forelegs straddled her sweating flanks—

—and *snap* and they were a couple of rutting timber wolves, and he clasped her sleek body with his strong front legs and stabbed at her with his long chisel-pointed member and howled over her bristling back—

—but *snap* again and once more they were just a man and a woman fucking on the ground. "I can't hold it," Margarita panted. *"Ayudame, querido*, help me—"

"Right," Luke said in her ear, clutching her hips, keeping

himself deep inside her, forming the words in his mind and wondering if he could really pull this off. "Just a second—"

And then, for a time, the snakes and jackrabbits and burrowing owls were treated to the sight of a pair of enormous snow-white buffalo coupling in the moonlight. Their hooves tore and pounded the earth; their bellowing could have been heard halfway to Mexico. Nothing like it had been seen in these parts since the last time the big ice came south. Even the tortoises woke up and waddled out to watch.

Luke's mind had shut down altogether; his whole consciousness was now a single raging red lust, radiating from the two melon-sized balls that hung between his great driving hind legs. His belly pressed hard against her shaggy rump as he rammed his huge shaft deep into her mighty vault. Horns tossing, she braced herself to take his incredible weight—later she said it was like being fucked by a hairy mountain—and blared her joy to the night.

At the moment of earth-shaking climax (that was no corny metaphor; they *did* make it shake, causing at least one minor rockslide on the side of the nearest mesa) he threw back his head and joined his roar to hers. Seconds later, still pumping into her, he felt the shift beginning and tried to fight it, but the buffalo brain just wasn't up to the job. "Shit!" he cried as they collapsed together onto the sand, humans again and right now a couple of pretty damn tired ones.

"*Ay,*" Margarita sighed beneath him. "That was good."

Too spent to reply, Luke lay on top of her, still in her, still emptying himself. When the last spurting spasm subsided he pulled out and rolled off and stretched out beside her. "Wham, bam," he offered, "and thank *you*, ma'am."

He wanted very badly to put his arms around her and go to sleep right there and then. But it wouldn't do; they weren't all that far from the town yet, and come morning El Jefe would be furiously following their all too easily followed trail—motorcycle tracks being, in this year of 1922, not exactly common in the New Mexico desert.

"Well," Luke said and got to his feet. That hurt; everything hurt. It had been a long time since he had done a major shape change and he had forgotten how sore you felt afterward. "We better get our clothes back on and get out of here. You see my shirt anywhere?"

Dwight came slithering out from a patch of prickly pear. "My," he said. "Quite *impressive,* one must admit."

He yawned, showing his fangs. A good-sized bulge now showed about halfway between his head and tail. "A young prairie dog of *no* breeding," he murmured, "but with a certain naive charm . . . of course," he went on, "normally one wouldn't dream of actually *watching.* But that little exhibition you two put on was hardly, well, *intimate.* I don't know if you noticed, but toward the end the jackrabbits were applauding."

A few minutes later, straddling the Henderson again—Dwight muttering, "God, I *hate* this thing!"—Luke looked back over his shoulder at Margarita. "Wonder if there's enough gas to make it to the next town."

"Only one way to find out," she told him. "Let's go, *Indio.*"

He twisted the throttle grip and off they went, bumping and banging over the moon-pale flat, laughing like maniacs. Behind them a long rooster-tail plume of dust hung white in the air for a little while before settling softly back to the desert floor.

AUTHOR'S NOTE

Some years ago a certain well-known editor invited me to contribute a story to an anthology of erotic fantasy which she was putting together. The bad news was that time had almost run out; deadline, in fact, was only a couple of days away.

I wandered around for the rest of the afternoon, trying to think what the hell I could do—erotic fantasy? What did I know from erotic fantasy? This was made more difficult because an irritating song had chosen that time to embed itself in my mind, on continuous-replay mode; a song I always disliked, about a man who had been in the desert on a horse with no name....

Until I finally realized I was going to have to put the man and his horse into the story, just to get rid of them. After that the story quickly came together, as did the protagonists.

I wrote the whole thing in one sitting, staying up all night to finish it. At about six in the morning I hit the "save" command—and the ancient computer I was using at the time ATE THE LAST SIX PAGES.

At that point I became somewhat incoherent. When I could talk again I called the famous editor up and told her what had happened. She was most sympathetic and said, "Don't worry about it. Get some sleep. I'll give you a few more days."

Which was nice of her, except I knew if I crashed I would never again be able to remember how those pages had gone. So I sat up for another five or six hours, stoking myself with strong black coffee and doughnuts—the poor freelancer's speed—and scrabbling around in my head for remembered bits and scraps of the missing text.

And by God I did it; I pulled it up and I nailed it, and I printed it and sent it in to the famous editor, feeling very proud of myself, and then I drank a dangerous quantity of Jim Beam, as an antidote to all that caffeine and sugar, and went to bed.

The famous editor bounced the story. She said it didn't have enough of a plot. (Plot? In an erotic fantasy story? When did this happen? Nobody ever tells me anything.)

And so Tenbears and his nameless horse went into my files, never to be seen by public eyes until now. Lucky you.

As for the famous editor, she did the same thing to me a couple of years later, turning down a story I had written at her express invitation for another anthology. Subsequently I learned that this was normal procedure for the famous editor—who, if she ever gets another story from me, had better be wearing thick woolen undies, because Hell will have frozen over. But I digress.

GOING AFTER
OLD MAN ALABAMA

CHARLIE BADWATER was the most powerful medicine man in all the eastern Oklahoma hill country. Or the biggest witch, depending on which person you listened to; among Cherokees the distinction tends to be a little hazy.

Either way, when Thomas Cornstalk finally decided that something had to be done about Old Man Alabama, he didn't need to think twice before getting in his old Dodge pickup truck and driving over to Charlie Badwater's place. Thomas Cornstalk was no slouch of a medicine man himself, but in a situation like this you went to the man with the power.

Charlie Badwater lived by himself in a one-room log cabin at the end of a really bad dirt road, up near the head of Butcherknife Hollow. There was nobody in sight when Thomas Cornstalk drove up, but as he got down from the pickup cab a big gray owl fluttered down from the surrounding woods and disappeared into the deep shadows behind the cabin. A moment later the cabin door opened and Charlie Badwater stepped out into the sunlight. "'Siyo, Tami, dohiju?" he called.

Thomas Cornstalk half-raised a hand in casual greeting. He and Charlie Badwater went back a long way. "'Siyo, Jali. Gado haduhne? Catching any mice?" he added dryly.

Charlie Badwater chuckled deep in his chest without moving his lips. "Hey," he said, "remember old Moses Otter?" And they both chuckled together, remembering.

Moses Otter had been a mean old man with a permanent case of professional jealousy, especially toward anybody who might have enough power to make him look bad. Since Moses Otter had never in his life been more than a second-rate witch, this included a lot of people.

One of his nastier tricks had been to turn himself into an owl—he could do that all right, but then who can't?—and fly over the woods until he spotted a clearing where a possible rival was growing medicine tobacco. Now of course serious tobacco has to be grown absolutely unseen by anyone except the person who will be using it, so this had meant a great deal of frustration and ruined medicine all over the area. Quite a few people had tried to witch Moses Otter and put a stop to this crap, but his protective medicine had always worked.

Charlie Badwater, then a youthful and inexperienced unknown, had gone to Moses Otter's place and told him in front of several witnesses that if he enjoyed being a bird he could have a hell of a good time from now on. And had turned him on the spot into the mangiest, scabbiest turkey buzzard ever seen in Oklahoma; and Moses Otter, after a certain amount of flopping around trying to change himself back, had flown away, never to be seen again except perhaps as an unidentifiable member of a gang of roadkill-pickers down on the Interstate.

That, Thomas Cornstalk recalled, had been the point at which everybody had realized that Charlie Badwater was somebody special. Maybe they hadn't fully grasped just how great he would one day become, but the word had definitely gone out that Charlie Badwater was somebody you didn't want to screw around with.

Now, still chuckling, Charlie Badwater tilted his head in the direction of his cabin. "*Kawi jaduli*? Got a pot just made."

They went inside the cabin and Thomas Cornstalk sat down at the little pineboard table while Charlie Badwater poured a couple of cups of hell-black coffee from a blue and white speckled metal pot. "Ought to be ready to walk by now," Charlie Badwater said. "Been on the stove a long time."

"Good coffee," Thomas Cornstalk affirmed, tasting. "Damn near eat it with a fork."

They sat at the table, drinking coffee and smoking hand-rolled cigarettes, not talking for the moment: a couple of fifty-some-odd-year-old full-bloods, similarly dressed in work shirts and Wal-Mart jeans and cheap nylon running shoes made in Singapore. Charlie Badwater had the classic lean, deep-chested, no-ass build of the mountain Cherokee, while Thomas Cornstalk was one of those heavyset, round-faced types who may or may not have some Choctaw blood from way back in old times. Their faces, however, were similarly weathered, the hands callused and scarred from years of manual labor. Charlie Badwater was missing the end joint of his left index finger. There were only three people who knew how he had lost it and two of them were dead and nobody had the nerve to ask the third one. Let alone Charlie.

They talked a little, finally, about this and that: routine inquiries about the health of relatives, remarks about the weather, the usual pleasantries that a couple of properly raised Cherokee men will exchange before getting down to the real point of a conversation. But Thomas Cornstalk, usually the politest of men, was worried enough to hold the small talk to the bare minimum required by decency.

"*Gusdi nusdi*," he said finally. "Something's the matter. I'm not sure what," he added, in response to the inquiry in Charlie Badwater's eyes. "It's Old Man Alabama."

"That old weirdo?" Charlie Badwater wrinkled his nose very slightly, as if smelling something bad. "What's he up to these days? Still nutty as a *kenuche* ball, I guess?"

"Who knows? That's what I came to talk with you about," Thomas Cornstalk said. "He's up to something, all right, and I think it's trouble."

Old Man Alabama was a seriously strange old witch—in his case there was no question at all about the definition—who lived on top of a mountain over in Adair County, not far from the Arkansas line. He wasn't Cherokee; he claimed to be the last surviving descendant of the Alabama tribe, and he often gibbered and babbled in a language he claimed was the lost Alabama tongue. It could have been; Thomas Cornstalk couldn't recognize a word of it, and he spoke sixteen Indian languages as well as English and Spanish—that was his special medicine, the ability to speak in different tongues; he could also talk with animals. On the other hand it might just as easily have been a lot of meaningless blather, which was what Thomas Cornstalk and a good many other people suspected.

There was also the inconvenient fact that there were still some Alabamas living on a reservation down in Texas, big as you please; but it had been along time since anybody had pointed this out in Old Man Alabama's hearing. Not after what had happened to the last bigmouth to bring the subject up.

Whatever he was—Thomas Cornstalk had long suspected he was some kind of Creek or Seminole or maybe Yuchi, run off by his own people—Old Man Alabama was as crazy as the Devil and twice as nasty. That much was certain.

He was skinny and tall and he had long arms that he waved wildly about while talking, or for no apparent reason at all. Everything about him was long: long matted hair falling past his shoulders, long beaky nose, long bony fingers ending in creepy-looking nails. He walked with a strange angling gait, one shoulder higher than the other, and he spat constantly, tuff tuff tuff, so you could follow him down a dirt road on a dry day by the little brown spots in the dust.

It was widely believed that he had a long tongue like a moth's, that he kept curled up in his mouth and only stretched out at night during unspeakable acts. That was another story people weren't eager to investigate first hand.

He also stank. Not the way a regular man smelled bad, even a very dirty regular man—though Old Man Alabama was sure as hell dirty enough—but a horrible, eye-watering stench that reminded you of things like rotten cucumbers and dead skunks on the highway in hot weather. That alone would have been reason enough for people to give him a wide berth, even if they hadn't been afraid of him.

And oh, yes, people were afraid of him. Mothers hid their pregnant daughters indoors when they saw him walking by the house, afraid that even a single direct look from those hooded reptilian eyes might cause monstrous deformities to the unborn.

Most people, in face, avoided talking about him at all; it was well known that witches knew when they were being talked about, and the last thing people wanted was to draw the displeased attention of a witch as powerful and unpredictable as Old Man Alabama. It was a measure of the power of both Charlie Badwater and Thomas Cornstalk that they were willing to talk freely about him. Even so, Thomas Cornstalk would have been just as comfortable if Charlie Badwater hadn't spoken quite so disrespectfully about the old man.

"All I know," Thomas Cornstalk said, "he's been cooking up some kind of almighty powerful medicine up on that mountain of his. I go over that way pretty often, you know, got some relatives that call me up every time one of their kids gets a runny nose . . . anyway, sometimes you can hear these sounds, up where your ear can't quite get ahold of them, like those dog whistles, huh? And people see strange lights up on the mountain at night, and sometimes in the daytime the air looks sort of shimmery above the mountaintop, the way it does over a hot stove. Lots of smoke too, that's another thing. I got a smell or two when the wind was right and I don't know what the old man's burning up there but it's nothing I'd want in *my* medicine bag."

He paused, sipping his coffee, his eyes wandering about the interior of the cabin. Lots of medicine men live surrounded by all sorts of junk, their houses littered and smelly, walls and ceiling hung with bundles of dried herbs and feathers and skins and bones and other parts of birds and animals. Charlie Badwater's cabin, however, was as neat as a white doctor's office, everything stowed carefully away out of sight.

"I went up to see him, finally," Thomas Cornstalk said. "Or tried to, but he was either gone or hiding. I couldn't get close to the cabin. He's got the place circled—you know? You get to about ten or fifteen steps from the cabin and it starts to be harder and harder to walk, like you're stepping in molasses, till finally you can't go any farther. By then the cabin looks all runny, too, like it's melting. I had my pipe with me, and some good tobacco, and I tried every *igawesdi* I know for getting past a protective spell. Whatever Old Man Alabama has around that cabin, it's no ordinary medicine."

"Huh." Charlie Badwater was beginning to look interested. "See anything? I mean anything to suggest what's going on."

"Not a thing." Thomas Cornstalk pulled his shoulder blades together for a second. "Place made my skin crawl so bad, I got out pretty quick. Went home and smoked myself nearly black. Burned enough cedar for a Christmas-tree lot before I felt clean again."

"Huh," Charlie Badwater said again. He sat for a minute or so in silence, staring out through the open cabin door, though there was nothing out there but a stretch of dusty yard and the woods beyond.

"All right," he said at last, and got to his feet. "We better go pay Old Man Alabama a visit."

Thomas Cornstalk stood up too. "You want to go right now?" he said, a little surprised.

"Sure. You got something else you have to do?"

"No," Thomas Cornstalk admitted, after a moment's hesitation. He wasn't really ready for this, he thought, but maybe it was better to get on with it. The longer they waited, the better the chance that Old Man Alabama would find out they were coming, and do something unusually bad to try and stop them.

Charlie Badwater started toward the door. Thomas Cornstalk said, "You're not taking any stuff along? You know, medicine?"

Charlie Badwater patted his jeans pockets. "Got my pipe and some tobacco on me. I don't expect I'll need anything else."

Going out the door, following Charlie Badwater across the yard, Thomas Cornstalk shook his head in admiring wonder. That Charlie, he thought. Probably arm-wrestle the Devil left-handed, if he got a chance. Probably win, too.

They rode back down the dirt road in Thomas Cornstalk's old pickup truck. Charlie Badwater didn't own any kind of car or truck. He didn't have a telephone or electricity in his cabin, either. It was some mysterious but necessary part of his personal medicine.

The dirt track came out of the woods, after a mile or so of dust and rocks and sun-hardened ruts, and joined up with a winding gravel road that dipped down across the summer-dry bed of Butcherknife Creek and then climbed up the side of Turkeyfoot Ridge. On the far side of the ridge, the gravel turned into potholed county blacktop. Several miles farther along, they came out onto the Stilwell road. "Damn, Charlie," Thomas Cornstalk said, hanging a left, "you think you could manage to live further back in the woods?"

"Not without coming out on the other side," Charlie Badwater said.

The road up the side of Old Man Alabama's mountain was even worst than the one to Charlie Badwater's place. "I was here just this morning," Thomas Cornstalk said, fighting the wheel, "and I swear this mule track is in worse shape than it was then. And look at that," he exclaimed, and stepped on the brake pedal. "I know that wasn't there before—"

A big uprooted white oak tree was lying across the road. The road was littered with snapped-off limbs and still-green leaves. The two men in the pickup truck looked at each other. There hadn't been so much as a stiff breeze all day.

"Get out and walk, then," Charlie Badwater said after a minute. "We can use the exercise, I guess."

They got out and walked on up the road, climbing over the fallen tree. A little way beyond, the biggest rattlesnake Thomas Cornstalk had ever seen was lying in the road, looking at them. It coiled up and rattled its tail and showed its fangs but Charlie Badwater merely said, *"Ayuh jaduji,"* and the huge snake uncoiled and slid quietly off into the woods while Charlie and Thomas walked past.

"I always wondered," Thomas Cornstalk said as they trudged up the steep mountainside. "You suppose a rattlesnake really believes you're his uncle, when you say that?"

"Who knows? It doesn't matter how things work, Thomas. It just matters that they do work." Charlie Badwater grinned. "Talked to this professor from Northeastern State once, showed up at a stomp dance down at Redbird. He said Cherokees are pragmatists."

"What's that mean?"

"Beats me. I told him most of the ones I know are Baptists, with a few Methodists and of course there's a lot of people getting into those holy-roller outfits—" Charlie Badwater stopped suddenly in the middle of the road. "Huh," he grunted softly, as if to himself. Thomas Cornstalk couldn't remember ever seeing him look so surprised.

They had rounded the last bend in the road and had come in sight of Old Man Alabama's cabin. Except the cabin itself was barely in sight of all, in any normal sense. The whole clearing where the cabin stood was walled off by a kind of curtain of yellowish light, through which the outlines of the cabin showed only vaguely and irregularly. The sky looked somehow darker directly above the clearing, and all the surrounding trees seemed to have taken on strange and disturbing shapes. There was a high-pitched whining sound in the air, like the singing of a million huge mosquitoes.

"You were right, Thomas," Charlie Badwater said after a moment. "The old turd's gotten hold of something heavy. Who'd have thought it?"

"It wasn't like this when I was here this morning," Thomas Cornstalk said, looking around him and feeling very uneasy. "Not so extreme, like."

"Better have a look, then." Charlie Badwater took out a buckskin pouch and a short-stemmed pipe. Facing toward the sun, he poured a little tobacco from the pouch into his palm and began to sing, a strange-sounding song that Thomas Cornstalk had never heard before. Four times he sang the song through, pausing at the end of each repetition to blow softly on the tobacco. Then he stuffed the tobacco into the bowl of the pipe. It was an ordinary cheap briar pipe, the kind they sell off cardboard wall displays in country gas stations. In Cherokee medicine there is no particular reverence or importance placed on the pipe itself; the tobacco carries all the power, and then only if properly doctored with the right *igawesdi* words. Charlie Badwater could, if he had preferred, have simply rolled the tobacco into a ciga-rette and used that.

He lit the pipe with a plastic butane lighter and walked to-ward the cabin, puffing. Thomas Cornstalk followed, rather re-luctantly. He didn't like this, but he would have followed Charlie Badwater to hell. Which, of course, might very well be where they were about to go.

Charlie Badwater pointed the stem of the pipe at the shim-mering wall of light that blocked their way. Four times he blew smoke at the barrier, long dense streams of bluish white smoke that curled and eddied back strangely as they hit the bright cur-tain. On the fourth puff there was a sharp cracking sound and suddenly the curtain was gone and the humming stopped and there was only a weed-grown clearing and a tumble-down gray board shack badly in need of a new roof. Somewhere nearby a bird began singing, as if relieved.

"*Asuh*," Thomas Cornstalk murmured in admiration.

"Make me think, I'll teach you that one some time," Charlie Badwater said, "It's not hard, once you learn the song . . . well, let's have a look around."

They walked slowly toward the cabin. There wasn't much to see. The yard was littered with an amazing assortment of junk—broken crockery and rusting pots and pans, chicken feathers and unidentifiable bones, bottles and cans, a wrecked chair with stuffing coming out of the cushions—but none of it suggested anything except that you wouldn't want Old Man Alabama living next door. A big pile of turtle shells lay on the sagging front porch. There was a rattlesnake skin nailed above the door.

"No smoke," Charlie Badwater said, studying the chimney. "Reckon he's gone? Well, one way to find out."

He stepped up onto the porch, and turned to look back at Thomas Cornstalk, who hadn't moved. "Coming?"

"You go," Thomas Cornstalk said. "I'll wait out here for you. If it's all the same to you." He wouldn't have gone inside that cabin for a million dollars and a lifetime ticket to the Super Bowl. "Need to work on my tan," he added.

Charlie Badwater chuckled and disappeared through the cabin door. There was no sound of voices or anything else from within, so Thomas Cornstalk figured he must have been right about Old Man Alabama being gone. That didn't make much sense; why would the old maniac have put up such a fancy protective spell if he wasn't going to be inside? Come to think of it, how could he have laid on that barrier from the outside? As far as Thomas Cornstalk knew, a spell like that had to be worked from inside the protective circle. But nothing about this made any sense. . . .

Charlie Badwater's laugh came through the open cabin door. "You're not going to believe this," he called. "I don't believe it myself."

"What did you find?" Thomas Cornstalk said as Charlie came back out.

"About what you'd expect, mostly. A whole bunch of weird stuff piled every which way and hanging from the ceiling, all of it dirty as a pigpen and stinking so bad you can hardly breathe in there. Nothing unusual—considering who and what lives here—except these."

He held up a stack of books. Thomas Cornstalk stared. "Books?" he said in amazement. "What's Old Man Alabama doing with books? I know for a fact he can't read."

"Who knows? Maybe got them to wipe his ass with. Ran out of pine cones or whatever he uses." Charlie Badwater sat down on the edge of the porch and began flipping through the books. "Looks like he stole them from the school over at Rocky Mountain. Old bastard's a sneak thief on top of everything else."

"What kind of books are they? The kind with pictures of women? Maybe he's been out in the woods by himself too long."

"No, look, this is a history book. And this one has a bunch of pictures of old-time sailing ships, like in the pirate movies. Now why in the world—"

Charlie Badwater sat staring at the books for a couple of minutes, and then he tossed them aside and stood up. "I'm going to look around some more," he said.

Thomas Cornstalk followed him as he walked around the cabin. The area in back of the cabin looked much the same as the front yard, but then both men saw the blackened spot where a small fire had been burning. Large rocks had been placed in a circle around the fire place, and some of the rocks were marked with strange symbols or patterns. A tiny wisp of smoke, no greater than that from a cigarette, curled up from the ashes.

Charlie Badwater walked over the held his hand above the ashes, not quite touching the remains of the fire. Then he crouched way down and began studying the ground closely, slowly examining the entire area within the circle of stones and working his way back toward where Thomas Cornstalk stood silently watching. This was one of Charlie Badwater's most famous specialties: reading sign. People said he could track a catfish across a lake.

"He came out here," he said at last, "barefoot as usual, and he walked straight to that spot by the fire and walked around it—at least four times, it's pretty confused there—and then, well . . .."

"What? Where'd he go?"

"Far as I can tell, he just flew away. Or disappeared or something. He didn't walk back out of that circle of rocks, anyway. And whatever he did, it wasn't long ago that he did it. Those ashes are still warm."

A small dry voice said, "Looking for the old man?"

Thomas Cornstalk turned around. A great big blue jay was sitting on the collapsing eaves of Old Man Alabama's shack.

"Because," the jay said, speaking in that sarcastic way jays have, "I don't think you're going to find him. Not anytime soon, anyway. He left sort of drastic."

"Did you see what happened?" Thomas Cornstalk asked the jay.

Charlie Badwater had turned around too by now. He was looking from Thomas Cornstalk to the say and back again. There was an odd look on his face; he seemed almost wistful. For all his power, all the fantastic things he could do, he had never been granted the ability to talk with animals—which is not something you can learn; you have the gift or you don't—and there are few things that can make a person feel quite as shut out as watching somebody like Thomas Cornstalk having a conversation with bird or beast.

"Hey," the jay said, "I got trapped in here when the old son of a bitch put that whatever-the-hell around the cabin. Tried to fly out, hit something like a wall in the air, damn near broke my beak. Thought I was going to starve to death in here, till you guys showed up. Tell your buddy thanks for turning the damn thing off."

"Ask him where Old Man Alabama went," Charlie Badwater said.

"I saw the whole thing," the jay said, not waiting for the translation. Thomas Cornstalk noticed that; he had suspected for some time that blue jays could understand Cherokee, even if they pretended not to. "Old guy walked out there mumbling to himself, stomped around the fire a little, made a lot of that racket that you humans call singing—hey, no offense, but even a boat-tailed grackle can sing better than that—and then all of a sudden he threw a bunch of stuff on the fire. There was a big puff of smoke and when it cleared away he was just as gone as you please."

"I knew it," Charlie Badwater said, when this had been interpreted for him. He squatted down by the fire and began picking up handfuls of ashes and blackened twigs and dirt, running the material through his fingers and sniffing it like a dog and occasionally putting a pinch in his mouth to taste it. "Ah," he said finally. "All right, I know what he used. Don't understand why—there are some combinations in there that shouldn't work at all, by any of the rules I know—but like I said, what works is what works."

He stood up and looked at the jay. "Ask him if he can remember the song."

"Sure," the jay said. "No problem. Not sure I can sing it, of course—"

"I'll be right back," Charlie Badwater said, heading for the cabin. A minute later Thomas Cornstalk heard him rummaging around inside. The jay said, "Was it something I said?"

In a little while Charlie Badwater came back, his arms full of buckskin bags and brown paper sacks. "Lucky for us he had plenty of everything," he said, and squatted down on the ground and took off his old black hat and turned it upside down on his knees and began taking things out of the bags: mostly dried leaves and weeds and roots, but other items too, not all of them easily identifiable. At one point Thomas Cornstalk was nearly certain he recognized a couple of human finger bones.

"All right," Charlie Badwater said, setting the hat carefully next to the dead fire and straightening up. "Now how does that song go?"

That part wasn't easy. The jay had a great deal of trouble forming some of the sounds; a crow would have been better at this, or maybe a mockingbird. The words weren't in any language Thomas Cornstalk had ever heard, and Charlie Badwater said he'd never heard a song remotely like this one.

At last, after many false starts and failed tries, Charlie Badwater got all the way through the song and the jay said, "That's it. He's got it perfect. No accounting for tastes, I guess."

Charlie Badwater was already piling up sticks from the pile of wood beside the ring of stones. He got out his lighter and in a few minutes the fire was crackling and flickering away. "*Ehena*," he said over his shoulder. "Ready when you are."

"You want me in on this?"

"Of course. Let's go, Thomas. *Nula.*"

Thomas Cornstalk wasn't at all happy about this, but he walked across the circle to stand beside Charlie Badwater, who had picked up his hat and was holding it in front of him in both hands.

"This I've got to see," the jay commented from its perch on the roof. It had moved up to the ridgepole, probably for a better view. "You guys are crazier than the old man."

Charlie Badwater circled the fire four times, counterclockwise, like a stomp dancer, with Thomas Cornstalk pacing nervously behind him. After the fourth orbit he stopped, facing the sun, and began singing the song the jay had taught him. It sounded different now, somehow. The hair was standing up on Thomas Cornstalk's neck and arms.

Suddenly Charlie Badwater emptied the hat's contents onto the fire. There was a series of sharp fizzing and sputtering noises, and a big cloud of dense gray smoke surged up and surrounded both men. It was so thick that Thomas Cornstalk couldn't see an inch in front of his face; it was like having his head under very muddy water, or being covered with a heavy gray blanket.

Other things were happening, too. The ground underfoot was beginning to shift and become soft; it felt like quicksand, yet he wasn't sinking into it. His skin prickled all over, not painfully but pretty unpleasantly, and he felt a little sick to his stomach.

The grayness got darker and darker, while the ground fell away completely, until Thomas Cornstalk felt himself to be floating through a great black nothingness. For some reason he was no longer frightened; he simply assumed that he had died and this was what it was like when you went to the spirit world. *"Ni, Jali,"* he called out.

"Ayuh ahni, Tami." The voice sounded close by, but strange, as if Charlie Badwater had fallen down a well.

"Gado nidagal'stani? What's going to happen?"

"Nigal'stisguh," came the cheerful reply. "Whatever . . ."

Thomas Cornstalk had no idea how long the darkness and the floating sensation lasted. His sense of time, the whole idea of time itself, had vanished in that first billow of smoke. But then suddenly the darkness turned to dazzling light and there was something solid under his feet again. Caught by surprise, he swayed and staggered and fell heavily forward, barely getting his arms up in time to protect his face.

He lay half-stunned for a moment, getting the breath back into his lungs and the sight back to his eyes. There was hard smooth planking against his hands; it felt like his own cabin floor, in fact, and at first he thought he must somehow be back home. Maybe the whole thing was a dream and he'd just fallen out of bed . . . but he rolled over and saw bright blue sky above him, crisscrossed by a lot of ropes and long poles. He sat up and saw that he was on the deck of a ship.

It was a ship such as he had only seen in books and movies: the old-fashioned kind, made of wood, with masts and sails instead of an engine. Off beyond the railing, blue water stretched unbroken to the horizon.

Beside him, Charlie Badwater's voice said, "Well, I have to admit this wasn't what I expected."

Thomas Cornstalk turned his head in time to see Charlie Badwater getting to his feet. That seemed like a good idea, so he did it too. The deck was tilted to one side and the whole ship was rolling and pitching, gently but distinctly, with the motion of the sea. Thomas Cornstalk's stomach began to feel a trifle queasy. He hadn't been aboard a ship since his long-ago hitch in the marines, but he remembered about seasickness. He closed his eyes for a second and forced his stomach to settle down. This was no time to lose control of any part of himself.

He said, "Where the hell are we, Charlie?"

From behind them came a harsh cackle. "Where? Wrong question."

The words were in English. The voice was dry and high-pitched, with an old man's quaver. Both men said, "Oh, shit," and turned around almost in unison.

Old Man Alabama was standing on the raised deck at the stern of the ship, looking down at them. His arms were folded and his long hair streamed and fluttered in the wind. His mouth was pulled back at the corners in the closest thing to a smile Thomas Cornstalk had ever seen on his face.

"Not *where*," he went on, and cackled. "You ought to ask, *when* are we? Of course there's some *where* in it too—"

The horrible smile disappeared all at once. "Say," Old Man Alabama said in a different voice, "how did you two get here, anyway?"

"Same way you did," Charlie Badwater said, also in English. "It wasn't very hard."

"You're a liar." Old Man Alabama spat hard on the deck. "It took me years to learn the secret. How could you two stupid Cherokees—"

"A little bird told us," Thomas Cornstalk interrupted. He knew it was too easy but he couldn't resist.

"I used the same routine you did," Charlie Badwater said, "only I put in a following-and-finding *igawesdi*. You ought to have known you couldn't lose me, old man. What are you up to, anyway?"

Old Man Alabama unfolded his long arms and waved them aimlessly about. It made him look remarkably like a spider monkey Thomas Cornstalk had seen in the Tulsa zoo.

"Crazy Old Man Alabama," he screeched. "I know what you all said about me behind my back—"

"Hey," Charlie Badwater said, "I said it to your face too. Plenty of times."

"Loony old witch," Old Man Alabama went on, ignoring him. "Up there on his mountain, doing nickel-and-dime hexes and love charms, comes into town every now and then and scares the little kids, couldn't witch his way out of a wet paper sack. Yeah, well, look what the crazy old man went and did."

He stopped and shook himself all over. "I did it, too," he said. His voice had suddenly gone softer; it was hard to understand the words. "Nobody else ever even tried it, but I did it. Me."

He stared down at them for a minute, evidently waiting for them to ask him what exactly he'd done. When they didn't, he threw his hands way up over his head again and put his head back and screamed, "*Time!* I found out how to fly through time! Look around you, damn it—they don't have ships like this in the year we come from. Don't you know what you're looking at, here?"

Thomas Cornstalk was already glancing up and down the empty decks, up into the rigging and . . . empty decks? "What the hell," he said. "What happened to the people? The sailors and all?"

"Right," Charlie Badwater said. "You didn't sail this thing out here by yourself. Hell, you can't even paddle a canoe. I've seen you try."

Old Man Alabama let off another of his demented laughs. "There," he said, gesturing out over the rail. "There they are, boys. Fine crew they make now, huh?"

Thomas Cornstalk looked where the old man was pointing, but he couldn't see anything but the open sea and sky and a bunch of seagulls squawking and flapping around above the ship's wake. Then he got it. "Aw, hell," he said. "You didn't."

"Should have been here a little while ago," Old Man Alabama chortled, "when they were still learning how to fly. Two of them crashed into the water and a shark got them. Hee hee."

"But why?" Charlie Badwater said. "I mean, the part about traveling into the past, okay, I hate to admit it but I'm impressed. But then fooling around with this kind of childishness, turning a lot of poor damn sailors into sea birds? I know you hate white people, but—"

"Hah! Not just any bunch of sailors," Old Man Alabama said triumphantly. "Not just any white people, either. This is where it all started, you dumb blanket-asses! And I'm the one who went back and fixed it!"

He began to sing, a dreadful weird keening that rose and fell over a four-tone scale, without recognizable words. Charlie Badwater and Thomas Cornstalk looked at each other and then back at the old man. Thomas Cornstalk said, "You mean this ship—"

"Yes! It's old *Columbus's* ship! Now the white bastards won't come at all!" Old Man Alabama's face was almost glowing. "And it was me, me, me that stopped them! Poor cracked Old Man Alabama, turns out to be the greatest Indian in history, that's all—"

"Uh, excuse me," Thomas Cornstalk said, "but if this is Columbus's ship, where are the other two?"

"Other two what?" Old Man Alabama asked irritably.

"Other two ships, you old fool," Charlie Badwater said. "Columbus had three ships."

"That's right," Thomas Cornstalk agreed. "I remember from school."

Old Man Alabama was looking severely pissed off. "Are you sure? Damn it, I want to a lot of trouble to make sure I got the right one. Gave this white kid from Tahlequah a set of bear claws and a charm to make his girlfriend put out—little bastard drove a hard bargain—for finding me the picture in that book. Told me what year it was and everything. I'm telling you, this is it." Old Man Alabama stomped his bare feet on the deck. "Columbus's ship. The *Mayflower*."

"You ignorant sack of possum poop," Charlie Badwater said. "You don't know squat, do you? Columbus's ship was named the *Santa Maria*. The *Mayflower* was a totally different bunch of *yonegs*. Came ashore up in Maine or somewhere like that."

"These schoolkids nowadays, they're liable to tell you anything," Thomas Cornstalk remarked. "Half of them can't read any better than you do. My sister's girl is going with a white boy, I swear he don't know any more than the average fencepost."

Old Man Alabama was fairly having a fit now. "No," he howled, flailing the air with his long skinny arms. "No, no, it's a lie—"

Charlie Badwater sighed and shook his head. "I bet this isn't even the *Mayflower*," he said to Thomas Cornstalk. "Let's have a look around."

They walked up and down the deserted main deck, looking. There didn't seem to be anything to tell them the name of the ship.

"I think they put the name on the stern," Thomas Cornstalk said. "You know, the hind end of the ship. They did when I was in the Corps, anyway."

They climbed a ladder and crossed the quarterdeck, paying no attention to Old Man Alabama, who was now lying on the deck beating the planks with his fists. "Hang on to my belt or something, will you?" Thomas Cornstalk requested. "I don't swim all that good."

With Charlie Badwater holding him by the belt, he hung over the railing and looked at the name painted in big letters across the ship's stern. It was hard to make out at that angle, and upside down besides, but finally he figured it out. "*Mary Celeste*," he called back over his shoulder. "That's the name. The *Mary Celeste.*"

Charlie Badwater looked at Old Man Alabama. "*Mayflower.* Columbus. My Native American ass," he said disgustedly. "I should have let those white guys hang him, back last year."

Thomas Cornstalk straightened up and leaned back against the rail. "Well," he said, "what do we do now?"

Charlie Badwater shrugged. "Go back where we came from. When we came from."

"Can you do it?"

"Anything this old lunatic can do, I can figure out how to undo."

Thomas Cornstalk nodded, feeling much relieved. "Do we take him along?"

"We better. No telling what the consequences might be if we left him." Charlie Badwater stared at the writhing body on the deck at his feet. "You know the worst part? It was a hell of a great idea he had. Too bad it had to occur to an idiot."

"*Nasgi nusdi*," Thomas Cornstalk said. "That's how it is."

He looked along the empty decks once again. "You think anybody's ever going to find this boat? Come along in another ship, see this one floating out here in the middle of the ocean, nobody on board . . . man," he said, "that's going to make some people wonder."

"People need to wonder now and then," Charlie Badwater said. "It's good for their circulation."

He grinned at Thomas Cornstalk. "Come on," he said. "Let's peel this old fool off the deck and go home."

AUTHOR'S NOTE:

There really was an Old Man Alabama; he was a famous and greatly feared sorcerer in the old Creek Nation, in the early part of the 20th century. My adopted grandfather, the late Louis Littlecoon Oliver, saw him several times as a boy. The original article, however, was a much less whimsical figure.

This one was originally written for *Tales From the Great*

Turtle, which was supposed to be a collection of American Indian fantasy stories. The anthology itself was a disappointment to me—contrary to what I had been told, almost all the stories were by white authors, quite a few were seriously inauthentic, and several were actually offensive—and I was pretty upset about it; but when I talked with Roger he said, "That's just something that happens, in this business. Take the money and quit worrying about it. Your story will be remembered after the anthology is forgotten."

Which proved to be the case; GAOMA subsequently appeared in *Year's Best Science Fiction* and got a bit of critical notice in surprising places (*"Quel humor devastateur!"* cried one French critic; I am not either making this up) and now here it is again.

ELVIS BEARPAW'S LUCK

Grandfather Ninekiller said, "A man always has the right to try to change his luck."

He said that right after I told him how my cousin Marvin Badwater had suddenly dumped Madonna Hummingbird, after both families had all but officially agreed on the match, and brought home a Comanche girl whose name nobody could even pronounce. Grandfather never had been one for that sort of gossip, but it was two years since he'd died and naturally he was interested in any news I might bring him when I came to put tobacco on his grave.

"The right to try to change his luck," he said again, in a kind of distant satisfied way, as if he liked the sound of what he had said. That's one thing about ancestors: they can be awfully repetitious. I guess they've got a lot of time on their hands in the spirit world, with nothing much to do but study up these wise-sounding little one-liners.

Anyway I said, "I don't know about that, *eduda*. What about what happened to Elvis Bearpaw?"

"I said a man's got the right to *try*," Grandfather said, not a bit bothered by my disrespectful interruption. There was a time when he'd have taken my head off, but being dead seems to have mellowed him some. "Whether he succeeds or not, now, that's another patch of pokeweed."

He laughed, an old man's spidery-dry cackle. "And then, too, it's not always easy to know whether you're changing it upwards or down. As in the case of the said Elvis Bearpaw . . . remember that, do you, *chooch*?"

"How could I forget?" I said, surprised.

"Hey," Grandfather said, "you were just a kid."

I was, too, but I'd have gotten mad as a wet owl if anybody had said so at the time. I was all of twelve years old that spring, and I saw myself as for all valid purposes a full-grown Cherokee warrior—hadn't the great Harley Davidson Oosahwe killed those three Osage slave-raiders when he was only thirteen? Warrior hell, I figured I was practically Council material, barring a few petty technicalities.

I might or might not have heard, in the days leading up to

Game time, that Elvis Bearpaw was to be the Deer Clan's player that year. If I did, it wasn't something I paid much attention to. For one thing, being of the *Anijisqua*—Bird Clan—I had no personal interest in the matter; and for another, my mind was on a different aspect of the approaching Game days. This was the last year I was going to be eligible for the boys' blowgun contest; next year I'd be in the young men's class, and, unless Redbird Christie stepped on a rattlesnake in the next twelve months, getting my brains beat out like everybody else. So I was determined to win this year, and I was practicing my ass off every spare moment.

But for all my puckering and puffing, I wasn't exactly unaware of the goings-on around me. That would have been pretty damn difficult to say the least; back then, Game time still meant something, things were happening. Not like now. . . .

Well, maybe I shouldn't say that. Maybe everything just seems larger and more exciting when you're a kid; or maybe a man's memory likes to improve on reality. But it does seem to me that the Game time isn't what it used to be. It's almost as if people are merely going through the motions. Is it just me?

"Is it just me," I said to Grandfather Ninekiller, "or has Game time gone downhill in the last few years? Of course I'm not talking about the Game itself," I added hastily. You don't want to seem to disparage sacred matters when you're talking with an ancestor. "I mean, that's still the center of the whole year, always has been, always will be—"

"Wasn't always," Grandfather interrupted. "Back in the old days, in the Yuasa times, it wasn't at all like it is now. You know that, *chooch*."

"Well, yes." I knew, all right; he'd told me often enough, along with the other stories about the history of the People. Though there's always been a sort of not-quite-real quality to those old tales, for me at least; I've never been sure how much of that Yuasa business to take seriously. They even say there was a time when the People didn't have the Game at all, and who can imagine that?

"Anyway," I went on, "I meant the whole affair—the dances, the contests, the feeds and the giveaways—all the stuff that goes on when the People get together for the Game. I can't help feeling like there used to be a lot more to it, you know? But then I've noticed a lot of things seem to sort of shrink as you get older."

Grandfather snorted. "Tell me about it, *chooch*," he said bitterly. "You don't know the half of it yet."

Whatever . . . and be all that as it may, I recall that Game season as possibly the best of my lifetime. The sky was clear and the sun bright every day, with no sign of the storms and drizzly spells that so often come with the spring in the Cherokee hill country. Even the wind was at least reasonably warm—though of course it never stopped blowing, this being, after all, Oklahoma.

The weather was so fine, in fact, that some of the elders came to confer with Grandfather Ninekiller about whether it was really necessary to set out the broken glass and the ax heads to turn aside possible tornadoes. He told them probably not, but they went ahead and did it all the same; they said tradition was tradition and you couldn't be too careful about tornadoes, but I figured it was mainly because they'd already made the trip over to the ruins of Old Tahlequah to get the glass.

The tornadoes never showed up, but the people sure did. Oh, my, yes, the people, the People. . . .

They came from all directions, all day every day and sometimes at night, too. They began coming as much as half a moon before the Game days began, hoping to get good spots to camp— or, if they had the right connections, houseguest privileges with Cherokee families—but it wasn't long before all the regular campgrounds were full and you began finding people making camp in the damnedest places. Like this family of Pawnees my father found sleeping amid the broken walls of the old Park Hill post office.

They came from the Five Nations and the Seven Allied Tribes, but they also came from other tribes that had their Games at other times of the year. It was widely known that it was worth the journey just to enjoy Cherokee hospitality and sample the entertainment and do some wagon-tailgate trading.

Mostly they came from the Plains tribes to the west: Comanches and Kiowas and Apaches and Caddos and a few Cheyennes and Arapahos, all riding splendid horses and wearing beaded finery and the mysterious emblems of the peyote church. But there were also Quapaws and Otoes and Kaws and Poncas and lots of others. Osages, too, five of the big bastards, riding in a wagon made from the body of an old Cadillac car, come down to see how the enemy lived and do a little scouting, their lives safe during the Game-time truce.

There was even a delegation from the Washita Nation, of the far-off Arkansas hills, decked out in really weird outfits—fringed vests and pants, goofy-looking high-topped moccasins, quartz crystals big as your penis hanging around their necks—and spouting loony crap about "previous lives" and "channeling" to anybody they could corner. General opinion was that there wasn't a single drop of the real People's blood among the lot of them, and looking at them I could believe it, but nobody really objected all that much. If nothing else they were good for a laugh.

And after all, though nobody talks much about it, the truth is that most of the People have more white blood than they like to admit.

"It's not only because we took in so many of the surviving whites, after things went to hell for them," Grandfather Ninekiller said, the only time I ever raised the subject with him. "Clear back in Yuasa times, there were lots of mixed-bloods. Toward the end they outnumbered the full-bloods in a lot of tribes. Cherokees damn near screwed ourselves white, in fact, before it was over. How do you think your Grandmother Badwater got that red hair?"

"What about you, *eduda*?" I asked.

"Oh, I'm full-blood Cherokee," he said immediately. "And so were both of my parents. But my grandmother on my father's side, now, she was part white."

"Elvis Bearpaw is playing for the Deer Clan."

That was my uncle Kennedy Badwater, speaking to Grandfather Ninekiller. It was the day before the beginning of the Game period, and that was the first I can actually recall hearing about the honor that had fallen upon Elvis Bearpaw.

Grandfather said, "Well, he's always been an ambitious young man. This could be the big breakthrough for him."

They both laughed, and I joined in, in a quiet sort of way, from where I sat on the hard-packed ground next to Grandfather's seat. I wasn't, as I've said, all that interested in the subject, but there wasn't much else to do but listen in on the old men's conversation while I waited for Grandfather to need my assistance.

He'd been blind for three years by that time, and I'd lived with him the whole while, brought him the food that my mother cooked for him, filled and lit his pipe, helped him find various things around his cabin—not very often; he had a memory like a wolf trap—and generally served as his eyes and an extra set of hands. I'd helped him with certain items when he made medicine, too; and I'd led him, or rather accompanied him, around the village and to and from the various ceremonies and official functions where his duties took him. I'd sat at his feet at more Council meetings than I could have added up, hearing speech after speech on questions of war and peace and tribal politics, getting myself an unmatchable education but bored silly by it all at the time. . . .

"Word is he went to see Old Man Alabama as soon as they gave him the news," my uncle said. "Wonder what he did that for."

Old Man Alabama was a famous medicine man—a lot of people said witch—who lived on an island down on Lake Tenkiller, a little way above the old dam. He claimed to be the last living member of the Alabama tribe. His power was said to be tremendous and most people were afraid to even talk about him.

"Huh," Grandfather grunted. "Wonder why anybody would go to see that old nutcase. Old Man Alabama's the kind who give mad sorcerers a bad name."

I took a hardwood dart from the cane-joint quiver at my waist and held it up and sighted along it, checking for straightness. Not that there was any chance of finding anything wrong, as many times as I'd inspected those darts in the last few days, but it was something to do. My blowgun lay across my lap and I could have taken a few practice shots at some handy target while the old men talked, but it would have been a little impolite and I was trying to make a good impression on my uncle, who always gave me some sort of present at Game time.

"Looking for an angle," my uncle said.

"You know the old Cherokee saying," Grandfather said. "'Watch out what you look for. You might find it.'"

"Is that an old Cherokee saying?" my uncle said, grinning.

"Must be," Grandfather said, straight-faced. "I said it, and I'm an old Cherokee."

The following morning, out at the great field, they had the opening ceremony. As the ball of the sun cleared the horizon, the Master of the Fire, old Gogisgi Wildcat, lit the sacred fire. Smoke rose against the brightening sky and Grandfather Ninekiller raised his voice in a song so ancient that even he didn't know what half the words meant; and when he finished, to a shouted chorus of "*Wado!*" from the assembled Cherokee elders, the Game days had at last begun.

Grandfather and I watched the start of the cross-country foot race, and the first heats of the shorter races—all right, I watched and gave Grandfather a running description—and then drifted over to take in the opening innings of the women's softball series. After that we walked slowly back across the fields to the outskirts of the town, where women tended fires and steam rose from big pots and the air was fairly edible with the smells of food. People called out invitations to come sample this or that—*kenuche*, corn soup, chili—and Grandfather generally tried to oblige; I couldn't see where he put it all in that skinny old frame. I didn't dare load up, myself, what with the blowgun competition coming up in the afternoon; but I did allow myself to be tempted by some remarkably fine wild grape dumplings, or maybe by the pretty Paint Clan girl who offered them to me. I was starting to take an interest in that girl business, those days.

I might as well have gone ahead and stuffed myself, for all the difference it made. That was how I felt, anyway, after a sudden puff of wind made me miss the swinging target completely in the final round of the blowgun shoot and I wound up losing out to Duane Kingfisher from up near Rocky Ford. Now, looking back, second place doesn't seem so bad—especially when I remember that the Osages killed Duane four years later, when he went on that damn fool horse-stealing raid—but at the time all I could see was that I'd lost. I felt as if I'd been booted in the stomach.

I was still feeling pretty rotten that night at the stomp dance. I don't even think I'd have gone if I hadn't had to accompany Grandfather Ninekiller. Sitting beside him under the Bird Clan arbor, watching the dancers circling the fire and listening to the singing and the *shaka-shaka-shaka* of the turtle shell rattles on the women's legs, I felt none of the usual joy, only a dull mean dog-kicking anger—at the wind, at Duane Kingfisher, mostly at myself.

After a while my Uncle Kennedy appeared from out of the darkness and sat down beside me. "*'Siyo, chooch*," he said to me, after exchanging greetings with Grandfather.

I said, "*'Siyo, eduji*," in a voice about as cheerful and friendly as an open grave. But he didn't appear to notice.

"Damn," he said, watching the dancers, "there's Elvis Bearpaw leading, big as you please."

Now he mentioned it, I saw that Elvis Bearpaw was in fact leading this song, circling the fire at the head of the spiral line of dancers, calling out the old words in a strong high voice. His face shone in the firelight as he crouched and turned and waved his hands. He was a husky, good-looking young guy, supposed to be something of a devil with the women. I don't guess I'd ever even traded greetings with him; his family and mine moved in a different circles. Watching him now, though, I had to admit that he could sure as hell sing and dance.

"Don't think I ever saw him lead before," Uncle Kennedy said. "How about that?"

On the other side of me Grandfather made a noise that was part snort and part grunt. He wasn't a big admirer of the Bearpaws, whom he considered pushy assholes who'd lucked into more wealth and power than they knew what to do with.

"Saw you in the blowgun shoot today, *chooch*," my uncle remarked. "Tough luck there. But hell, you still came in second. Better than I ever did."

He was taking something from his belt, from up under the tail of his ribbon shirt. "Here," he said. "Didn't figure to give you this till later on, but you look like you could use some cheering up."

It was a knife, a fine big one with a deer horn handle and a wide businesslike blade; a man's knife, not a kid's whittler like the one I'd been carrying, and somebody had done some first-class work putting a glass-smooth finish on that lovely steel. . . . I said, "*Wado, eduji*," but my voice didn't come out entirely right.

"Got some good stiff saddle leather at home," my uncle said. "Make you a sheath for that thing, you bring it by sometime. Boy," he added admiringly. "Look at old Elvis go."

Out by the fire Elvis Bearpaw was getting down and winding up, his body rocking from side to side. There was something strange in his face, I thought, or maybe that was just a trick of the firelight. He called out a phrase and the other men responded: "*Ho-na-wi-ye, ho-na-wi-ye.*" And *shaka-shaka-shaka* went the turtle shells.

The next few days were a regular whirlwind of feasting and dancing and singing and sports, sports, sports: all the things needed to make a twelve-year-old boy decide that when he dies he wants to go some place where it's like this all the time.

I went to everything I could, with or without Grandfather, who was having to make a lot of heavy medicine in preparation for the approaching Game. I played stickball with the other Cherokee boys, of course, and even scored a couple of goals, though in the end the Choctaws beat us by one. I watched Uncle Kennedy win the rifle shoot and then saw him lose everything he'd won, betting on a horse race between the Seminoles and the Kickapoos. I went to the cornstalk shoot—going to have to try that myself next year, now I was big enough to pull a serious bow—and the tomahawk throw, the horseshoe matches and the wild-cow-roping contest, even the canoe race down on the river. And the bicycle race, the very last year they ever had it; it was getting impossible to find parts to keep those old machines rolling, and the leather-rope tires they had to use kept coming off in the turns and causing mass crashes. What was the name of that Wichita kid who won? I forget.

And every night at the stomp dance ground there was Elvis Bearpaw out by the fire, singing and dancing his ass off, always with that funny strained expression on his face. Uncle Kennedy said he looked like he thought something might be gaining on him.

There was no stomp dance the night before Game day, naturally; too many of the dance leaders and other important persons would be spending the night taking medicine and making smoke and otherwise purifying themselves, getting ready for their parts in the Game.

That included Grandfather Ninekiller, who had to do some things so secret and dangerous that I wasn't even allowed to be in the cabin while he did them. I helped him lay out a few medicine items, made sure there was plenty of firewood in the box, and got the hell out without having to be told twice. That sort of business always scared me half to death. Still does.

I was supposed to be staying at my parents' cabin that night, but I didn't really want to go, not any sooner than I could help anyway. I'd never gotten along with them worth a damn; that might have been why they'd been so happy to send me off to live with the old man.

I stood for a moment thinking about it, and then I turned the other way and walked away from the town, off across the moon white fields, following the distant *boom-boom* of a big Plains drum. Some of our Western visitors were having one of their pow-wow dances that night. I wasn't all that fond of that damn howling racket the Plains People call singing, but it would beat sitting around all evening listening to questions about the old man's health and complaints about my failure to visit more often and stories about how smart my younger brothers were.

I stayed at the powwow till pretty late, having more fun than I'd expected—all right, that Kiowa music has a good beat, you can dance to it—and hanging out with some of my buddies who'd sneaked off from their own families. Along about midnight I met a Creek girl named Hillary Screechowl and after a certain amount of persuasive bullshit on my part she took a little walk with me off into the woods. Where nothing really major took place, but we did get far enough to clear up a few questions I'd been wondering about lately.

It was really late, maybe halfway between midnight and daybreak, when I finally left the powwow area and headed back toward town. The moon had almost gone down but the stars were big and white, and I had no trouble finding my way across the darkened fields. The town itself was invisible against the blackness of the tree line, but a good many fires still burned there.

I took a shortcut through a narrow stand of trees and found myself near the Game grounds. For no particular reason—still in no hurry to get to my parents' place, I guess—I changed course and walked along next to the south border of the grounds. I'd never before seen the place on the night before a Game, with everything laid out in readiness and nobody around. It was an interesting sight, but a little on the spooky side.

The long tables and benches shone faintly in the starlight, their wood scrubbed white over the years by generations of laboring women and wagonloads of wood ash soap. Everything was already in place for the players, of course, as was the ceremonial equipment up on the big packed-earth platform at the eastern end of the grounds. It had all been smoked and doctored late the previous day, in a ceremony closed to everyone except the chief medicine men of the twelve participating tribes, and covered with sheets of white cloth that would have paid for a whole herd of horses at any trade meet in Oklahoma.

All the people had gone home now, except for a couple of guards who were supposed to be keeping an eye on things. I wondered why they hadn't challenged me already. Sitting on their butts somewhere nearby, no doubt, having a smoke or even asleep.

I felt a surge of righteous twelve-year-old indignation at the thought. Not that there was any serious risk of intruders, let alone thieves—even Osage raiders wouldn't dare cross that sacred line—but still, when you had the honor of standing guard over the grounds, on the night before a Game at that . . . .

Then I saw Elvis Bearpaw coming out of the woods.

I didn't recognize him at first; he was no more than a vague shadow, half a bow shot away. For a moment I thought it was one of the guards, but then the starlight fell on his face and I recognized him. Without quite knowing why, I stepped back into the deep shadow beneath the trees, watching.

He was moving fast, almost at a run, and he was crouched down low like a bear dancer. He crossed the white lime medicine line without so much as an instant's hesitation and dived in between the nearest rows of playing tables. The sacrilege was so enormous that the breath went out of me and my vision went blurry, and when I could see and breathe again Elvis Bearpaw had disappeared.

I don't know why I didn't call out for the guards; the idea never even occurred to me. Instead I stood there for what felt like a long time, scanning the rows of tables and the open ground all around trying to figure out where he'd gone and what he was up to.

And I'd almost decided that I'd lost him, that he'd left the grounds as sneakily as he'd come, but then I finally thought to watch the Cherokee players' table, up in the middle of the front row and directly in front of the big platform. Sure enough, I was just in time to spot him when he popped up.

He didn't pop very high. All I could see was the top half of his head, silhouetted against the whiteness of the tabletop, and his hands as they reached up and then vanished beneath the white cloth.

By now my heart was trying to bang a hole in my chest and the blood was roaring in my ears like a buffalo stampede. I watched in paralyzed horror, waiting for lightning to strike or the earth to open or whatever was going to happen. Yet nothing did, even though now I saw that Elvis Bearpaw was doing something so unspeakably blasphemous that my mind couldn't take it in. A moment later he ducked back out of sight, and then after almost no time he appeared again from among the tables, running flat out back the way he'd come, into the shelter of the trees. He didn't make a sound the whole time.

It took a little while before I could move. At last I got my feet unstuck and began walking again, toward the town and my parents' cabin. When I got there the place was dark and I let myself in as quietly as I could, but my mother was waiting for me and she woke my father up and they both gave me a good deal of shit. Under the circumstances I hardly noticed.

Early next morning I went back to Grandfather's cabin. I hadn't slept much even after my parents finally let me go to bed. My feet felt like somebody else's and the light hurt my eyes.

"Damn, *chooch,*" Grandfather said, "what's happened to you? You look like you were rode hard and put up wet."

So I told him about Elvis Bearpaw and what I'd seen him do. I'd been planning to tell him anyway; I just hadn't been sure when.

"*Doyuka?*" he said when I was finished. "You're sure?"

"No," I answered honestly. "I mean, I know I saw him and I know he went onto the grounds and in among the tables, and he did something. Whether he did what I thought I saw him do— well, the light was bad and I wasn't very close. And," I added, "I don't really want to believe it."

"Huh." His lined old face was as unreadable as ever, but there was something a little strange in the way he stood. His hands made a quick restless motion. "You tell anybody else?" he asked.

"No."

"Good." He turned his blind eyes toward me and gave me a toothless smile. "You always did have sense, *chooch.* Too bad certain other people don't have as much."

I said, "What are you going to do, *eduda?*"

He looked surprised. "Do? Why, you know perfectly well what I'm fixing to do, *chooch*. Right up there on that stage, in front of the whole world."

"I mean about Elvis Bearpaw," I said, a little impatiently. "Will you tell the Chief and the other elders? Will they stop the Game, or—" I flapped my hands. "Or what?"

"Oh, no, no. Can't do that, *chooch*. Too late now," he said. "No telling what might happen. All we can do is let things go on, the way they're supposed to. Afterward—" He shrugged. "Come on. Time we got ourselves out to the grounds."

We began walking in that direction. We weren't the only ones. People were pouring out of the town and the campgrounds like swarming bees, all of them heading toward the Game grounds. They all recognized Grandfather Ninekiller, though, and gave us plenty of respectful space so that despite the crowds around us we were able to talk freely.

"Anyway," Grandfather said as we passed the council house, "you forget my position. Once the sun's come up on Game day, I'm not allowed to talk to anybody, even the Chief, about the Game or the players. If I try to tell your story, I'll be in the shit nearly as deep as you-know-who. Shouldn't even be talking with you about it, strictly speaking." He rested his hand on my shoulder. "But what the hell."

It seemed pretty strange to be picking at fine points of Game protocol, after Elvis Bearpaw had practically pissed on everything and everybody. But I didn't say so.

Grandfather's hand tightened on my shoulder. "Don't worry too much about it, *chooch*," he said in a softer voice. "These things have a way of working themselves out."

At the Game grounds we waited outside the medicine line until Grandfather's two young assistants came and led him away toward the big platform. I watched them help him up the steps, and felt thankful that I wasn't allowed to go with him. Once inside the line, nobody was allowed to leave, or eat food, or drink anything but water, until the Game was ended.

By this time the surrounding area was covered with people, from the medicine line—or rather a little way back; most people had enough sense to leave a couple of bowstring lengths' worth of safe space—clear back to the edge of the woods. And into the woods, too; there were kids of all sizes, and quite a few grown men, sitting perched up in the trees like a flock of huge weird birds.

Most of the people sat on the ground, or on whatever seats they'd brought along; it was considered ill-mannered to stand, since that could block somebody's view. For the most part they sat in bunches of family and friends, and nearly every group had a couple of big baskets of food and water, because the no-eating rule didn't apply to the people watching from outside the line, and there was no reason to pass up the chance to make a little picnic of the occasion. There was a lot of laughing and talking and passing food and water gourds around; in fact the noise was pretty intense if you let yourself notice it.

Uncle Kennedy and his bunch had saved me a place, down near the southeast corner of the grounds, close enough to hear and see everything. I sat down, accepted a roasted turkey leg from Aunt Diana, wiggled my skinny young rump into a reasonably comfortable fit with the ground, and had myself a good long look around.

There was plenty to see, for sure. Out on the playing field, the players were already standing at their places behind the long tables, facing the platform and, roughly, the still-rising sun. Front and center, naturally, was the table of the Host Nation, manned by the seven players who represented the seven clans of the Cherokee nation. Elvis Bearpaw was right in there, standing straight as a bowstring. I couldn't make out any particular expression on his face, but then all the players were looking very straight-faced and serious, in accordance with the Game manners.

On their left stood the Seminole players, in their bright patchwork jackets, while on the other side of the Cherokees were the players from the Creek clans. Directly behind were the tables of the Choctaws and the Chickasaws.

Behind the tables of the Five Nations were those of the Seven Allied Tribes: Shawnee, Delaware, Sac and Fox, Potawatomie, Kickapoo, Ottawa, and Miami. I didn't know anything about their clan arrangements or how they chose their players, though no doubt they used some form of blind lot drawing like everybody else.

Each table was flanked by a pair of senior warriors, dressed all in black and carrying long hardwood clubs. The Deacons—I've never known why they were called that—would be watching the players constantly all through the game, for even the smallest violation of the rules.

Up on the big platform, looking out over the playing tables, sat the chiefs and senior medicine men and other leading persons of the twelve tribes. Our Chief, for example, was accompanied by the Clan Mothers of the seven clans. There was also the Crier of the Game, fat old Jack Birdshooter, and, down at the south end of the stage, Grandfather Ninekiller and his assistants.

Now that was how it was done when I was a boy. Later on a lot of things got changed. I can't say whether the changes were for good or bad. I only know I liked the old days.

When the sun was high over the fields, the Crier stepped to the front of the stage and called for attention. The Chief of the Cherokee Nation was about to speak.

Come to think of it, that's one thing I wasn't too sorry to see dropped from the ceremonies—that long-winded speech, or rather recitation, that the Chief always used to deliver to start things off. Not that the speech itself was so bad, but when you had to hear the damn thing every year, word-for-word the same every time . . . .

"Long ago there were only the People."

Marilyn Blackfox was a pretty good Chief in her day, but she never had much of a speaking voice. But it didn't matter, since the Crier immediately repeated everything she said in English, in a voice that carried like the bellow of a bull alligator. That was out of courtesy to the people of the other tribes, but it was also handy for the large number of Cherokees who couldn't understand their own language—not, at any rate, the pure old-style Cherokee that Chief Marilyn was speaking.

That didn't matter either, seeing that most of us had heard the speech so many times we could have recited it from memory in either language. I leaned back on my elbows and let my mind wander, while she droned on and on about how the People tried to treat the whites right, when they first showed up, only to learn too late that this was the most treacherous bunch of humans the Creator ever let live. And about the massacres and the hunger and the diseases and the forced marches and the rest of it: old stuff, though no doubt it was all true.

"But even in the days when it seemed the People would vanish from the world," Chief Marilyn went on, "our wise elders were given a prophecy—"

Well, here came the bullshit part. According to Grandfather, who should know, the prophecy was that fire would come from the sky and destroy the whites, leaving only the People.

Which, as everybody surely knows, wasn't how it happened. Oh, there was fire enough, when the whites and the black people began fighting each other—I've seen the blackened ruins of the cities, and the pictures in the old books—until the whole Yuasa nation was at war within itself.

But what finally finished the whites was that mysterious sickness that rushed across the land like a flash flood, striking both the whites and the black people too, even faster than their diseases had once wiped out the People.

The legend is that the Creator sent the sickness to punish the whites and free the People. But Grandfather once told me a story he'd heard from his own grandfather: the whites, or certain of their crazier medicine men, created that sickness on purpose, meaning to use it against the black people. Only somebody screwed up and it wound up taking the whites, too.

Some parts of the story are pretty hard to believe, like the business about people breeding little invisible disease bugs the way you'd breed horses. But I think there must be something to it, all the same. Because, after all, there are still a fair number of whites left; but have you ever met anyone who's ever seen a black person in the flesh?

Nobody knows why the People—and the ones with similar blood, like the Meskins—were the only ones the sickness didn't affect. Maybe the Creator has a peculiar sense of humor.

"And so at last the People reclaimed their lands." Chief Marilyn was raising her voice now as she got close to the end. "And life was hard for many generations, and they found that they had forgotten many of the old ways. But they still remembered one thing above all from their traditions, the one great gift from the Creator that had held their grandmothers and grandfathers together through the evil times of the past; and they knew that the Game could save them, too, if they remained faithful. And so it was, and so it is today, and so it always will be."

She stretched out both arms as far as they would go. In a

high clear shout she spoke the words everybody had been waiting for:

"Let the Game begin!"

"Players," the Crier roared, "take your seats!"

Out on the field, the assembled players of the Five Nations and the Seven Tribes did so, all together and with as little noise as possible. They *better*; the hard-faced Deacons were already fingering their clubs, and even simple clumsiness could be good for a rap alongside the head. I mean, those guys loved their work.

While the players bowed their heads and studied the polished hardwood boards in front of them, one of Grandfather's assistants began beating on a handheld water drum, the high-pitched *ping-ping-ping* sounding very loud in the hush that had settled over the whole area. The other assistant led Grandfather—who was perfectly capable of managing by himself, but the routine was meant to remind everyone that he was truly blind—to the wooden table at the front of the stage. With one hand the assistant raised the lid of the big honeysuckle vine basket that took up the whole top of the table, while with the other he guided Grandfather's hand toward the opening.

Grandfather reached into the basket. The drummer stopped drumming. You could have heard a butterfly fart.

Grandfather stood there a moment, groping around inside the basket, and then he pulled his hand back out and held up a little wooden ball, smaller than a child's fist, painted white. You couldn't really see it at any distance, but everybody there knew what it was. There was a soft rustling sound that ran across the field, as the people all drew their breaths.

Without turning, Grandfather passed the little ball to Jesse Tiger, the Seminoles' elder medicine man, who stood beside him. And Jesse Tiger, having looked at the ball, passed it on to the Creek medicine man on his left; and so the little ball went down the line of waiting medicine men, till all twelve had examined it. At the end of the line, the Ottawa elder—I didn't know his name—handed it to Jack Birdshooter, the Crier. Who took a single careful look at the ball and shouted, in a voice that would have cracked obsidian:

"*AY, THIRTY-TWO!*"

There was another soft windy sound as several hundred People let out their breaths. Everybody was craning and staring, now, watching the players. None appeared to have moved.

The drummer was already pinging away again. Grandfather had his hand and most of his forearm down into the huge basket this time, and he didn't fool around before pulling out the second ball. The ball went down the line as before and the Crier took it and looked and blared:

"OH, SEVENTEEN!" And, after a pause, *"ONE-SEVEN!"* just to make sure some idiot didn't mistake the call for seventy.

Still no action on the field. The players' heads were all bent as if praying. Which, of course, most if not all of them were. I wondered what was going through Elvis Bearpaw's mind.

There went the drummer again, *ping-ping-ping*. There went Grandfather's hand, in and out, and there went the third little ball down the line of dark-spotted old hands. And there went Jack Birdshooter:

"ENN, SIX!"

A number that low, this early? That was a lucky sign. And sure enough, over toward the other side of the field, the Deacons were watching one of the Shawnee players as he reached out and carefully placed a polished black stone marker on one of the squares of the walnut board in front of him.

There was a muffled cheer from the watching crowd. Even the dignitaries up on the stage permitted themselves a soft chorus of pleased grunts. This Game was off to an unusually good start.

My uncle said, "Want some more of that turkey, *chooch?*"

"Here," my aunt said, handing me a big buckskin-covered cushion. "Might as well get comfortable. It's liable to be a long day."

Up on the stage the drummer was at it again.

It was a warm day for spring, and there was no shade out on the open ground around the playing field. My eyes were sore from my nearly sleepless night, so I kept them closed a good deal. Aunt Di claimed I fell asleep for a little while there, but I was just resting my eyes and thinking.

I lost track of the progress of the Game soon enough; it wasn't long before all the players had at least a few markers on their boards, and nobody could have keep an eye on all of them. That, after all, was part of what the Deacons were there for.

As best I could see from where I sat, Elvis Bearpaw had a good many markers down, though nothing all that unusual. His face, when he raised his head to listen for a call, was still giving nothing away.

The morning turned to afternoon and the sun began her descent toward the western rim of the sky. The shadow of the sun pole, in front of the platform, grew longer and longer. There was a big brush-covered roof above the stage, to shade the dignitaries, but it was no longer doing them any good. Most of them were squinting and shading their eyes with their hands. Grandfather Ninekiller, of course, didn't have that problem. He kept reaching into the basket and pulling out the little balls, all the while staring straight and blind-eyed toward that hard white afternoon sun. From time to time he would pause while his assistants put the lid back on the great basket and lifted it between them, on its carrying poles, and gave it a good shaking, rocking it from side to side to mix up the balls. By now I figured it must be a good deal lighter. I wondered if this Game would go on long enough for the basket to have to be refilled. That was something I'd never seen, but I knew it occasionally happened.

This one was starting to look like one of the long Games, too. Already a couple of the senior Deacons were checking the supply of ready-to-light torches in the cane racks beside the platform, in case the play went on into the night.

"*BEE, TWENTY-TWO!*" shouted the Crier. And down at the end of the front row, not far from where I sat, one of the Seminole players reached up and put another marker on his board.

The sun was going down in a big bloody show off beyond the trees, and the torches were already being lit and placed in their holders, when it finally happened.

By then I was so tired I was barely listening, and so I missed the call; and to this day I couldn't tell you what ball it was. I was sitting there next to Uncle Kennedy, munching honeycake and trying to stay awake, and my ears picked up the Crier's voice as he boomed out yet another string of meaningless sounds, but all my mind noticed was that he seemed to be getting a little hoarse.

But then my uncle made a sudden surprised grunt. "*Ni,*" he said sharply, and I sat up and looked, while all around us people began doing the same, and a low excited murmur passed through the crowd.

Down on the field, Elvis Bearpaw had gotten to his feet. The two nearest Deacons were already striding toward him, their clubs swinging, ready to punish this outrageous behavior, but Elvis wasn't looking at them. He was staring down at his board as if it had turned into a live water moccasin.

The Deacons paused and looked at the board too. One of them said something, though his voice didn't carry to where I sat.

All the people in the crowd began getting to their feet. Somehow they did it in almost-complete silence. There wasn't even the cry of a baby.

Other Deacons were converging on the spot, now, and after a moment one of them left the growing bunch of black-clad figures and trotted over to the stage. Again I couldn't hear what was said, but all the people on the stage obviously did. Their faces told us onlookers that our guess had been right.

The group of Deacons split and stepped back, except for the original pair, who were now standing on either side of Elvis Bearpaw. One of them jabbed him in the side with the end of his club.

Elvis Bearpaw's mouth opened. A strange croaking sound came out, but it wasn't what you'd call human speech.

The Deacon poked him again, harder. Elvis straightened up and faced the stage and seemed to shake himself. "Bingo," he said, so softly I barely heard him. Then, much louder, "*Bingo!*"

Everybody breathed in and held it and then breathed out, all together.

Old Jack Birdshooter had been doing this too long to forget his lines now. "Deacons," he cried formally, "do we have a Bingo?"

The Deacon on Elvis Bearpaw's right raised his club, saluting the stage. "Yes," he shouted, "we do have a Bingo."

And, needless to say, that was when the crowd went absolutely bat-shit crazy, as always, jumping up and down and waving their arms in the air, yelling and hooting and yipping till it was a wonder the leaves didn't fall off the trees, while the Deacons led Elvis Bearpaw slowly toward the platform. His face, in the dying red light, was something to see.

A long, long time afterward, Grandfather Ninekiller told me the inside story. That was after he had gone on to the spirit world, where he learned all sorts of interesting things.

"What happened," Grandfather said, "Elvis Bearpaw did go to see Old Man Alabama, just like we heard. Wanted some kind of charm or medicine for the Game. Old Man Alabama told him no way. Fixing the Game, that was too much even for a crazy old witch."

"How'd you learn all this?" I asked, a little skeptically. Grandfather hadn't been dead very long at the time, and I was still getting used to talking with him in his new form.

"Old Man Alabama told me," Grandfather said. "Hell, he died a couple of years ago. He's been here longer than me."

"Oh."

"Anyway," Grandfather went on, "Elvis Bearpaw went on and on, offered all kinds of stuff for payment. Finally Old Man Alabama said he could do one thing for him and that was all. He could tell him where the Bingo was going to fall."

"*Doyuka?*"

"Would I shit you? And you and I know what the silly bastard went and did."

"I was right, then," I said. "About what he was up to that night. He switched his game board with his neighbor's. With what's-his-name, that guy from the Wolf Clan."

"*Uh-uh.* Only he didn't understand how that kind of a prophecy works," Grandfather said. "Old Man Alabama told him where the Bingo was going to fall, and that was where it fell. Like I told you that morning," he added, "these things have a way of working themselves out."

But as I say, that was a lot of years later. That night, I could only guess and wonder, while they brought Elvis Bearpaw up onto the stage and the medicine men and then the chiefs came by one at a time to shake his hand, and Chief Marilyn with her own hands tied the winner's red cloth around his head. She was a short woman and she had to stand on tiptoe, but she managed. Then they did the rest of it.

He screamed a lot while they were doing it to him. They all do, naturally, but I don't think I've ever heard a Game winner scream as loud and as long as Elvis Bearpaw did. Some Seneca kids I talked with next day said they heard him clear over at their camp, on the far side of the ball field. Well, they do say that that's the sign of a good strong sacrifice.

And you know, they must be right, because it rained like a son of a bitch that year.

AUTHOR'S NOTE:

This was the story that started my short-fiction career. Roger Zelazny called me up and wanted me to write something for a new anthology he was working on. "Gambling stories," he said. "Anything to do with gambling. Maybe you could do something about Native American Gambling traditions."

I knew what he was getting at; he was thinking of those ancient, often semi-sacred games still practiced by some tribes, such as the Kiowa "guessing game." Cherokees don't have anything like that, but I didn't tell him. I knew immediately what I had to do—and Roger, when he saw the results, didn't seem disappointed.

This story is perhaps properly classed as science fiction rather than fantasy, since it does have a future setting. Of course it could be argued that there are supernatural elements as well, notably the conversation with the deceased grandfather; but why should it be considered fantastic that dead Cherokees can speak to the living? After all, they manage to vote in every tribal election. . . .

THE SCUTTLING

Or, Down by the Sea with Marvin and Pamela

The Bradshaws got back from their vacation late Friday evening and discovered right away that they were not alone.

Marvin Bradshaw was coming up the front walk, having gone across the road to pick up their accumulated mail from the neighbors, when he heard his wife scream. He ran up the stairs and into the house, cursing and wishing he had tried a little harder to get that pistol permit; but there were no intruders to be seen, only his wife standing white-faced and trembling in the kitchen, pointing in the direction of the sink. "Look," she said.

He looked, wondering what he was supposed to see. Everything was as he remembered, but then he had never given much attention to the kitchen area, which after all wasn't his department. He said, "What?" and then he saw something small and dark moving rapidly along the sink's rim. Now he saw another one, slightly larger, going up the wall behind the faucets.

"Son of a bitch," Marvin Bradshaw said. "Cockroaches."

"I came in here to get a drink of water." Pamela Bradshaw's voice was almost a whisper, as if that one scream had used up all her volume reserves. "I turned on the light and Marvin, they were *everywhere*. They went running in all directions." She shuddered. "I think one ran over my foot."

Marvin Bradshaw stepped toward the sink, but the cockroaches were too fast for him. The one on the sink dived off into space, hit the floor, and slipped into a barely visible crack beneath the baseboard. The one on the wall evaded Marvin's slapping hand and disappeared into the cupboard space above the sink. Marvin swore in frustration, but he felt a little relieved too; he hadn't really been eager to crush a cockroach with his bare hand.

"Cockroaches," he said. "Wonderful. Bust your ass for years, finally get out of the city, away from the dirt and the coloreds, into a two-hundred-grand house on one of the best pieces of ocean-front property on Long Island. And then you go away for a couple weeks, and when you get home you got cockroaches. Jesus."

He glared at his wife. "You know who's responsible, don't you? You had to go hire that God-damned Mexican maid."

"Inez is Guatemalan," Pamela protested. "And we don't know—"

"Mexican, Guatemalan, who gives a fuck?" Marvin had never seen the point of these picky-ass distinctions between people who said *sí* when they meant yes. Maybe you needed to know the difference between Japs and Chinamen and other slopes, since nowadays you had to do business with the yellow assholes; but spics were spics, whatever hell-hole country they came from.

"The fact remains," he said, "we never had cockroaches here, and then two months ago you hired her, and now we do. I'm telling you, you let those people in, you got roaches. Didn't I run that block of buildings in Spanish Harlem for your father, back before we got married? Cockroaches and Puerto Ricans, I saw enough of both. Don't tell *me*."

"I'll speak to her when she comes in tomorrow."

"No you won't." He took a sheet of folded paper from the stack of mail in his left hand. "That was what I was coming to tell you. Look what your precious Inez left us."

She took the paper and unfolded it. The message was printed in pencil, in large clumsy block capitals:

NO MAS. YOU NO PAY ME 5 WIKS NOW. GO LIV SISTER
IN ARIZONA. PLES SEN MY MONY MARGARITA FLORES
72281 DEL MONTE TUCSON AZ 85707.
INEZ

Marvin took the note back and wadded it up and hurled it at the kitchen wastebasket, missing. "Comes in here, turns our home into a roach motel, runs out on us when our backs are turned, then she expects to get paid. Lots of luck, you fat wetback bitch."

Pamela sighed. "I'll miss her, all the same. You know, I was working with her, trying to help her remember her past lives. I believe she was a Mayan princess—"

Marvin groaned. "Christ sake," he said, "not now, all right?"

He hadn't had much fun over the last two weeks. He hadn't liked Miami, which had been swarming with small brown people, and where there had been nothing to do but swim—which in his book was something you did only to keep from drowning—or lie around getting a tan, if you were asshole enough to want to look colored. The flight home had been delayed again and again. All in all, this was no time to have to listen to Pamela and her New Age crap.

"Okay," he told her, "we'll go out, get something to eat. Monday I'll call an exterminator. Antonio's okay? I could go for seafood."

Driving away from the house, he considered that at least there was one good side to the situation: eating out would give him a chance to have some real food, rather than that organic slop that Pamela tended to put on the table. He suspected this was merely a cover for her basic incompetence in the kitchen; chopping up a lot of raw vegetables was as close to real cooking as she could manage.

"Marvin," Pamela said suddenly, "you said an exterminator. You mean someone who'll kill the cockroaches?"

He glanced at her, wondering what the hell now. "What, you're worried about chemicals, poisons, like that?"

"Well, that too." Pamela paused, frowning. Marvin realized he'd just handed her something else to be a pain in the ass about. "But what I was going to say," she went on, "isn't there some other way? Besides killing them?"

"Christ." Marvin ground his teeth. "You want to get rid of the roaches but you don't want the poor little things hurt? What's that, more Oriental mumbo-jumbo? The roaches might be somebody's reincarnated souls?"

"I wish you wouldn't be so negative about reincarnation," she said stiffly. "I suppose it's not part of the religion you were brought up in."

Actually Marvin Bradshaw's parents had never shown any interest in any religion at all, and he had followed their lead; churches were places you went for funerals and weddings, and then only if you couldn't get out of it. All he had against reincarnation was that it was believed in by people from India—such as the one who collected fat payments for sitting around in a sheet spouting this shit to Pamela and a bunch of other goofy middle-aged women—and Hindus, after all, were just another variety of little brown bastards who ought to go back where they came from. (Which, in the case of the said Baba Lal Mahavishnu, Marvin suspected would be somewhere in New Jersey; but that was another matter.)

"In any case," Pamela added, "it's not true that human beings can be reborn as insects. That's a Western misconception."

"Then—"

"Still and all, Marvin." Pamela bashed right on over him, an avalanche-grade unstoppable force. "Babaji says it's always best to avoid harming any living creature. The karma accumulates. All those roaches, there must be hundreds, even thousands—disgusting to our our eyes, of course, but so many lives. I can't imagine the karmic consequences of killing them all."

"Then what do you want me to do about the fucking things? Ask them nicely to leave? Get them their own place? How about you go talk to them," he said, enraged beyond control. "That would make any self-respecting insect hit the road."

She didn't answer. From the tone of her silence Marvin figured one of them would be sleeping in the guest bedroom tonight. Well, that was another bonus.

Pamela kept up the silent treatment almost all the way through dinner. Marvin knew it was too good to last. Sure enough, as he was finishing up his lobster, she started in again. "My God," he said, "couldn't you wait till we're out of here? Talking about roaches, what are you, trying to make me sick?"

He leaned back and looked at the remains of his meal. He didn't really like lobster all that well; he'd just ordered this one to jerk Pamela's chain. Antonio's was one of those places with live lobsters in a big glass tank, so you could pick yours out and have them boil his ass alive. Marvin had enjoyed saying "boil his ass alive" and watching Pamela cringe. She hadn't been too horrified, he noticed, to clean her own plate. Probably thought all those clams and scallops had died naturally. Ocean roadkill, maybe, run over by a submarine.

He got up, tossing his napkin on the table, and headed for the men's room. As he was coming back the proprietor stepped not quite into his path. "Mr. Bradshaw," Antonio said. "I hope your dinner was satisfactory."

Marvin nodded and tried to smile. Antonio was small and dark and his black hair was a little too glossy; but he came from a Portuguese family that had been in the area for a couple of centuries at least, and he ran a hell of a good restaurant. Marvin thought that Antonio was okay for, well, an Antonio.

"No offense," Antonio said, glancing around and lowering his voice, "but I couldn't help overhearing your conversation just now."

"You and everybody else in the place," Marvin said. "Sorry if she upset your customers, talking about cockroaches. She's been kind of weird, last year or so. Think she's getting change of life."

"Oh, that's all right." Antonio made a quick no-problem gesture. "No, what I was going to say, you're not the only one with roaches. I've heard a lot of people complaining, the last couple of weeks. It's like they just moved into the area." He made a face. "In my business it's something you worry about."

Marvin thought it over. So it wasn't just his house. Must be the new people moving in, bringing the pests with them. The standards had really gone to hell around here since that housing-discrimination lawsuit.

"Point is," Antonio went on, "it won't be easy getting an exterminator any time soon. You'll do well to get one by the end of next week."

"Shit!" Marvin said, louder than he meant to. "Hey, Antonio, I can't live with those things in the house for a week. You must know some people, guy in your line. You know anybody might be willing to make a special call? I'll make it worth their while."

Antonio shook his head. "Believe me, all the ones I know are already making 'special calls' and charging through the nose, too." He rubbed his chin. "Now there's one possibility, maybe . . . "

"Talk to me. Come on, Antonio. Help me out here."

"Well—one of my bus boys," Antonio said, "the one doing that table by the door, see? He's got this grandfather, supposed to be good at getting rid of roaches and rats and the like."

Marvin saw a short, chunky, very dark kid in a white apron. Coarse, badly-cut black hair. Huge cheekbones, heavy eyebrows, big nose. "What's he," Marvin said, "Mexican?" Thinking, *no way.*

Antonio laughed. "Actually, he's an Indian."

"From India?" No way in *hell.* "Doesn't look it."

"No, no. American Indian. Some small tribe I can't even pronounce, got a reservation upstate."

"Huh." Marvin stared, amazed. As far as he knew he had never seen an Indian in these parts before. That was one thing you had to say for Indians, compared to other kinds of colored people: they kept to themselves, lived out in the sticks on reservations, didn't come pushing themselves in where they weren't wanted.

"I don't really know much about it," Antonio admitted. "Some people I know in Amityville, the old man did a job for them and they were very pleased. But they didn't tell me a lot of details."

"Huh," Marvin said again. "A redskin exterminator. Now I've heard everything."

"He's not an exterminator, strictly speaking." Antonio gave Marvin an odd grin. "This is the part your wife's going to like. He doesn't kill anything. He just makes the pests go away."

Marvin turned his stare onto Antonio. "This is a gag, right? You're going to tell me he blows a horn or something and they follow him away, like the Pied fucking Piper? Hey, Antonio, do I look like I'm in the mood for comedy?"

"No, this is for real." Antonio's face was serious. "I'm not sure how he does it—what I heard, he sort of smokes them out. Indian secret, I guess."

"I'll be damned." For a moment Marvin considered the idea. Indians did know a lot of tricks, everybody knew that. "Nah. Thanks, but I'll wait till Monday and hit the yellow pages. Hell, I can stand anything for a few more days."

But later that night, about to go to bed—in the guest bedroom, sure enough—he felt a sudden thirst, and went down to the kitchen to get himself a beer; and when he turned on the light, there they were.

Pamela hadn't been exaggerating. The cockroaches were everywhere. They swarmed over the sink and the counter and the dishwasher, the refrigerator and the walls and the floor: little flat brown oblongs that began running, all at once, when the light came on, so that the whole room appeared to squirm sickeningly for a moment. In almost no time most of the roaches had vanished, but a few remained, high on the walls or in other inaccessible places. Through the glass doors of the china cupboard Marvin could see a couple of them perched on top of a stack of antique bone-china dishes.

Then he glanced up and saw that there was a large roach on the ceiling directly above his head. Its long feelers waved gently as if in greeting. It seemed to be looking at him, considering a drop.

"Jesus Christ!" Marvin shouted, and ran from the kitchen without stopping to turn off the light.

His hands were shaking as he picked up the phone. The restaurant was closed for the night, and when he dialed Antonio's home phone he had to listen to a lot of rings before Antonio picked it up.

"Listen," Marvin said over Antonio's sleepy protest, "you know that old Indian you were telling me about? How fast do you think you could get hold of him?"

Next morning when Marvin went nervously into the kitchen for his coffee, there were no roaches to be seen. He knew they were still there, hiding during the daylight hours; still, it wasn't so bad as long as he couldn't see them.

He poured himself a cup of black coffee and went out through the sliding glass doors to the sun deck. The sun was well up above the eastern horizon and the light hurt his eyes; he wished he'd brought a pair of shades. He sat down at the little table at the north end of the sun deck, keeping his back to the sun.

The Bradshaws' house was built at the edge of a rocky bluff, sixty or seventy feet above the ocean. If Marvin cared to look straight down, through the cracks between the planks of the sun deck, he could see the white sand of what Pamela liked to call "our beach." It wasn't much of a beach, just a narrow strip of sand that sloped steeply to the water. At high tide it was almost entirely submerged.

He tested his coffee cautiously. As he had expected, it was horrible. Have to start interviewing replacement help; Pamela's efforts in the kitchen were going to be almost as hard to live with as the cockroaches.

Cockroaches. He made a disgusted face, not just at the bitter coffee. He had really lost it last night. Now, sitting in the bright morning sunlight with the cool clean wind coming off the sea, he couldn't believe he'd gone into such a panic over a few bugs. Calling Antonio up in the middle of the night, for God's sake, begging him to bring in some crazy old Indian. Going to be embarrassing as hell, eating at Antonio's, after this.

Marvin raised the cup again and took a mouthful of coffee. God, it tasted bad. Even more gruesome than Pamela's usual coffee-making efforts, which was saying something. There even seemed to be something solid—

He jerked suddenly back from the table, dropping the cup, spilling coffee over himself and not noticing. He raised his hand to his mouth and spat onto his palm the soggy cadaver of a drowned cockroach.

Marvin leaped to his feet and dashed for the railing and energetically emptied his stomach in the direction of the Atlantic Ocean. When the retching and heaving at last subsided he hung there for several minutes, clutching the rail to keep from collapsing to the deck, breathing noisily through his mouth.

It was then that Pamela appeared in the kitchen doorway. "Marvin," she said, "a couple of men are out front in a pickup truck. They say you sent for them."

The kid from Antonio's was standing on the front porch, hands jammed into his ass pockets. With him was a little old man—no more than five feet tall, not much over a hundred pounds—with a face like a sun-dried apple. They both wore faded jeans and cheap-looking checkered work shirts. The old man had on a mesh-backed cap with a Dolphins emblem on the front and some kind of feather dangling from the crown. Behind them in the driveway sat an old pickup truck, its paint so faded and scabbed with rust that it was impossible to tell what color it had originally been.

The kid said, "Mr. Bradshaw? Mr. Coelho said you had a roach problem."

The old man said something in a language that sounded like nothing Marvin had ever heard. The kid said, "My grandfather needs to have a look around before he can tell you anything."

Marvin nodded weakly. He still felt dizzy and sick. "Sure," he said, and led the way back to the kitchen.

Pamela came and stood in the kitchen doorway beside Marvin. They watched as the old Indian walked slowly about the kitchen, bending down and studying the baseboards, running his fingers under the edge of the counter and sniffing them, peering behind the refrigerator. Suddenly he squatted down and opened the access doors and reached up into the dark space beneath the sink. A moment later he was standing up again, holding something small and wiggly between his thumb and forefinger. His wrinkled dark face didn't really change expression—it hadn't been wearing any recognizable expression to begin with—but there was something like satisfaction in his eyes.

He spoke again in that strange-sounding language. The kid said, "He needed to know what kind of roaches you had. He says no problem. This kind is easy."

The old man went out on the sun deck and flipped the cockroach over the rail. He came back and said something brief. "He says one hundred dollars," the kid translated.

For once Marvin was in no mood to argue. He could still taste that coffee-logged cockroach. "When can he start?"

"Right now," the kid said. "If that's okay."

The kid went back up the hall—Marvin thought he should have had Pamela go along to make sure he didn't steal anything, but it was too late now—while the old man continued to study the kitchen. A few minutes later the kid was back with a pair of nylon carry-on bags, which he set on the counter beside the sink. The old man nodded, grunted, unzipped one of the bags, and began rummaging inside.

While he was rummaging the kid said, "Any animals in the house? Dogs, cats?"

Pamela shook her head. Marvin said, "Hell, no." That was something he couldn't understand, people keeping dirty hairy animals in the house. Maybe a good guard dog, but even he belonged outside, behind a fence.

"It would be better," the kid said, "if you could go somewhere, like out of the house, till this is over."

"Yeah?" Marvin grinned. "You'd like that, wouldn't you?"

Pamela kicked his ankle. To the Indian kid she said, "Is this going to involve any toxic chemicals?"

"No, no, nothing like that." The kid gestured at the pile of stuff the old man was taking out of the bag. "See, we don't even use respirators. No, it's just, well, better if you're not here."

"Uh huh," Marvin said. "Forget it, Geronimo. Nice try."

The kid shrugged. "Okay." He turned and began unzipping the other bag.

By now the old man had laid out several bundles of what looked like dried weeds. Now he selected four of these and twisted them together to form a single long bundle. From the bag he took a roll of ordinary white twine and began wrapping the bundle tightly from end to end, compressing it into a solid cylinder about the size and shape of a rolled-up newspaper. He put the rest of the stuff back into the bag and spoke to the kid.

The kid had taken out a small drum, like a big tambourine without the metal jingles, and a long thin stick with one end wrapped in what looked like rawhide. He gave the drum a tap and got a single sharp *poong* that filled the kitchen and floated off down the hallway.

The old man produced a throwaway butane lighter, which he lit and applied to one end of the herb bundle. Marvin expected a quick flare-up, but the stuff showed some reluctance to ignite. The old man turned the bundle in his fingers, blowing gently, until at last the end of the bundle was a solid glowing red coal.

By now smoke was pouring from the bundle in thick white clouds, billowing up to the ceiling and then rolling down to fog the whole room. Marvin started to protest, but then he decided that the smell wasn't bad at all. He recognized cedar in there— for an instant he recalled the time he had been allowed to burn the family tree after Christmas because his father was too drunk—and something that might be sage, and other things he couldn't guess at.

Hell, he thought, you could probably market this shit for some serious bucks. The old ladies in particular would go big for a new house scent.

Now the old Indian was turning this way and that, waving the smoldering bundle, getting the smoke into all the corners of the room. The kid started beating his drum, *poong poong poong poong,* and the old man commenced to sing. At least that was what he seemed to think he was doing, though for sure he was no Tony Bennett. It was a weird monotonous tune, maybe half a dozen notes repeated over and over, and the words didn't sound like words at all, just nonsense syllables such as a man might sing if he'd forgotten the lyrics.

Whatever it was, Marvin Bradshaw didn't like it a damn bit. He started to speak, to tell the old man to get on with the fumigating and never mind the musical production number. But the two Indians were already walking past him and up the hallway, trailing clouds of smoke and never missing a beat or a hey-ya. Marvin said, "Oh, fuck this," and turned to follow, to put a stop to this crap before it went any farther.

Pamela, however, moved to block the doorway. "Marvin," she said, very quietly but in a voice like a handful of razor blades.

He recognized the tone, and the look in her eyes. There were times when you could jerk Pamela around, and then there were times when simple survival required you to back off. There was no doubt which kind of time this was.

"All right," Marvin said crankily, "let me go after them anyway, keep an eye on them. God knows what the redskin sons of bitches are liable to walk off with . . . is that liquor cabinet locked?"

*   *   *

The drumming and singing and smoking went on for the rest of the morning. The old man insisted on doing every room in the house, upstairs and down, as well as the basement, attic, and garage.

At one point Marvin paused on the stairs, hearing his wife on the hall phone: "No, really, Theresa, I swear, a real Native American shaman, and he's doing a smoke ceremony right here in our house. It's so exciting . . . "

There was a lengthy pause. Lengthy for Pamela, anyway. "Oh," she said at last, "I used to feel guilty about them, too. I mean, all the terrible things that were done to them. But you know, Babaji explained that really, the Native Americans who have it so hard nowadays—poverty and alcoholism and so on— they're the reincarnated spirits of white soldiers who killed Native people in earlier times, and that's how they're working off their karma."

Upstairs the kid was banging the drum and the old man was chanting and smoke was rolling back down the stairs, but Marvin stayed to listen a moment longer.

"I wish you'd been there," Pamela was saying. "Jessica told about giving some change to this poor homeless Negro she saw in the city, and Babaji said that giving was always good for one's own karma but after all, in a previous life, that man was probably a slave-ship captain."

There was a happy sigh. "It's just as Babaji says, Theresa. Once you understand how karma works, you realize that everything really *is* for the best."

Marvin snorted loudly and went on up the stairs. "Space," he mumbled, "the final fucking frontier."

A little before noon, having smoked up the garage until you could barely find the cars without feeling around, the old man stopped singing and held the smoke bundle up over his head. The kid quit drumming and said, "That's all."

"That's it?" Marvin folded his arms and stared at the kid. "And for this you expect me to cough up a hundred bucks?"

The old man was bent over, grinding the glowing end of the bundle against the floor to extinguish it. Without looking up he said something in Algonquin or whatever the hell language it was.

The kid said, "You don't have to pay now. We'll come back to-morrow. If you're not satisfied with the results by then, you don't have to pay at all."

Marvin started to tell him not to waste his time. But the old man turned and looked at Marvin with dark turtle eyes and Marvin heard himself say, "Okay. Sure. See you then."

When they were gone Marvin went back into the house and got out the key to the liquor cabinet. It wasn't often that he had a drink this early in the day but his nerves were just about shot.

The smoke had thinned a good deal inside the house, but the scent was still strong; he could even smell it out on the sun deck, where he took his drink. He leaned against the railing and looked out over the ocean, enjoying the salt breeze and the swishing mutter of small waves over the sand below. Saturday morning shot to hell, but at least it was over. Maybe there'd be a good game on TV in the afternoon, or a fight. Even a movie, as long as there weren't any Indians in it.

He became aware that his fingertips were tapping steadily on the railing, thumping out a medium-fast four-four beat that was, he realized then, the same rhythm the Indian kid had been beating on his drum.

"Jesus H. Christ," he said aloud. And downed his drink in one long shuddering gulp.

Pamela stayed on the phone for the rest of the afternoon, telling her big story to one cuckoo-clock friend after another. Since this kept her off Marvin's back, he figured the whole thing had almost been worth it.

He went into the kitchen and stuck a frozen dinner into the microwave. The smoke smell was still very pronounced, though the air looked clear and normal now. He took the cardboard tray out to the sun deck and ate his lunch, letting the sound of the ocean drown out the Indian music that kept running through his head.

Later, he tried without success to find a game on television. All the sports shows were taken up with silly crap like tennis. That would just about make it perfect, spend the afternoon watching a couple of bull dykes batting a stupid ball back and forth across a net. Finally he found a Bronson movie he hadn't seen before, and after that, over on PBS, Louis Rukeyser had some really interesting things to say about the stock market; and so Marvin made it through the afternoon, and most of the time he hardly noticed the smoke smell at all. And only a few times, maybe once or twice an hour, did he catch himself tapping a foot or finger to the beat of the Indian kid's drum.

When they went out to dinner that evening, Marvin drove clear to the next town up the coast, to a not particularly good and way to hell overpriced steak house, rather than eat at Antonio's. He was feeling particularly pissed off at Antonio, whom he suspected of setting the whole thing up as a practical joke. Ought to drown the grinning little greaseball, Marvin thought, in his own fucking lobster tank.

A little after eleven that night, Marvin was sitting in the living room, trying to read Rush Limbaugh's latest book, when Pamela called him from the head of the stairs.

He had the radio on, tuned to a New Jersey station that played country and western—which he hated, but he was trying to use one irritation against another; a bunch of Gomers singing through their noses might cancel out that God-damned Indian racket that wouldn't get out of his mind. Pamela had to call several times before he got up and came to the foot of the stairs. "What?"

"You'd better go out and have a look, Marvin," she said calmly. "There are people down on our beach."

"Oh, fuck." He'd always known it would happen sooner or later, but why did it have to happen now? "Get me my shotgun," he said, "and phone the cops."

Pamela didn't move. "Don't overreact, Marvin. I don't think there are more than two of them, and they don't seem to be doing anything. They're not even close to the house. Probably just walking along the beach in the moonlight."

"Sure." Marvin threw up his hands. "Right, I'll just go see if they'd like a complimentary bottle of *champagne*. Maybe a little violin music."

He went down the hallway and through the kitchen, muttering. Probably some gang of crack-head punks from the city, looking for white people to rob and rape and murder. Pamela wouldn't be so God-damned serene when they tied her up and took turns screwing her in the ass before they killed her. He hoped they'd let him watch.

The glass door slid silently open and Marvin stepped sockfooted out onto the deck. The tide was out and the sea was calm, and in the quiet he could definitely hear voices down on the beach.

He reached back through the door and flipped a switch. Suddenly the area beneath him was flooded with light, bright as day. One of the voices made a sound of surprise and Marvin grinned to himself. It hadn't cost much to have those big lights installed underneath the deck, and held known they'd come in handy some night like this.

He walked quickly across the deck and peered over the railing. It was almost painful to look down; the white sand reflected the light with dazzling intensity. He had no trouble, though, in seeing the two men standing on the beach, halfway between the house and the water. Or in recognizing the two brown faces that looked up at him.

"Hi, Mr. Bradshaw," the Indian kid called. "Hope we didn't disturb you."

The old man said something in Indian talk. The kid said, "My grandfather wants to apologize for coming around so late. But it was a busy night at the restaurant and Mr. Coelho wouldn't let me off any sooner."

"What the fuck," Marvin said, finally able to speak.

"You ought to come down here," the kid added. "You'll want to see this."

The logical thing to do at this point, of course, was to go back in the house and call the police and have these two arrested for trespassing. But then it would come out, how Marvin had gotten involved with the red bastards in the first place. The local cops didn't like Marvin, for various reasons, and would probably spread the story all over the area, how he had hired an Indian medicine man to get the cockroaches out of his home.

And if he simply shot the sons of bitches, he'd go to jail. There was no justice for a white man any more.

Marvin went back through the house. Pamela was still standing on the stairs. "It's those damn Indians," he told her as he passed. "If they scalp me you can call nine-one-one. No, you'll probably bring them in for tea and cookies."

He went out the front door and around the house and down the wooden stairway to the beach. The two Indians were still there. The old man was down in a funny crouch, while the kid was bent over with his hands on his knees. They seemed to be looking at something on the ground.

"Here, Mr. Bradshaw," the kid said without looking up. "Look at this."

Marvin walked toward them, feeling the sand crunch softly beneath his feet, realizing he had forgotten to put on any shoes. Socks full of sand, great. He came up between the old man and the kid and said, "All right, what's the," and then in a totally different voice, "Jesus God Almighty!"

He had never seen so many cockroaches in all his life.

The sand at his feet was almost hidden by a dark carpet of flat scuttling bodies. The light from the floodlamps glinted off their shiny brown backs and picked out a forest of waving antennae.

Marvin leaped back and bumped into Pamela, who had followed him. "Look out, Marvin," she said crossly, and then she screamed and clutched at him.

The cockroaches, Marvin saw now, were not spreading out over the beach, or running in all directions in their usual way. They covered a narrow strip, maybe three feet wide, no more; and they were all moving together, a cockroach river that started somewhere in the shadow of the house and ran straight as Fifth Avenue across the sandy beach, to vanish into the darkness in the direction of the ocean. Marvin could hear a faint steady rustling, like wind through dry leaves.

"You wanted them out of your house," the kid said. "Well, there they go."

"How . . ." Pamela's voice trailed off weakly.

"They're going home," the kid said. "Or trying to."

Marvin barely heard the words; he was watching the cockroaches, unable to pull his eyes away from the scurrying horde. He walked toward the house, studying the roaches, until he came up against the base of the bluff. Sure enough, the roaches were pouring straight down the rock face in a brown cataract that seemed to be coming from up under the foundation of the house.

"See," the kid was saying, "the kind of roaches you got, the little brown cockroaches like you see in houses in this part of the country—they're not native. Book says they're German cockroaches, some say they came over with those Hessian mercenaries the King hired to fight Washington's guys. I don't know about that, but anyway the white people brought them over from Europe."

Marvin turned and stared at the kid for a moment. Then he looked down at the cockroaches again. "Fucking foreigners," he muttered. "I should have known."

"Now down in Florida and around the Gulf," the kid added, "you get these really big tropical roaches, they came over from Africa on slave ships. Then there's a kind that comes from Asia, very hard to kill."

Pamela said, "And your grandfather's, ah, medicine—?"

"Makes them want to go back where they came from. Well, where their ancestors came from. Makes them *have* to. Look."

Marvin was tracking the cockroach stampede in the other direction now, out across the beach. The moon was up and full, and even beyond floodlight range it was easy to see the dark strip against the shiny damp low-tide sand.

At the water's edge the cockroaches did not hesitate. Steadily, without a single break in the flow, they scurried headlong into the sea. The calm water of the shallows was dotted with dark specks and clumps that had to be the bodies of hundreds, maybe thousands of roaches. Marvin found himself remembering something he'd heard, how you could line all the Chinamen up and march them into the ocean and they'd never stop coming because they bred so fast.

The old man spoke as Marvin came walking back across the sand. The kid said, "He says he'll leave it on the rest of the night, in case you got rats or mice."

"It works on them too?" Pamela asked.

"Sure." The kid nodded. "No extra charge."

"The hell," Marvin said, "you're going to claim you people didn't have rats or mice either, before Columbus?"

"Some kinds. Woods and field mice, water rats, sure. But your common house mouse, or your gray Norway rat, or those black rats you see in the city, they all came over on ships."

"I don't see any," Pamela observed.

"Oh, you wouldn't, not yet. The bigger the animal, the longer the medicine takes to work. Matter of body weight. You take a real big gray rat, he might not feel it for the rest of the night. Along about daybreak, though, he'll come down here and start trying to swim back to Norway or wherever."

The old man spoke again. "My grandfather says we'll come back tomorrow, so he can turn the medicine off. Can't leave it on too long. Things . . . happen."

At their feet the cockroaches streamed onward toward oblivion.

Marvin slept badly that night, tormented by a persistent dream in which he ran in terror across an endless empty plain beneath a dark sky. A band of Indians pursued him, whooping and waving tomahawks and beating drums, while ranks of man-sized cockroaches stood on their hind legs on either side, shouting at him in Spanish. Pamela appeared in front of him, naked. "It is your karma, Marvin!" she cried. He saw that she had long antennae growing from her head, and an extra set of arms where her breasts had been.

He sat up in bed, sweating and shaking. The smoke smell in the room was so strong he could hardly breathe. "Gah," he said aloud, and fought the tangled covers off him and got up, to stand on wobbly legs for a moment in the darkness.

On her side of the bed Pamela mumbled, "Marvin?" But she didn't turn over, and he knew she wasn't really awake.

He went downstairs, holding tight to the banister, and got a bottle of Johnny Walker from the liquor cabinet. In the darkened hallway he took a big drink, and then another, straight from the bottle. The first one almost came back up but the second felt a lot better.

He carried the bottle back upstairs, to the guest bedroom, where he cranked the windows wide open and turned on the big ceiling fan and stretched out on the bed. He could still smell the smoke, but another belt of Scotch helped that.

He lay there drinking for a long time, until finally the whiskey eased him off into a sodden sleep. He dreamed again, but this time there were no Indians or cockroaches; in fact it was a pleasant, restful dream, in which he found himself strolling across gently rolling pasture land. Big oak trees grew along the footpath where he walked, their branches heavy with spring-green leaves. Sheep grazed on a nearby hillside.

In the distance, at the crest of a high hill, rose the gray walls and battlements of an ancient-looking castle. A winding dirt road led up to the castle gate, and he saw now that a troop of soldiers in red coats were marching along it, headed in his direction. The *poong poong poong poong* of their drum carried across the fields to Marvin, and he could hear their voices raised in song:

hey ya hey yo hey ya
yo hey ya hey na wey
ah ho ha na yo
ho ho ho ho

He awoke again with the sun shining through the windows. He lay for a long time with a pillow over his face, knowing he wasn't going to enjoy getting up.

When he finally emerged from the guest bedroom, sweaty and unshaven, it was almost midday. Passing the main bathroom, he heard the shower running. Pamela would have been up for hours; she always got up ridiculously early, so she could do her silly meditation and yoga exercises on the deck as the sun came up.

Marvin was sitting in the living room drinking coffee when the doorbell rang. He lurched to his feet, said, "Shit!", and headed for the front door. Sunlight stabbed viciously at his eyes when he opened the door and he blinked against the pain. He opened his eyes again and saw the two Indians standing on his porch.

"Sorry if we're a little early," the kid said. "I have to be at work soon."

Marvin regarded them without warmth. "The fuck you want now?"

"Well, you know, Mr. Bradshaw. My grandfather did a job for you."

Marvin nodded. That was a mistake. When the agony in his head receded he said, "And now you want to get paid. Wait here a minute."

There was no way these two clowns could make a claim stick, but he didn't feel up to a nasty scene. His wallet was upstairs in the bedroom, but he knew Pamela kept a little cash in a vase on the mantlepiece, for paying delivery boys and the like. He dug out the roll and peeled off a twenty and went back to the front door. "There you are, Chief. Buy yourself a new feather."

The old man didn't touch the twenty. "One hundred dollars," he said. In English.

Marvin laughed sourly. "Dream on, Sitting Bull. I'm being a nice guy giving you anything, after you stank up my house. Take the twenty or forget it."

The old man jabbered at the kid. He didn't take his eyes off

Marvin. The kid said, "You don't pay, he won't turn the medicine off."

"That's supposed to worry me? If I believed in this crap at all, I wouldn't want it 'turned off.' Leave it on, keep the roaches away forever."

"That's not how it works," the kid said. "It won't affect anything that wasn't in the house when the medicine was made."

Marvin thought of something. "Look, I tell you what I'll do. You give me some of that stuff you were burning yesterday, okay? And I'll write you out a check for a hundred bucks, right now."

After all, when you cut past the superstitious bullshit, there had to be something in that smoke that got rid of roaches better than anything on the market. Screwed up their brains, maybe, who knew? Take a sample to a lab, have it analyzed, there could be a multi-million-dollar product in there. It was worth gambling a hundred. Hell, he might not even stop payment on the check. Maybe.

But the old man shook his head and the kid said, "Sorry, Mr. Bradshaw. That's all secret. Anyway, it wouldn't work without the song."

Marvin's vision went even redder than it already was. "All right," he shouted, "get off my porch, get that rusty piece of shit out of my driveway, haul your red asses out of here." The kid opened his mouth. "You want trouble, Tonto? You got a license to run a pest-control business in this county? Go on, *move!*"

When the rattling blat of the old pickup's exhaust had died away, Marvin returned to the living room. Pamela was standing on the stairs in a white terry robe. Her hair was wet. She looked horribly cheerful.

"I thought I heard voices," she said. "Was it those Native Americans? I hope you paid them generously."

Marvin sank onto the couch. "I gave them what they had coming."

"I'm just disappointed I didn't get to see them again. Such an honor, having a real shaman in my house. Such an inspiring ceremony, too. Remember that lovely song he sang? I can still hear it in my mind, over and over, like a mantra. Isn't that wonderful?"

Singing happily to herself, *hey ya hey yo hey ya*, she trotted back up the stairs. And *poong poong poong poong* went the drum in Marvin's head.

* * *

He spent the rest of the day lying on the living room couch, mostly with his eyes closed, wishing he could sleep. He made no move toward the liquor supply. He would have loved a drink, but his stomach wouldn't have stood for it.

The hangover didn't get any better; at times it seemed the top of his skull must surely crack open like an overcooked egg. His whole body ached as if he'd fallen down a flight of stairs. Even the skin of his face felt too tight.

Worst of all, he was still hearing Indian music, louder and clearer and more insistent than ever. Up to now it had been no more than a nuisance, one of those maddening tricks the brain occasionally plays, like having the *Gilligan's Island* theme stuck in your mind all day. Now, it had become a relentless clamor that filled the inside of his head with the savage boom of the drum and the endless ululation of the old man's voice; and from time to time Marvin put his hands over his ears, though he knew it would do no good. He might even have screamed, but that would have hurt too much.

Pamela had vanished around noon; off to visit her crazy friends, Marvin thought dully, never mind her poor damn husband. But around four he tottered into the kitchen—not that he had any appetite, but maybe some food would settle his stomach—and happened to glance out through the glass doors, and there she was, down on the beach. She wore a long white dress and she appeared to be dancing, back and forth along the sand, just above the line of the incoming tide. Her hands were raised above her head, clapping. He couldn't hear the sound, but his eyes registered the rhythm: *clap clap clap clap*, in perfect synch with the drumming in his head and the boom of blood in his throbbing temples.

The sun went down at last. Marvin left the lights off, finding the darkness soothing. He wondered if Pamela was still down on the beach. "Pamela!" he called, and again; but there was no answer, and he decided he didn't give enough of a damn to go look for her.

But time went by and still no sign of her, and finally Marvin got to his feet and shuffled to the door. It wasn't safe, a white woman out alone on a beach at night. Besides, he needed some fresh air. The stink of smoke was so bad it seemed to stick to his skin; he itched all over.

He went slowly down the wooden steps to the little beach. The moon was up and full and the white sand fairly gleamed. He could see the whole beach, clear out to the silver line that marked the retreating edge of the sea.

He couldn't see Pamela anywhere.

He walked out across the sand, with no real idea what he expected to find. His feet seemed to move on their own, without consulting him, and he let them. His body no longer hurt; even his headache was gone. The drumming in his head was very loud now, a deafening POONG POONG POONG POONG, yet somehow it didn't bother him any more.

The damp sand below the high-tide mark held a line of small shoeless footprints, headed out toward the water. Marvin followed without haste or serious interest. He saw something ahead, whiter than the sand. When he got there he was not greatly surprised to recognize Pamela's dress.

The footprints ended at the water's edge. Marvin stood there for a while, looking out over the moonlit ocean. His eyes were focused on nothing nearer than the invisible horizon. His toes tapped out a crunchy rhythm on the wet sand.

He took a step forward.

Up at the top of the bluff, sitting on a big rock, the Indian kid from Antonio's said, "There he goes."

Beside him his grandfather grunted softly. "How long's it been?"

"Since she went in?" The kid checked his cheap digital watch. The little bulb was broken but the moonlight was plenty strong. "Hour and a half. About."

"Hm. Didn't think he was that much bigger than her."

"She had small bones."

"Uh huh." The old man grinned. "I saw you when she took off her dress. Thought you were going to fall off the bluff."

"She did have a good shape," the kid said. "For a woman her age."

They watched as Marvin Badwater walked steadily into the sea. By now the water was up to his waist, but he kept going.

"Guess he can't swim," the kid remarked.

"Wouldn't do him much good if he could. Come on, son. Time we were leaving."

As they walked back to the truck the kid said, "Will you teach me to make that medicine?"

"Some day. When you're ready."

"Does it have a name? You know, what we—you—did, back there. What do you call it?"

"A start."

The kid began laughing. A moment later the old man joined in with his dry wispy chuckle. They were still laughing as they drove away, up the coast road and toward the distant glow of the main highway.

Behind them the sea stretched away flat and shining in the moonlight, its surface broken only by the small dark spot that was the head and shoulders of Marvin Bradshaw, wading toward Europe.

AUTHOR'S NOTE:

Originally written, as will surprise no one, during the presidential campaign of 1990, as a response to the xenophobic utterances of the ineffable Mr. Patrick Buchanan.

This is the story *nobody* wanted. If you will examine it closely you will find it is covered with little round marks from being touched with eleven-foot poles. Most of the editors who bounced it seemed not to have gotten the point of the story. Or maybe at some level they *did* get it, and it made them uncomfortable. One wonders.

Anyway, their loss is your gain.

NINEKILLER AND THE NETERW

JESSE NINEKILLER was five thousand feet above the Egyptian desert when his grandfather spoke to him. He was startled but not absolutely astonished, even though his grandfather had been dead for almost thirty years. This wasn't the first time this had happened.

The first time had been way back in '72, near Cu Chi, where a brand-new Warrant Officer Ninekiller had been about to put a not-so-new Bell HU-1 into its descent toward a seemingly quiet landing zone. He had just begun to apply downward pressure on the collective pitch stick when the voice had sounded in his ear, cutting clear through the engine racket and the heavy *wop-wop-wop* of the rotor:

"*Jagasesdesdi, sgilisi*! You don't want to go down there right now."

Actually it was only later, thinking back, that Jesse recalled the words and put them together. It was a few seconds before he even realized it had been Grandfather's voice. At the moment it was simply the shock of hearing a voice inside his helmet speaking Oklahoma Cherokee that froze his hands on the controls. But that was enough; by the time he got unstuck and resumed the descent, the other three Hueys in the flight were already dropping rapidly earthward, leaving Jesse well above and behind, clumsy with embarrassment and manhandling the Huey like a first-week trainee as he struggled to catch up. Badly shaken, too; he didn't think he'd been in Nam long enough to be hearing voices . . . .

Then the tree line at the edge of the LZ exploded with gunfire and the first two Hueys went up in great balls of orange flame and the third flopped sideways into the ground like a huge dying hummingbird, and only Jesse, still out of range of the worst of the metal, was able to haul his ship clear. And all the way back to base the copilot kept asking, "How did you know, man? How did you *know?*"

That was the first time, and the only time for a good many years; and eventually Jesse convinced himself it had all been his imagination. But then there came a day when Jesse, now flying for an offshore oil outfit out of east Texas, got into a lively

afternooner with a red-headed woman at her home on the outskirts of Corpus Christi; and finally she got up and headed for the
bathroom, and Jesse, after enjoying the sight of her naked white
bottom disappearing across the hall, decided what he needed
now was a little nap.

And had just dropped off into pleasantly exhausted sleep
when the voice woke him, sharp and urgent: "Wake up, *chooch!*
Grab your things and get out of there, *nula!*"

He sat up, blinking and confused. He was still blinking when
he heard the car pull into the driveway; but he got a lot less confused, became highly alert in fact, when the redhead called from
the bathroom, "That'll be my husband. Don't worry, he's cool."

Not buying that for a second, Jesse was already out of bed
and snatching up his scattered clothes. He sprinted ballocky-
bare-assed down the hall and out the back door and across the
scrubby lawn, while an angry shout behind him, followed by a
metallic *clack-clack* and then an unreasonably loud bang, indi-
cated that the husband wasn't being even a little bit cool. There
were more bangs and something popped past Jesse's head as he
made it to his car, and after he got back to his own place he discovered a couple of neat holes, say about forty-five-hundredths of
an inch in diameter, in the Camaro's right rear fender.

In the years that followed there were other incidents, not
quite so wild but just as intense. Like the time Grandfather's
voice woke him in the middle of the night in time to escape from a
burning hotel in Bangkok, or when it stopped him from going
into a Beirut cafe a couple of minutes before a Hezbollah bomb
blew the place to rubble. So even though Grandfather's little visi-
tations never got to be very frequent, when they did happen
Jesse tended to pay attention.

As in the present instance, which bore an uneasy similarity
to the first. The helicopter now was a Hughes 500D, smaller than
the old Huey and a hell of a lot less work to drive, and Egypt definitely didn't look a bit like Nam, but it was still close enough to
make the hairs on Jesse's neck come smartly to attention when
that scratchy old voice in his ear (his left ear, for some reason it
was always the left one) said, *"Ni, sgilisi!* This thing's about to
quit on you."

Jesse's eyes dropped instantly to the row of warning lights at
the top of the instrument panel, then to the dial gauges below.
Transmission oil pressure and temperature, fuel level, battery

temperature, engine and rotor rpm, turbine outlet temperature, engine oil pressure and temperature—there really were a hell of a lot of things that could go wrong with a helicopter, when you thought about it—everything seemed normal, all the little red and amber squares dark, all the needles where they were supposed to be. Overhead, the five-bladed rotor fluttered steadily, and there was no funny feedback from the controls.

Beside him, in the right seat, the man who called himself Bradley and who was supposed to be some kind of archaeologist said, "Something the matter?"

Jesse shrugged. Grandfather's voice said, "Screw him. Listen. Make about a quarter turn to the right. See that big brown rock outcrop, off yonder to the north, looks sort of like a fist? Take a line on that."

Jesse didn't hesitate, even though the lights and needles still swore there was nothing wrong. He pressed gently on the cyclic stick and toed the right tail-rotor pedal to bring the nose around. As the Hughes wheeled to the right the man called Bradley said sharply, "What do you think you're doing? No course changes till I say—"

Just like that, just as Jesse neutralized the controls to steady the Hughes on its new course, the engine stopped. There was no preliminary loss of power or change of sound; one second the Allison turbine was howling away back there and the next it wasn't. Just in case nobody had noticed, the red engine-out light began blinking, while the warning horn at the top of the instrument console burst into a pulsating, irritating hoot.

Immediately Jesse shoved the collective all the way down, letting the main rotor go into autorotation. Under his breath he said, "Damn, *eduda*, how come you always cut it so close?"

"What? What the hell?" Bradley sounded more pissed off than seriously scared. "What's happening, Ninekiller?"

Jesse didn't bother answering. He was watching the airspeed needle and easing back on the cyclic, slowing the Hughes to its optimum speed for maximum power-off gliding range. When the needle settled to eighty knots and the upper tach showed a safe 410 rotor rpm he exhaled, not loudly, and glanced at Bradley.

"Hey," he said, and pointed one-fingered at the radio without taking his hand off the cyclic grip. "Call it in?"

"Negative." Bradley didn't hesitate. "No distress calls. Maintain radio silence."

Right, Jesse thought. And that flight plan we filed was bogus as a tribal election, too. Archaeologist my Native American ass.

But there was no time to waste thinking about spooky passengers. Jesse studied the desert floor, which was rising to meet them at a distressing rate. It looked pretty much like the rest of Egypt, which seemed to consist of miles and miles and *miles* of simple doodly-squat, covered with rocks and grayish-yellow sand. At least this part didn't have those big ripply dunes, which might look neat but would certainly make a forced landing almost unbearably fascinating.

"Get set," he told Bradley. "This might be a little rough."

For a minute there it seemed the warning had been unnecessary. Jesse made a school-perfect landing, flaring out at seventy-five feet with smooth aft pressure on the cyclic, leveling off at about twenty and bringing the collective back up to cushion the final descent. As the skids touched down he thought: *damn*, I'm good.

Then the left skid sank into a pocket of amazingly soft sand and the Hughes tilted irresistibly, not all the way onto its side but far enough for the still-moving rotor blades to beat themselves to death against the ground; and things did get a little rough.

When the lurching and slamming and banging finally stopped Bradley said, "Great landing, Ninekiller." He began undoing his safety harness. "Oh, well, any landing you can walk away from is a good one. Isn't that what you pilots say?"

Jesse, already out of his own harness and busy flipping switches off—there was no reason to do that now, but fixed habits were what kept you alive—thought of a couple of things one pilot would like to say. But he kept his mouth shut and waited while Bradley got the right door open, his own being jammed against the ground. They clambered out and stood for a moment looking at the Hughes and then at their surroundings.

"Walk away is what we get to do, I guess," Bradley observed. He took off his mesh-back cap and rubbed his head, which was bald except for a couple of patches around the ears. Maybe to compensate, he wore a bristly mustache that, combined with a snubby nose and big tombstone teeth, made him look a little like Teddy Roosevelt. His skin was reddish-pink and looked as if it would burn easily. Jesse wondered how long he was going to last in the desert sun.

He climbed back into the Hughes—Jesse started to warn him about the risk of fire but figured what the hell—and rummaged around in back, emerging a few minutes later with a green nylon duffel bag, which he slung over his shoulder. "Well," he said, jumping down, "guess we better look at the map."

Grandfather's voice said, "Keep going the way you were. Few miles on, over that rise where the rock sticks out, there's water."

Jesse said, "*Wado, eduda,*" and then, as Bradley looked strangely at him, "Come on. This way."

Bradley snorted. "Long way from home, aren't you, to be pulling that Indian crap? I mean, it's not like you're an Arab." But then, when Jesse started walking away without looking back, "Oh, Christ, why not? Lead on, Tonto."

Grandfather's few miles turned out to be very long ones, and, despite the apparent flatness of the desert, uphill all the way. The ground was hard as concrete and littered with sharp rocks. Stretches of yielding sand slowed their feet and filled their shoes. It was almost three hours before they reached the stony crest of the rise and saw the place.

Or *a* place; it didn't look at all as Jesse had expected. Somehow he had pictured a movie-set oasis, a little island of green in the middle of this sandy nowhere, with palm trees and a pool of cool clear water. Maybe even some friendly Arabs, tents and camels and accommodating belly dancers . . . okay, he didn't really expect that last part, but surely there ought to be something besides more God-damned rocks and sand. Which, at first, was all he could see.

Bradley, however, let out a dry-lipped whistle. "How did you know, Ninekiller? Hate to admit it, but I'm impressed."

He started down the slope toward what had looked like a lot of crumbling rock formations and sand hillocks, but which Jesse now realized had too many straight lines and right angles to be natural. Ruined buildings, buried by sand?

Jesse said, "Does this do us a lot of good? Looks like nobody lives here any more."

"Yeah, but there's only one reason anybody would live out here."

"Water?"

"Got to be." Brad nodded. "This is a funny desert. Almost no rain at all, but the limestone bedrock holds water like a sponge. Quite a few wells scattered around, some of them pretty old."

"Maybe this one went dry," Jesse suggested. They were getting in among the ruins now, though it was hard to tell where they began. "Maybe that's why the people left."

"Could be. But hey, it's the best shot we've got." Bradley glanced back and grinned. "Right, guy?"

He stepped over what had to be the remains of a wall—not much, now, but a long low heap of loose stone blocks, worn almost round by sand and wind. The whole place appeared to be in about the same condition; Jesse saw nothing more substantial than a few knee-high fragments of standing masonry, and most of the ruins consisted merely of low humps in the sand that vaguely suggested the outlines of small buildings. These ruins were certainly, well, *ruined*.

But Bradley seemed fascinated; he continued to grin as they picked their way toward the center of the village or whatever it had been, and to look about him. Now he stopped and bent down. "Son of a bitch," he said, very softly, and whistled again, this time on a higher note. "Look at this, Ninekiller."

Jesse saw a big block of stone half buried in the sand at Bradley's feet. Looking more closely, he saw that the upturned surface was covered with faint, almost worn-away shapes and figures cut into the stone.

"Hieroglyphics," Bradley said. "My God, this place is Egyptian."

Egyptian, Jesse thought, well, of *course* it's Egyptian, you white asshole, this is *Egypt*. No, wait. "You mean ancient Egypt? Like with the pyramids?"

Bradley chuckled. "I doubt if these ruins are contemporaneous with the pyramids, guy. Though it's not impossible." He straightened up and gazed around at the ruins. "But yes, basically, those Egyptians. I'd hate to have to guess how old this site is. Anywhere from two to four thousand years, maybe more."

"Holy shit," Jesse said, genuinely awed. "What were they doing out here? I thought they hung out back along the Nile."

"Right. But there was a considerable trade with the Libyans for a long time. They had regular caravan routes across the desert. If there was a first-class well here, it would have been worth maintaining a small outpost to guard the place from marauding desert tribes."

He flashed the big front teeth again. "Kind of like Fort Apache, huh? Probably a detachment of Nubian mercenaries under Egyptian command, with a force of slaves for labor and housekeeping. They often sent prisoners of war to places like this. And, usually, worked them to death."

He took off his cap and wiped his sweaty scalp. "But we're going to be mummies ourselves if we don't find some water. Let's look around."

The well turned out to be square in the center of the ruined village, a round black hole fifteen feet or so across and so deep Jesse couldn't see if there was water at the bottom or not. Hell's own job, he thought, sinking a shaft like that in limestone bedrock, with hand tools and in this heat. He kicked a loose stone into the well and was rewarded with a deep muffled splash.

"All *right*," Bradley said. "I've got a roll of nylon cord in my bag, and a plastic bottle we can lower, so at least we're okay for water."

Jesse was studying the ground. "Somebody's been here. Not too long ago."

"Oh, shit," Bradley said crankily, "are you going to start with that Indian routine again?" Then he said, *"Hah!"*

Next to the well, lying there in plain sight, was a cigarette butt.

"Should have known," Bradley said after a moment. "No doubt the nomadic tribes and caravan guides know about this place. Good thing, in fact, because the well would have filled up with sand long ago if people hadn't kept it cleaned out."

"Bunch of tracks there." Jesse pointed. "These desert Arabs, do they go in for wearing combat boots?"

"Could be." Bradley was starting to sound unhappy. "We better check this out, though."

It didn't take an expert tracker to follow the trail away from the well and through the ruined village. There had been a good deal of booted traffic to and from the well, and the boot wearers had been pretty messy, leaving more butts and other assorted litter along the way. "Hasn't been long," Bradley said. "Tracks disappear fast in all this sand and wind. You're right, Ninekiller." He stopped, looking uneasily around. By now they were at the western edge of the ruins, where the ground began to turn upward in a long rock-strewn slope. "Somebody's been here recently."

A few yards away, Jesse said, "Somebody's still here."

On the ground, in the sliver of black shade next to a low bit of crumbling wall, lay a man. He was dressed in desert-camo military fatigues, without insignia. A tan Arab headcloth had been pulled down to cover his face. He wasn't moving and Jesse was pretty sure he wasn't going to.

"Jesus," Bradley said.

The dead man wasn't a pleasant sight. There had been little decomposition in the dry desert air, but the right leg was black and enormously swollen. The camo pants had been slashed clear up to the hip and what looked like a bootlace had been tied just above the knee. It hadn't helped.

"Snakebite," Bradley declared. "Sand viper, maybe. Or even a cobra."

"More tracks over here," Jesse reported. "Somebody was with him. Somebody didn't stick around."

The footprints climbed a little way up the slope and then ended. In their place was a very clear set of tire tracks—a Jeep, Jesse figured, or possibly a Land Rover—leading off across the slope and disappearing out into the desert. The driver had thrown a lot of gravel when he left. Lost his nerve, Jesse guessed. Found himself out here in the empty with no company but a dead man and at least one poisonous snake, and hauled ass.

A large camouflage net, lying loose on the ground beside the tire tracks as if tossed there in a hurry, raised interesting questions. Jesse was about to remark on this when he realized that Bradley was no longer standing beside him, but had moved on up the slope and was now looking at something else, something hidden by a pile of rocks and masonry fragments. "Come look," he called.

Jesse scrambled up to join him and saw another hole, this one about the size and proportions of an ordinary doorway. A rectangular shaft, very straight-sided and neatly cut, led downward into the ground at about a forty-five-degree angle. Some kind of mine? Then he remembered this was Egypt, and then he remembered that movie. "A tomb?" he asked Bradley. "Like where they put those mummies?"

"Might be." Bradley was scrabbling around in his duffel bag, looking excited. "It just might be—ah." He pulled out a big flashlight, the kind cops carry. "Watch your step, guy," he said, stepping into the hole. "You don't want to be the next snakebite fatality."

Bradley seemed to assume Jesse was coming along. That wasn't a very sound assumption; screwing around with any kind of grave was very high on the list of things Indians didn't do.

And yet, without knowing why, he climbed over the heap of scree and rubble and stepped down into the shaft after Bradley.

Bradley was standing halfway down the stone steps that formed the floor of the shaft. He was shining his flashlight here and there on the walls, which were covered with colored pictures. The paint was faded and flaking, but it was easy to make out lively scenes of people eating and paddling boats and playing musical instruments—some naked dancing girls in one panel, complete with very candid little black triangles where their legs joined—as well as other activities Jesse couldn't identify. Animals, too, cats and baboons, crocodiles and hippos and snakes; and, in among the pictures, lines of hieroglyphic writing.

There were also some extremely weird figures, human bodies with bird or animal heads. "What are they," Jesse asked, pointing, "spirits?"

"Gods," Bradley said. "*Neterw*, they were called. The one with the jackal head, for example, is Anubis, god of burials and the dead."

"This one's got a boner."

"Oh, yes. Ithyphallic figures weren't unusual." Bradley headed down the steps, swinging his flashlight. "But we can look at the art later. Let's see what we've got down here."

The shaft leveled off into a narrow passageway. The walls here were covered with murals too, but Bradley barely spared them a glance as he strode down the corridor. "Ah," he said as the hall suddenly opened into a larger and very dark space. "Now this is—oh, my God."

Behind him, Jesse couldn't see at first what Bradley was ohing his God about. He looked over Bradley's shoulder into a low-ceilinged chamber, about the size of a cheap motel room. The flashlight beam showed more paintings on the walls and ceiling. It also showed a stack of wooden boxes against the back wall.

Bradley crossed the room fast and began yanking at one of the boxes. The lid came off and thudded to the stone floor. "Shit," Bradley cried, shining his light into the box. He reached in and hauled out what Jesse instantly recognized as an AK-47 assault rifle. Kalashnikov's products tend to make an indelible impression on anyone who has ever been shot at with them.

Bradley leaned the rifle against the wall and opened another box. This time it was a grenade he held up. "Bastards," he said, almost in a whisper.

Another corridor led off to the rear. Bradley charged down it, cursing to himself, and Jesse hurried after him, disinclined to wait alone in the dark.

The corridor was a short one, ending in another room about the size of the first. It contained an even bigger stack of boxes and crates, piled to the ceiling. Some wore red *danger-explosives* markings in Arabic and English. There were also a number of plastic jerricans full of gasoline. No wonder they went outside to do their smoking, Jesse thought. What the hell was this all about?

Bradley ripped off the top of a cardboard box. "Great," he said sourly, and pulled out a small oblong packet. "U.S. Army field rations. Good old Meals, Ready to Eat. Possibly the most lethal item down here. Wonder where they got them?"

He flashed the light around the room. The chamber was fancier than the other one. Somebody had even painted fake columns along the walls.

"Bastards," he said again. "A priceless treasure of art and knowledge, and they used it for a God-damned terrorist supply dump."

"What do you suppose they did with the mummy?" Jesse asked, thinking about those stories about the mummy's curse. And that snake-bit guy lying outside.

"Oh, that was probably disposed of centuries ago, along with any portable valuables. Tomb robbing is a very ancient tradition in this country." Bradley made a disgusted sound in his throat. "Here." He tossed the MRE packet to Jesse and fished out another. "We better do lunch. We've got a burial detail waiting for us, and I don't think we'll have much appetite afterwards."

They buried the dead man in a shallow grave, using a couple of shovels that they found in the outer chamber of the tomb, piling rocks on top. "Rest in peace," Bradley said. "You poor evil little son of a bitch." He wiped his forehead with his hand. The heat was incredible. "Let's get out of this sun," he said. "Back to the tomb."

Back in the outer chamber, he tossed his shovel into a corner and sat down on a crate. He took off his cap and hoisted the water bottle and poured the contents over his head. "Needed that," he said. "I'll go get a refill in a minute."

"Don't bother," Jesse told him. "There's a big plastic jug of water over here, nearly full." He was poking around in a clutter of odds and ends by the front wall. "You can save your flashlight, too." He picked up a big battery lantern and switched it on.

"Sons of bitches made themselves at home, didn't they?" Bradley clicked his flashlight off. "Ninekiller, I'm about to commit a major breach of security. But the situation's pretty unusual, and there's no way to keep you out of it, so you'd better know the score."

He leaned back against the wall, his head resting just beneath a painting of an archer taking aim from a horse-drawn chariot. "Does the name Nolan mean anything to you?"

"Isn't he the American . . . renegade, I guess you'd say, supposed to be working for the Libyans? Running some kind of commando operation?" Jesse sat down on the floor next to the entrance. "I heard a few rumors, nothing solid. They say he's hiring pilots."

"Yes. Quite a few Americans are working for Khaddafi now," Bradley said, "fliers mostly, young soldier-of-fortune types gone bad. But Nolan is an entirely different, higher-level breed of turncoat. It's not easy to impress people in this part of the world when it comes to terrorism, sabotage, and assassination, but Nolan is right up there with the best native talent. The Colonel values his services very highly."

A circuit closed in Jesse's head. "So that's what this business is all about. Archaeology hell, you were hunting Nolan."

"A preliminary reconnaissance," Bradley said. "Word was he had something going on in this area. You wouldn't have been involved in any real action."

"Nice to know this was such a safe job," Jesse said dryly. "Why not just let the Egyptians do it?" Another realization hit him. "That's right, I remember what I heard. Nolan's a rogue CIA officer, isn't he? You guys want him out of the way without any international embarrassment."

"That, of course, I couldn't tell you," Bradley said calmly. "Your need to know extends only to the immediate situation."

He picked up one of the AK-47s from the open box. "Sooner or later, somebody is going to show up here. Too much to hope that it'll be Nolan himself, but at least it'll be somebody from his outfit. If the odds aren't too bad, and we make the right moves, we'll have a handle on Nolan and a ride out of here." He hefted the AK-47. "Know how to use one of these?"

"The hell," Jesse said angrily. "I'm a pilot, not a gunfighter. Do your own bushwhacking. You're the one who works for the CIA."

"Oh? Who do you think owns Mideast Air Charter and Transfer Services?" Bradley paused, letting that sink in. "You're a pilot? Okay, I'm an archaeologist. No shit," he said, and glanced around the tomb chamber. "Got my degree from the University of Pennsylvania, did my field work over at Wadi Gharbi. That's where they recruited me . . . and there was a time when I'd have given a leg and a nut to find something like this. Well, as it turns out, I've made myself a valuable discovery of a different kind."

He looked at Jesse. The Teddy Roosevelt grin didn't even try to make it to his eyes. "But you're welcome to sit on your ass and play conscientious objector while I take the bastards on alone. Then if they kill me you can tell them all about what an innocent bystander you are. I'm sure they'll believe you."

"Son of a bitch."

"So I've been told." He got up and walked over and held out the AK-47. "Take it, Ninekiller. It's the only way either of us is going to get out of this place alive. Or even dead."

Bradley insisted they maintain a constant watch, taking turns up at the crest of the rise, hunkering in the inadequate shade of the fist-shaped rock outcrop and staring out over the empty desert. "Have to, guy," he said. "Can't risk getting caught down in that tomb when the bad guys arrive."

When the sun finally went down, in the usual excessively spectacular style of tropical sunsets, Jesse assumed they'd drop the sentry-duty nonsense for the night. Bradley, however, was unyielding. "Remember who these people are," he pointed out, "and what they're up to. Moving by night would make good sense."

He thumbed his watch, turning on the little face light. It was getting really dark now. "I'll go below and catch a few Z's, let you take the evening watch. You wake me up at midnight and I'll take over for the graveyard shift. That okay with you, guy?"

Jesse didn't argue. He hardly ever turned in before midnight anyway. Besides, he didn't mind spending a few hours away from Bradley and the God-damned tomb. Both were starting to get on his nerves.

Alone, he slung the AK-47 over his shoulder and walked up the slope, taking his time and enjoying the cool breeze. It wasn't so bad now the sun was down. The stars were huge and white and a fat half-moon was climbing into the black sky. In the silvery soft light the desert looked almost pretty.

A dry voice in his left ear said, "'*Siyo, chooch.*"

Jesse groaned. "'*Siyo, eduda.* What's about to happen now?"

There was a dusty chuckle. "Don't worry, *chooch*. No warnings this time. Turn around—and keep your hands off that war gun."

Jesse turned. And found himself face to face with Wile E. Coyote.

That was who it looked like at first, anyway: the same long pointy muzzle, the same big bat ears and goofy little eyes. But that was just the head; from the neck down, Jesse saw now, the body was that of a man about his own size.

Jesse said, "Uh."

Grandfather's voice said, "This is Anpu. Anpu, my grandson Jesse."

"Hi," Coyote said.

That's it, Jesse thought dazedly. Too much time out in the sun today, God *damn* that Bradley. Talking coyotes—no, hell, no coyotes in Egypt, must be a jackal. Sure looks like a coyote, though. Then memory kicked in and Jesse said, "Anubis. You're Anubis."

"Anpu." The jackal ears twitched. "The Greeks screwed the name up."

"Anpu wants you to meet some friends of his," Grandfather said.

"This way," Anpu said. "The way you were going, actually."

He walked past Jesse and headed up the slope, not looking back. Grandfather's voice said, "Don't just stand there, *chooch*. Follow him."

"I don't know, *eduda*," Jesse said as he started after the jackal-headed figure. "This is getting too weird. How did you get hooked up with this character?"

"He's the god of the dead, in these parts. And, in case you've forgotten," Grandfather pointed out, "I'm dead."

Anpu was standing at the base of the fist-shaped rock outcrop. "Here," he said, pointing.

Jesse saw nothing but a big cleft in the rock, black in the moonlight. He'd seen it dozens of times during the day. "So?" he said, a little irritably.

Anpu stepped into the cleft and disappeared, feet first. His head popped back out long enough to say, "Watch your step. It's pretty tricky."

Jesse bent and stuck his arm down into the crack. His fingers found an oval shaft, just big enough for a man's body, angling steeply down into the rock. It was so well camouflaged that even now he knew it was there, he couldn't really see it.

"It's all right, *chooch*," Grandfather said. "Go on."

Jesse stuck a cautious foot into the hole. There were notches cut into the wall of the shaft for footholds, but they weren't very deep. Gritting his teeth, he let himself down into the darkness.

He couldn't tell how far down the shaft went, but the absolute blackness and the scariness of the climb made it feel endless. The rock seemed to press in on him from all sides; he gasped for breath, and might have quit except that going back up would be just as bad. The tunnel bent to one side and then there was nothing under his feet. He probed with one toe, lost his grip, and plummeted helplessly out of the shaft and into open space. Off balance, he hit cross-footed and fell on his ass onto very hard flat stone.

He opened his eyes—he didn't know when he'd closed them—and saw immediately that he was in another tomb. Or another underground chamber, anyway, complete with art work on the walls and ceiling. This one was filled with a soft, slightly yellowish light; he couldn't see the source.

Anpu was standing over him, reaching down a hand. "Are you all right?" the jackal-headed god asked anxiously. "I should have warned you about that last bit. Sorry."

Jesse took the hand and pulled himself to his feet. Suddenly a tall, beautiful woman in a flowing white dress came rushing up, shoving Anpu out of the way and putting her arms around Jesse's neck. "Oh, poor man," she cried, pulling Jesse's head down and pressing his face against her bosom. It was one hell of a bosom. "Did you hurt yourself? Do you want to lie down?"

"This is Hathor," Anpu said. His voice sounded muffled; Jesse's ears were wonderfully obstructed for the moment.

"Goddess of love and motherhood," Grandfather's voice said. "Get loose, *chooch*, there's others to meet. Later for the hot stuff."

Jesse managed to mumble something reassuring and Hathor reluctantly let him go. As she stepped back he realized she had horns. Not just little ones, either, like the ones on the Devil in the old pictures. These were big, curving horns like a buffalo's, white as ivory and tipped with little gold balls.

A deeper voice said, "Nasty bit of work, that access tunnel. We don't like it either. But the main entrance shaft is sealed, and buried by sand as well."

The speaker was another animal-faced figure, this one with the head of a shaggy gray baboon atop a short, skinny human body. He looked a little like Jesse's high school principal. "I am Thoth," he added.

"God of wisdom and knowledge," Grandfather explained in Jesse's left ear.

"And this," Anpu said, waving a hand at a fourth individual, "is Sobek."

Jesse would just as soon have missed meeting Sobek. From the shoulders down he looked like a normal man—though built like a pro wrestler—but above that grinned the head of a crocodile. The long jaws opened, revealing rows of sharp teeth, and a voice like rusty iron said, "Yo."

"I still don't get what he does," Grandfather admitted. "Got a feeling I don't want to know."

"Sorry we can't offer refreshments," Anpu apologized. "We didn't come prepared for social occasions."

"Excuse me," Jesse said, "but where did you all learn English?"

"Your grandfather taught us," Thoth replied. "This afternoon, in fact."

"That fast?" Talk about quick studies.

"Of course," Thoth said stiffly. "Simple brain-scan. I mean, we *are* gods."

"Yeah," Grandfather's voice said, "but I tried first to teach them Cherokee and they couldn't get it worth a damn."

Jesse looked around the chamber. It was larger than the ones the Arabs had been using, and finer. The ceiling was cut in an arching vault shape, and the pictures on the wall had been carved in low relief as well as painted. "Nice place," he said politely. "Somebody loot this one too? I don't see any mummies."

"As a matter of fact," Thoth said, "this tomb was never used. It was built for the last commander of this outpost, a nobleman named Neferhotep—"

"He screwed up bad back in Thebes," Sobek croaked, "and Pharaoh sent him to this shit-hole."

"—who was killed," Thoth went on, glaring at Sobek, "in a clash with Libyan raiders. His body was never recovered. Soon afterward the outpost was abandoned."

"So what are you, uh, gods doing here now?" Jesse was trying not to stare at Hathor. That gown was so thin you could see right through it, and she wasn't wearing a damn thing underneath. For that matter none of the *neterw* had exactly overdressed; the others wore only short skirts and assorted jewelry.

"A mistake," Anpu said. "Strange business. You see, the dead man, the one you buried today, happened to be a very distant but direct descendant of the Pharaoh Ramses the Great. Though of course it's unlikely he knew it."

"The death of one of royal blood," Thoth said, "so near an unused tomb, somehow resulted in a false reading in the House of the Dead."

"Osiris stepped on his dick," Sobek growled. "Old Green-Face is losing it."

"Even Osiris," Anpu protested, "could hardly have predicted such an improbable coincidence."

"Oh, I don't know." Thoth looked thoughtful. "Perhaps not such a farfetched chance as it might seem—"

He produced a polished wooden box, bound in gold, about the size and shape of an attache case. Sitting cross-legged on the floor, he flipped a jeweled catch and the box opened into two sections. The lower half, which rested flat on his lap, contained a long ebony panel with rows of carved ivory pegs. The upper section was entirely filled by a smooth rectangle of some dark crystalline stone. Thoth tapped his fingertips over the pegs and a row of hieroglyphics appeared on the surface of the crystal, glowing with a faint greenish light.

"Let's see," Thoth mused. "Ramses the Second lived thirty-two centuries ago. He had over one hundred known offspring by his various wives. Now assuming an average number of progeny—"

"At any rate," Hathor sighed, "the four of us were sent, and here we are." She gave Jesse a smile that would have given the Sphinx an erection. "Well, perhaps things could be worse."

"—and a conservative estimate of three point five generations per century—" Thoth's fingers were dancing on the pegs. The crystal was covered with hieroglyphics.

"But," Jesse said, "if it was all a mistake, why are you still here?"

"—allowing a reasonable factor for infertility and infant mortality—"

Anpu shrugged. "Come on. I'll show you."

He led the way to an arched doorway at the rear of the chamber. Hathor and Sobek followed behind Jesse. As they left the room Thoth was staring at the crystal and scratching his head with one finger. "That can't be right," he muttered.

"At the rear of this tomb," Anpu explained as they made their way down a long hallway, "is what you might call a portal. Every burial center in Egypt has at least one. It's—" He stopped and looked back at Jesse. "I can't really explain it to you. It's a place where we can pass back and forth between this world and ours. Mortals can't even see it, let alone penetrate it."

"Except when they die," Hathor added, "and we come and get them."

"Which hasn't happened for a long time," Anpu said, nodding. "It's been almost two thousand of your years since anyone was interred with the necessary procedures. We were really disappointed to find out this was a false alarm. We had hoped the people were returning to the old ways."

He turned and started walking again. Only a few paces along the corridor, he stopped again. "There," he said. "You see the problem."

A huge slab of stone, apparently fallen from the ceiling, totally blocked the passageway. It was as big as a U-Haul trailer.

"It happened just after we arrived," Anpu said. "Evidently, when the other man drove away, the vibration caused the fall. Of course it must have been badly cracked already."

"And now you can't get back? To—wherever you came from?"

Anpu shook his head. "The nearest other portals are off in the Nile valley. I'm not sure we could make the journey." He looked at the great stone slab and his ears drooped a little. "But we may have to try."

"Never," Hathor declared. "That sun, that wind. My skin. No."

Jesse noticed a strange, impractical-looking contrivance lying on the floor, an assemblage of improvised ropes and levers. He recognized a couple of machine-gun barrels, and twisted-together rifle slings. He said, "What's this?"

"Something Anpu invented," Sobek grunted. "He calls it an *akh-me*. Doesn't work for shit."

"It seemed worth a try." Anpu kicked dispiritedly at the device. He looked at Jesse. "Can you help us? Your grandfather says you know about machinery."

Jesse studied the barrier. "I don't know. It's not in my usual line—" He felt Hathor's eyes upon him. "Maybe," he said. "I'll think about it. Let me sleep on it."

They went back up the corridor. As they entered the burial chamber Thoth looked up. "It's right here, I tell you." He touched a fingertip to the glowing crystal. "There's no arguing with the numbers. Everyone in the world is a descendant of Ramses the Second."

At midnight Jesse walked back down to the other tomb to wake Bradley. Anpu walked with him, for no apparent reason but sociability. Halfway down the slope they met Bradley coming the other way, lugging his rifle. "Hey, guy," he said cheerfully. "Get some sleep, now. I'll wake you at daybreak."

He went on up toward the big rock. Anpu chuckled. "Your friend can't see me. Not if I don't want him to, anyway."

"He's not my friend," Jesse said, more emphatically than he meant to.

Anpu looked curiously around as they entered the tomb. "I haven't really taken the time to look at the other tombs around here," he remarked as Jesse switched on the battery lantern. "This one isn't bad, actually."

Jesse leaned his AK-47 against the wall by the door. "Other tombs?"

"Oh, yes. Quite a few nearby—all sealed and hidden, of course. You'd never find them if you didn't know where to look."

He leaned forward, examining a hieroglyphic inscription on the wall. Jesse said, "What's that say, anyway?"

Anpu tilted his head to one side. "A free translation," he said after a moment, "might be: 'There once was a goddess named Isis, whose breasts were of different sizes. One was dainty and small, almost no breast at all, but the other was huge and won prizes.'"

"Get out of here."

"All right," Anpu said. "Have a pleasant night, Jesse."

When he was gone Jesse looked around briefly and then picked up the battery lantern and went down the corridor to the rear chamber. The air felt cooler there and the floor was cleaner. He took a gray military blanket from a stack in one corner and made himself a pallet on the floor, rolling up another blanket for a pillow. Lying down and switching off the lantern, he wondered if he would be able to sleep in this place; but he did, almost immediately, and without dreams.

When he awoke—he didn't know how long he had been asleep; later, though, he thought it couldn't have been long—it was with the distinct feeling that he was no longer alone in the burial chamber. That might have been because somebody was trying to take his clothes off.

He said, "Wha," and fumbled for the battery lantern and switched it on.

Hathor was crouching over him, tugging at the waistband of his pants. "You must help me," she said urgently. "I don't understand these strange garments."

Jesse blinked and shook his head. "Well, that is, ah—"

"Don't worry, *chooch*," said the voice in his left ear. "She's not out to steal your soul or anything like that. She just wants to get laid. It's been a long time since she did it with anybody who wasn't at least a couple thousand years old."

Hathor was now yanking his shoes off. Jesse skinned his sweaty T-shirt up over his head and reached to undo his belt buckle. Grandfather's voice said, "I'll leave you two alone now."

As Jesse got rid of his briefs—wishing he'd worn a better pair—Hathor rose to her feet and undid a clasp at her shoulder, letting the white gown fall away, leaving her naked except for wide gold bracelets on her wrists. "I shall give you love," she announced. "I shall serve you a feast of divine pleasure."

Throbbingly ithyphallic, Jesse watched as she put a foot on either side of him. The horns, he decided, weren't so bad once you got over the first shock of seeing them. In fact they were kind of sexy.

She knelt, straddling him. "Yes," she said, bending forward, mashing those astonishing breasts against his chest, "impale me with the burning spear of your desire." Clasping with arms and thighs, she rolled onto her back, pulling him on top of her, heels spurring him. "Oh, fill my loins with your mighty obelisk," she cried, "come into me with the Nile of your passion. Do me like a hot baboon, big boy!"

Well, Jesse thought, you always did like horny women with big ones . . .

He awoke again to disturbing dreams of Vietnam; sounds of gunfire and rotors rattled in his ears. The room was still dark but his watch showed almost eight o'clock. Hastily he dressed, pausing as he felt the bracelet on his right wrist. Hathor's; she must have put it there as he slept. Memories of the night came rushing back, and he stood for a moment grinning foolishly to himself.

Then he heard it again, faint but unmistakeable: a rapid snapping, like popcorn in a microwave.

He jerked his shoes on, not bothering with socks, and ran down the corridor to the front chamber. He was halfway across the room, going for the gun he had left there, when a man appeared in the doorway: no more than a vague dark shape in the poor light that came down the entrance corridor, but Jesse knew immediately that it wasn't Bradley. He saw a dull glint that had to be a gun barrel.

Without hesitation he threw his hands in the air as high as they would go. "Don't shoot!" he yelled, wishing he knew how to say it in Arabic. "See? No gun. *Salaam aleykum*," he added somewhat desperately. "Friendly Indian. Okay?"

The gun swung his way and his insides went loose. But either the man got the idea or, more likely, he realized it wasn't a good idea to fire shots inside a room full of munitions. A harsh voice hawked up several syllables in what sounded like Arabic, and then, in a loud shout, "No-lan! No-lan!"

An answering shout came from outside. The man jerked his weapon and said, "*Yalla*. You come. Quick."

He backed slowly up the corridor, keeping Jesse covered. Jesse followed, hands still in the air, sphincter clenched. The sunlight blinded him as he reached the foot of the stone steps and he stumbled, and was yelled at. At the top of the steps the gunman said, "Stop."

Jesse stopped, blinking against the glare, trying to focus on the three backlit figures standing before him. A big booming voice, American by accent and cadence, said, "Well, what have we got here? Speak English, fella?"

Jesse thought about replying in Cherokee, just to confuse matters, but he didn't think that would do any good. He nodded. "Sure."

He could see all right, now. The man who had found him stood four or five feet away, a dark, skinny little bastard dressed in desert camo, like the snakebite victim they had buried yesterday. A face that was mostly nose and bad teeth stared unpleasantly at Jesse from the shade of a sand-tan headcloth. To his left stood another who was virtually his twin in build, ugliness, and attitude. Both men held AK-47s, pointed at Jesse's belt buckle.

It was the third man, the one who had just spoken, who got and held Jesse's attention. He wore the same unmarked camo-and-headcloth outfit as the others, but if he was an Arab Jesse was Princess Leia. He was taller than Jesse, six feet at least, with broad shoulders and a big beefy face. A rifle dangled casually from his right hand.

"Nolan," Jesse said without thinking.

The big man fixed him with bright blue eyes. "Do we know each other?"

"Everybody's heard of you." Shovel a little, never hurts. "All the pilots around this part of the world, anyway."

"Pilots? Ah." Nolan nodded. "You'll be the one who piled up that Hughes, down yonder beyond the ridge."

Before Jesse could reply a fourth man came down the slope, feet sliding in the loose rocks and sand. "Hey, Nolan," he began, and then stopped, seeing Jesse. "What the hell?" he said. "Who's this?"

"One of your professional colleagues," Nolan told him. "Apparently he was flying that Hughes."

The new arrival was about Jesse's height and rather slight of build, with small sharp pretty-boy features. He wore light-blue coveralls and a baseball cap. His hands were empty but a shoulder-holstered pistol bulged beneath his left armpit.

"No shit?" The accent was Southern. "How'd you do that, man?"

"Engine failure," Jesse said.

Looking past the Southerner, Jesse saw that there was another helicopter sitting on the ground on the far side of the rise. He could just see the tail and part of the main rotor. It looked like a French Alouette but he wasn't sure.

What he couldn't see, anywhere, was Bradley. That might be good. Probably it wasn't.

Nolan said, "Well, I wish you'd had it somewhere else. That wreck is liable to draw all sorts of attention. Can't believe it hasn't been spotted already." He gave Jesse a speculative look. "Just what were you doing around here, anyway?"

Jesse shrugged. "Flying this guy around." Play it dumb, that shouldn't be too much of a reach. "He said he was an archaeologist."

The pilot, if that was what he was, laughed. Nolan grimaced. "Maybe he should have been. He wasn't worth a damn at what he was trying to do."

"Is he all right?" Jesse asked innocently.

"Not so you'd notice," the pilot said. "In fact he's pretty damn dead."

"He tried to ambush us," Nolan told Jesse. "It was a stupid business. The odds were impossible and he didn't have a clue what he was doing."

Jesse felt sick. He hadn't liked Bradley but still . . . why hadn't the damn fool called him when he saw the helicopter coming? Maybe he had. Maybe he hadn't realized how little Jesse could hear, down in that tomb. Or maybe he'd just decided he was John Wayne.

One of the gunmen said something in Arabic. Nolan said, "He wants to know if you buried the man who was here."

Jesse nodded. "We didn't kill him. Looked like a snake got him."

"We know," Nolan said. "It's why we're here. That worthless punk who was with him took off and tried to make the border, only he happened to run into some of our people. They interrogated him and sent a message. I came at first light."

He jerked his head at the Arab who had spoken. "Gamal only wanted to thank you for burying his cousin. Don't be misled. He'll kill you just as quickly if you make a mistake."

"So," the pilot said, "what now?"

"Shut the place down," Nolan said. "We've got to assume it's been compromised. Why else would a CIA agent be sniffing around?" He rubbed his chin and sighed. "God, what a mess . . . . I'll take Gamal and Zaal and set some charges."

"Going to blow it all?"

"Yes. Damn shame, after all the effort and risk that went into bringing all that material here. But it's not as if there weren't plenty where it came from." He looked at Jesse. "You better keep an eye on this joker till we're done."

The pilot nodded and reached for his pistol. "Gonna take him back with us?"

"Oh, sure," Nolan said. "Major Hamid can ask him some questions—"

Suddenly the man called Gamal let out a high excited screech and grabbed Jesse's right arm. "*Shoof, shoof,*" he cried. "No-lan, *shoof!*"

The other Arab joined in, shouting and squawking, pushing for a better look. Nolan barked something short and pungent and both men fell silent. Then everybody stood and stared at the gold band on Jesse's wrist.

Nolan took the arm away from Gamal and bent his head, studying the bracelet closely. "Where did you get this?" he asked softly.

Jesse said, "Well, there was this old Egyptian lady—"

Nolan sighed again, straightened, and hit Jesse hard in the stomach with his fist. Jesse doubled up and fell to his knees, retching and fighting for air. "Now," Nolan said patiently, "stop being silly and tell me where you got that bracelet. Did you find it around here?"

Unable to speak, Jesse nodded. The pilot said, "What's going on, Nolan?"

"Look at it," Nolan said. "That gold, that workmanship. You've never seen anything like it outside the museum in Cairo."

"Old, huh?" The pilot whistled, like Bradley. "Worth money?"

"Worth a great deal, even by itself. If there's more around here—"

"God damn," the pilot said. "All right, bud. Where'd you find it?"

Still on his knees, clutching his midriff and trying to breathe, Jesse looked past the two renegades and up the slope. A dark prick-eared head had popped up out of the hole in the fist-shaped rock. Silhouetted against the bright sky, Anpu looked even more like that cartoon coyote.

"If Gamal and Zaal have to get it out of you," Nolan said, "you won't like it."

Anpu wiggled his ears. A skinny arm came up and waved.

Anpu pointed with exaggerated motions at the backs of Nolan and his men. Then he jabbed his finger downwards, toward the rock. He grinned and disappeared.

Jesse raised a hand. "Okay," he said weakly. "Let me up. I'll show you."

He got to his feet and started up the slope. "Be careful," Nolan warned, falling in behind him. "This better not be a trick."

Up by the rock outcrop Jesse stopped. The pilot said, "Shit, there ain't anything here."

"Over here." Jesse showed them the hole. Nolan bent down and felt around with one hand. His eyebrows went up. "It goes down to this tomb," Jesse said. "Lots of interesting stuff down there."

"I'll be damned." Nolan's voice was almost a whisper. "Ray, have you got a flashlight?"

"Sure." The pilot unclipped a small black cylinder from his belt and passed it over. "Not real big, but she's brighter than she looks."

"Come on, then." Nolan handed his AK-47 to the man called Zaal. He stepped into the shaft and began working his way downward. When he had vanished from sight the pilot, looking very dubious, climbed down after him.

That left Jesse and the two Arabs, who were still eyeing him and fingering their weapons. He stood still and didn't eye back. Inside his head he was trying to replay the climb down the shaft. By now they should be about halfway down. Now Nolan would have reached the bend in the tunnel. Big as he was, he'd have a tight time of it. Now he should be almost there. Now—

The scream that came up the shaft was like nothing Jesse had ever heard. Or ever wanted to hear again, but almost immediately there was another one just like it.

Both Arabs made exclamations of surprise. Zaal ran over, still clutching his own AK-47 and Nolan's, and stared down the shaft. Gamal simply stood there with his mouth open and his eyes huge.

That was about as good as it was likely to get. Jesse put his hands together in a double fist and clubbed Gamal as hard as he could on the side of the neck. The AK-47 came loose easily as Gamal's fingers went limp. Jesse turned and put a long burst into Zaal, who seemed to have gotten confused to find himself holding two rifles. He swung the AK-47 back and shot Gamal in the chest a couple of times, just in case he hadn't hit him hard enough. Then he went and looked down the tunnel, keeping the gun ready but not expecting to have to use it.

Sure enough, Anpu stuck his head out of the hole. "Are you all right?" he asked. "Well," he said, seeing the two bodies, "not bad. Your grandfather said you could take care of yourself."

Some muffled nightmare sounds floated up the shaft. Anpu cocked his head and winced. "That Sobek," he murmured. "Good at what he does, but so *crude* . . . . "

He looked at Jesse and cleared his throat. "I realize this isn't a good time," he said apologetically, "but about that matter we discussed—"

"I'll see what I can do," Jesse said. "Looks like I owe you."

A couple of hours later, standing by the rock outcrop, Jesse said, "Now you're certain this is going to work?"

"Hey, *chooch.*" Grandfather sounded hurt. "Don't question an elder about his medicine. Have I ever let you down?"

Jesse snorted. "Where were you this morning?"

"You mean why didn't I wake you up, so you could run out and get yourself killed along with that white fool? He didn't have a chance," Grandfather said, "and you wouldn't have either. Be glad you were in the back room, where you couldn't hear till it was too late."

Jesse nodded reluctantly. "I guess you're right," he said. "Let's do it."

He looked around one more time. The *neterw* were standing there, as they had been for an hour or so, watching him with expressions of polite patience. Hathor raised a hand and wiggled white fingers and smiled. Sobek fingered something out of his back teeth and belched. None of them spoke.

Jesse picked up the little black box from between his feet, being careful not to foul the two wires that ran down into the tunnel. "Fire in the hole," he called, and thumbed the red button.

The noise was much less than he expected, just a dull quick *boomp.* The ground jumped slightly underfoot. That was all.

Anpu was already moving past him, sliding feet-first into the shaft, ignoring the smoke and fumes pouring out of the hole. "You'd better stay here," he said to Jesse. "It might be hard for you to breathe down there."

He dropped out of sight. Grandfather said, "Like I say, this is my medicine. Ought to be, after three years in the Seabees and eight in that mine in Colorado. Not to mention the Southern Pacific—"

A high-pitched yipping came up the tunnel. Anpu sounded happy.

"One thing I know," Grandfather finished, "is how to shoot rock."

"Then why didn't you just tell them how to do it?" Jesse wanted to know. "Why bring me in?"

"Trust those four with explosives? I may be dead but I'm not stupid. The thing about gods," Grandfather said, "they got a lot of power, but when you get right down to it they're not very smart. I remember once—"

Anpu's head and shoulders emerged from the hole. He was grinning widely. His tongue hung out on one side.

"It worked," he said cheerfully. "It was perfect. Shattered the rock into small fragments without damaging anything else. As soon as we can clear away the rubble—nothing Sobek can't handle—we can reach the portal and be on our way."

He went back down the shaft. Thoth was right behind him, then Sobek. Hathor paused and touched Jesse's cheek. "Call me," she said, and stepped gracefully into the hole.

"How about that," Grandfather said. "It worked."

"For God's sake," Jesse said, "you weren't sure? I thought you said—"

"Listen," Grandfather said defensively, "it's been a long time. And that funny plastic explosive those A-rabs had, I never used anything like that before."

Jesse shook his head. He walked around the rock outcrop and started down the side of the ridge, toward Nolan's helicopter. An Alouette, all right. He'd never even ridden in one. This was going to be interesting.

Grandfather said, "Can you drive that thing, chooch?"

"Sure," Jesse said dryly. "It's my medicine."

It took three tries to get the Alouette started and off the ground. Lifting clear at last, struggling with the unfamiliar controls, Jesse heard: "You got it, *chooch*? I'm cutting out now."

"You're staying here, *eduda?*" The Alouette kept trying to swing to the left. Maybe it wanted to go home to Libya.

"Going back to the spirit world," Grandfather said. "That portal of theirs is a lot easier than the regular route."

Jesse got the Alouette steadied at last, heading northward, and let out his breath. What next? Try to make the coast, ditch the Alouette in a salt marsh, walk to the coastal highway and try to hitch a ride to the nearest town. He had a little cash, and if he could get to Alexandria he knew people who would be good for a no-questions one-way trip out of this country. If things got tight that gold bracelet ought to buy a lot of co-operation. It wasn't going to be easy, but the alternative was to land at some airfield, tell his story to the authorities, and spend the next lengthy piece of his life in an Egyptian prison.

"Take care, *sgilisi*," Grandfather said. "I'll be around."

Like that, he was gone. Jesse almost felt him leave.

After a minute Jesse sighed and settled back in the seat. Feeding in more throttle, pressing cautiously against the cyclic, he watched the airspeed needle climb. Below him, the Alouette's shadow flitted across the sand and the rocks, hurrying over Egypt.

AUTHOR'S NOTE:

This was written by invitation for *Lord of the Fantastic*, the Roger Zelazny memorial anthology. The original title was to have been *Friends of Roger*, the idea being that all the contributors were people who knew Roger personally, and I wish they'd stayed with that . . . several people suggested *Forever Amber*; I proposed *Roger, Over and Out*. (Avon was not amused.)

We were supposed to write something that reflected the influence Roger had had on our work. For me that was easy, since, as told elsewhere in this book, he was the one who got me started writing short stories in the first place; anything I did would pay tribute to that. Additionally, it was through talking and corresponding with Roger, and through reading his work—notably the novels *Eye of Cat* and *Creature of Light and Darkness*—that I began to see the possibilities of using ancient myth in modern contexts.

Roger and I went back a long, long way; to the mid-sixties, in fact, when I was playing guitar in a Baltimore establishment called the Peabody Bookstore and Beer Stube—once a hangout of H.L. Mencken's, but by my time a waterhole for tragically hip proto-yuppies.

Most of the regulars were pretty tiresome, in fact; but there was one skinny, long-nosed character who often came in by himself, and actually listened to the music, and tipped well and refrained from pinching the waitresses' bottoms. The only other thing I noticed about him was that he was inordinately fond of the song "Waltzing Matilda" and often requested it—twice on one night, when he had had a few more than usual.

One of the waitresses, with whom I was romantically involved, said his name was Roger.

Later on things went to hell for me. I lost the job, the lover, and the guitar, in that order, and next year found myself in Omaha, sweating a couple of California felony warrants. One night I picked up a new paperback titled *Lord of Light*—I wasn't into SF at the time, but I was very interested in Hindu mythology—and found myself saying "Holy shit!" every couple of pages; I'd never read anything like it. Still haven't. . . .

And later on I found and read more books by the same author, but it never occurred to me to connect "Roger Zelazny" with the elongated table-sitter who had loved the Antipodean anthem.

In Mickey Rooney's words: "The world turns, and so does the weenie." Almost a quarter of a century later, I was a Promising First Novelist; at the instigation of my editor, Roger Zelazny contributed a cover quote. (Roger was famous for his cover quotes; no one was quicker to help a struggling newcomer with a blurb.) I called to thank him and we got to talking, and at some point a circuit closed. "You mean that was you—" "Yeah, you must be the one who—" "Remember when—"

We stayed in touch; we became friends. Roger had an extremely rare quality: he *listened*. During one especially low time in my personal life, he was a lifeline. No matter how late it was, how drunk or incoherent I was, he never blew me off or hung up on me.

Without Roger's encouragement and guidance I would surely have dropped out of SF, and probably out of writing entirely, long ago. I might have done something more drastic than that.

When I heard he was dead I wandered about the house crying helplessly for hours; and then late that night I got very, very drunk, and at last got out my current guitar and played "Waltzing Matilda" over and over again in the dark.

WHEN THIS WORLD
IS ALL ON FIRE

"SQUATTERS," JIMMY Lonekiller said as he swung the jeep off the narrow old blacktop onto the narrower and older gravel side road. "I can't believe we got squatters again."

Sitting beside him, bracing himself against the bumping and bouncing, Sergeant Davis Blackbear said, "Better get used to it. We kick this bunch out, there'll be more."

Jimmy Lonekiller nodded. "Guess that's right," he said. "They're not gonna give up, are they?"

He was a husky, dark-skinned young man, and tall for a Cherokee; among the women of the reservation he was generally considered something of a hunk. His khaki uniform was neat and crisply pressed, despite the oppressive heat. Davis Blackbear, feeling his own shirt wilting and sticking to his skin, wondered how he did it. Maybe fullbloods didn't sweat as much. Or maybe it was something to do with being young.

Davis said, "Would you? Give up, I mean, if you were in their shoes?"

Jimmy didn't reply for a moment, being busy fighting the wheel as the jeep slammed over a series of potholes. They were on a really bad stretch now, the road narrowed to a single-lane dirt snaketrack; the overhanging trees on either side, heavy with dust-greyed festoons of kudzu vine, shut out the sun without doing anything much about the heat. This was an out-of-the-way part of the reservation; Davis had had to check the map at the tribal police headquarters to make sure he knew how to get here.

The road began to climb, now, up the side of a steep hill. The jeep slowed to not much better than walking speed; the locally-distilled alcohol might burn cooler and cleaner than gasoline but it had no power at all. Jimmy Lonekiller spoke then: "Don't guess I would, you put it that way. Got to go somewhere, poor bastards."

They were speaking English; Davis was Oklahoma Cherokee, having moved to the North Carolina reservation only a dozen years ago, when he married a Qualla Band woman. He could understand the Eastern dialect fairly well by now, enough for cop purposes anyway, but he still wasn't up to a real conversation.

"Still," Jimmy went on, "you got to admit it's a hell of a thing. Twenty-first century, better than five hundred years after Columbus, and here we are again with white people trying to settle on our land. What little bit we've got left," he said, glancing around at the dusty woods. "There's gotta be somewhere else they can go."

"Except," Davis said, "somebody's already there too."

"Probably so," Jimmy admitted. "Seems like they're running out of places for people to be."

He steered the jeep around a rutted hairpin bend, while Davis turned the last phrase over in his mind, enjoying the simple precision of it: running out of places for people to be, that was the exact and very well-put truth. Half of Louisiana and more than half of Florida under water now, the rest of the coastline inundated, Miami and Mobile and Savannah and most of Houston, and, despite great and expensive efforts, New Orleans too.

And lots more land, farther inland, that might as well be submerged for all the good it did anybody: all that once-rich farm country in southern Georgia and Alabama and Mississippi, too hot and dry now to grow anything, harrowed by tornadoes and dust storms, while raging fires destroyed the last remnants of the pine forests and the cypress groves of the dried-up swamplands. Not to mention the quake, last year, shattering Memphis and eastern Arkansas, demolishing the levees and turning the Mississippi loose on what was left of the Delta country. Seemed everybody either had way too much water or not enough.

He'd heard a black preacher, on the radio, declare that it was all God's judgment on the South because of slavery and racism. But that was bullshit; plenty of other parts of the country were getting it just as bad. Like Manhattan, or San Francisco—and he didn't even want to think about what it must be like in places like Arizona. And Africa, oh, Jesus. Nobody in the world wanted to think about Africa now.

The road leveled out at the top of the hill and he pointed. "Pull over there. I want to do a quick scout before we drive up."

Jimmy stopped the jeep and Davis climbed out and stood in the middle of the dirt road. "Well," Jimmy said, getting out too, "I wish somebody else would get the job of running them off now and then." He gave Davis a mocking look. "It's what I get, letting myself get partnered with an old 'breed. Everybody knows why Ridge always puts you in charge of the evictions."

Davis didn't rise to the bait; he knew what Jimmy was getting at. It was something of a standing joke among the reservation police that Davis always got any jobs that involved dealing with white people. Captain Ridge claimed it was because of his years of experience on the Tulsa PD, but Jimmy and others claimed it was really because he was quarter-blood and didn't look all that Indian and therefore might make whites less nervous.

In his own estimation he didn't look particularly Indian or white or anything else, just an average-size man with a big bony face and too many wrinkles and dark brown hair that was now getting heavily streaked with gray. He doubted that his appearance inspired much confidence in people of any race.

The dust cloud was beginning to settle over the road behind them. A black-and-white van appeared, moving slowly, and pulled to a stop behind the jeep. Corporal Roy Smoke stuck his head out the window and said, "Here?"

"For now," Davis told him. "I'm going to go have a look, scope out the scene before we move in. You guys wait here." He turned. "Jimmy, you come with me."

The heat was brutal as they walked down the road, even in the shady patches. At the bottom of the hill, though, Davis led the way off the road and up a dry creek bed, and back in the woods it was a little cooler. Away from the road, there wasn't enough sunlight for the kudzu vines to take over, and beneath the trees the light was pleasantly soft and green. Still too damn dry, Davis thought, feeling leaves and twigs crunching under his boot soles. Another good reason to get this eviction done quickly; squatters tended to be careless with fire. The last bad woods fire on the reservation, a couple of months ago, had been started by a squatter family trying to cook a stolen hog.

They left the creek bed and walked through the woods, heading roughly eastward. "Hell," Jimmy murmured, "I know where this is now. They're on the old Birdshooter place, huh? Shit, nobody's lived there for years. Too rocky to grow anything, no water since the creek went dry."

Davis motioned for silence. Moving more slowly now, trying to step quietly though it wasn't easy in the dry underbrush, they worked their way to the crest of a low ridge. Through the trees Davis could see a cleared area beyond. Motioning to Jimmy to wait, he moved up to the edge of the woods and paused in the shadow of a half-grown oak, and that was when he heard the singing.

At first he didn't even recognize it as singing; the sound was so high and clear and true that he took it for some sort of instrument. But after a second he realized it was a human voice, though a voice like none he'd ever heard. He couldn't make out the words, but the sound alone was enough to make the hair stand up on his arms and neck, and the air suddenly felt cooler under the trees.

It took Davis a moment to get unstuck; he blinked rapidly and took a deep breath. Then, very cautiously, he peered around the trunk of the oak.

The clearing wasn't very big; wasn't very clear, either, any more, having been taken over by brush and weeds. In the middle stood the ruins of a small frame house, its windows smashed and its roof fallen in.

Near the wrecked house sat a green pickup truck, its bed covered with a boxy, homemade-looking camper shell—plywood, it looked like from where Davis stood, and painted a dull uneven gray. The truck's own finish was badly faded and scabbed with rust; the near front fender was crumpled. Davis couldn't see any license plates.

A kind of lean-to had been erected at the rear of the truck, a sagging blue plastic tarps with guy-ropes tied to trees and bushes. As Davis watched, a lean, long-faced man in bib overalls and a red baseball cap came out from under the tarp and stood looking about.

Then the red-haired girl came around the front of the truck, still singing, the words clear now:

> "Oh, when this world is all on fire
> Where you gonna go?
> Where you gonna go?"

She was, Davis guessed, maybe twelve or thirteen, though he couldn't really tell at this distance. Not much of her, anyway; he didn't figure she'd go over eighty pounds or so. Her light blue dress was short and sleeveless, revealing thin pale arms and legs. All in all it didn't seem possible for all that sound to be com-

ing from such a wispy little girl; and yet there was no doubt about
it, he could see her mouth moving:

"Oh, when this world is all on fire" (she sang again)
"Where you gonna go?"

The tune was a simple one, an old-fashioned modal-sounding
melody line, slow and without a pronounced rhythm. It didn't
matter; nothing mattered but that voice. It soared through the
still mountain air like a whippoorwill calling beside a running
stream. Davis felt his throat go very tight.

"Run to the mountains to hide your face
Never find no hiding place
Oh, when this world is all on fire
Where you gonna go?"

The man in the baseball cap put his hands on his hips. "Eva
May!" he shouted.

The girl stopped singing and turned. Her red hair hung
down her back almost to her waist. "Yes, Daddy?" she called.

"Quit the damn fooling around," the man yelled. His voice
was rough, with the practiced anger of the permanently angry
man. "Go help your brother with the fire."

Fire? Davis spotted it then, a thin trace of bluish-white
smoke rising from somewhere on the far side of the parked truck.
"Shit!" he said soundlessly, and turned and began picking his
way back down the brushy slope.

"What's happening?" Jimmy Lonekiller said as Davis reap-
peared. "What was that music? Sounded like—"

"Quiet," Davis said. "Come on. We need to hurry."

"Go," Davis said to Jimmy as they turned off the road and up
the brush-choked track through the trees. "No use trying to
sneak up. They've heard us coming by now."

Sure enough, the squatters were already standing in the
middle of the clearing, watching, as the jeep bumped to a stop in
front of them. The man in the red baseball cap stood in the middle, his face dark with anger. Beside him stood a washed-out-
looking blond woman in a faded flower-print dress and, next to
her, a tall teenage boy wearing ragged jeans and no shirt. The

boy's hair had been cropped down almost flush with his scalp.

The woman was holding a small baby to her chest. Great, Davis thought with a flash of anger, just what a bunch of homeless drifters needed. Running out of places for people to be, but not out of people, hell, no....

The red-haired girl was standing off to one side, arms folded. Close up, Davis revised his estimate of her age; she had to be in her middle to late teens at least. There didn't appear to be much of a body under that thin blue dress, but it was definitely not that of a child. Her face, as she watched the two men get out of the jeep, was calm and without expression.

The van came rocking and swaying up the trail and stopped behind the jeep. Davis waited while Roy Smoke and the other four men got out—quite a force to evict one raggedy-ass family, but Captain Ridge believed in being careful—and then he walked over to the waiting squatters and said, "Morning. Where you folks from?"

The man in the red baseball cap spat on the ground, not taking his eyes off Davis. "Go to hell, Indian."

Oh oh. Going to be like that, was it? Davis said formally, "Sir, you're on Cherokee reservation land. Camping isn't allowed except by permit and in designated areas. I'll have to ask you to move out."

The woman said, "Oh, why can't you leave us alone? We're not hurting anybody. You people have all this land, why won't you share it?"

We tried that, lady, Davis thought, and look where it got us. Aloud he said, "Ma'am, the laws are made by the government of the Cherokee nation. I just enforce them."

"Nation!" The man snorted. "Bunch of woods niggers, hogging good land while white people starve. You got no right."

"I'm not here to argue about it," Davis said. "I'm just here to tell you you've got to move on."

The boy spoke up suddenly. "You planning to make us?"

Davis looked at him. Seventeen or eighteen, he guessed, punk-mean around the eyes and that Johnny Pissoff stance that they seemed to develop at that age; ropy muscles showing under bare white skin, forearms rippling visibly as he clenched both fists.

"Yes," Davis told him. "If necessary, we'll move you."

To the father—he assumed—he added, "I'm hoping you

won't make it necessary. If you like, we'll give you a hand—"

He didn't get to finish. That was when the boy came at him, fists up, head hunched down between his shoulders, screaming as he charged: *"Redskin motherfu—"*

Davis shifted his weight, caught the wild swing in a cross-arm block, grasped the kid's wrist and elbow and pivoted, all in one smooth motion. The boy yelped in pain as he hit the ground, and then grunted as Jimmy Lonekiller landed on top of him, handcuffs ready.

The man in the red cap had taken a step forward, but he stopped as Roy Smoke moved in front of him and tapped him gently on the chest with his nightstick. "No," Roy said, "you don't want to do that. Stand still, now."

Davis said, "Wait up, Jimmy," and then to the man in the red cap, "All right, there's two ways we can do this. We can take this boy to Cherokee town and charge him with assaulting an officer, and he can spend the next couple of months helping us fix the roads. Probably do him a world of good."

"No," the woman cried. The baby in her arms was wailing now, a thin weak piping against her chest, but she made no move to quiet it. "Please, no."

"Or," Davis went on, "you can move out of here, right now, without any more trouble, and I'll let you take him with you."

The girl, he noticed, hadn't moved the whole time, just stood there watching with no particular expression on her face, except that there might be a tiny trace of a smile on her lips as she looked at the boy on the ground.

"No," the woman said again. "Vernon, no, you can't let them take Ricky—"

"All right," the man said. "We'll go, Indian. Let him up. He won't give you no more trouble. Ricky, behave yourself or I'll whup your ass."

Davis nodded to Jimmy Lonekiller, who released the kid. "Understand this," Davis said, "we don't give second warnings. If you're found on Cherokee land again, you'll be arrested, your vehicle will be impounded, and you might do a little time."

The boy was getting to his feet, rubbing his arm. The woman started to move toward him but the man said, "He's all right, damn it. Get busy packing up." He turned his head and scowled at the girl. "You too, Eva May."

Davis watched as the squatters began taking down the tarp.

The girl's long red hair fairly glowed in the midday sun; he felt a crazy impulse to go over and touch it. He wished she'd sing some more, but he didn't imagine she felt like singing now.

He said, "Roy, have somebody kill that fire. Make sure it's dead and buried. This place is a woods fire waiting to happen."

Davis lived in a not very big trailer on the outskirts of Cherokee town. Once he had had a regular house, but after his wife had taken off, a few years ago, with that white lawyer from Gatlinburg, he'd moved out and let a young married couple have the place.

The trailer's air conditioning was just about shot, worn out from the constant unequal battle with the heat, but after the sun went down it wasn't too bad except on the hottest summer nights. Davis took off his uniform and hung it up and stretched out on the bed while darkness fell outside and the owls began calling in the trees. Sweating, waiting for the temperature to drop, he closed his eyes and heard again in his mind, over the rattle of the laboring air conditioner:

> "Oh, when this world is all on fire
> Where you gonna go?
> Where you gonna go?"

It was the following week when he saw the girl again.

He was driving through Waynesville, taking one of the force's antique computers for repairs, when he saw her crossing the street up ahead. Even at half a block's distance he was sure it was the same girl; there couldn't be another head of hair like that in these mountains. She was even wearing what looked like the same blue dress.

But he was caught in slow traffic, and she disappeared around the corner before he could get any closer. Sighing, making a face at himself for acting like a fool, he drove on. By the time he got to the computer shop he had convinced himself it had all been his imagination.

He dropped off the computer and headed back through town, taking it easy and keeping a wary eye on the traffic, wondering as always how so many people still managed to drive, despite fuel shortages and sky-high prices; and all the new restrictions, not that anybody paid them any mind, the government having all it could do just keeping the country more or less together.

An ancient minivan, a mattress roped to its roof, made a sudden left turn from the opposite lane. Davis hit the brakes, cursing—a fenderbender in a tribal patrol car, that would really make the day—and that was when he saw the red-haired girl coming up the sidewalk on the other side of the street.

Some asshole behind him was honking; Davis put the car in motion again, going slow, looking for a parking place. There was a spot up near the next corner and he turned into it and got out and locked up the cruiser, all without stopping to think what he thought he was doing or why he was doing it.

He crossed the street and looked along the sidewalk, but he couldn't see the girl anywhere. He began walking back the way she'd been going, looking this way and that. The street was mostly lined with an assortment of small stores—leftovers, probably, from the days when Waynesville had been a busy tourist resort, before tourism became a meaningless concept—and he peered in through a few shop windows, without any luck.

He walked a couple of blocks that way and then decided she couldn't have gotten any farther in that little time. He turned and went back, and stopped at the corner and looked up and down the cross street, wondering if she could have gone that way. Fine Indian you are, he thought, one skinny little white girl with hair like a brush fire and you keep losing her.

Standing there, he became aware of a growing small commotion across the street, noises coming from the open door of the shop on the corner: voices raised, a sound of scuffling. A woman shouted, "No you don't—"

He ran across the street, dodging an oncoming BMW, and into the shop. It was an automatic cop reaction, unconnected to his search; but then immediately he saw the girl, struggling in the grip of a large steely-haired woman in a long black dress. "Stop fighting me," the woman was saying in a high strident voice. "Give me that, young lady. I'm calling the police—"

Davis said, "What's going on here?"

The woman looked around. "Oh," she said, looking pleased, not letting go the girl's arm. "I'm glad to see you, officer. I've got a little shoplifter for you."

The girl was looking at Davis too. If she recognized him she gave no sign. Her face was flushed, no doubt from the struggle, but still as expressionless as ever.

"What did she take?" Davis asked.

"This." The woman reached up and pried the girl's right hand open, revealing something shiny. "See, she's still holding it!"

Davis stepped forward and took the object from the girl's hand: a cheap-looking little pendant, silver or more likely silver-plated, in the shape of a running dog, with a flimsy neck chain attached.

"I want her arrested," the woman said. "I'll be glad to press charges. I'm tired of these people, coming around here ruining this town, stealing everyone blind."

Davis said, "I'm sorry, ma'am, I don't have any jurisdiction here. You'll need to call the local police."

She blinked, doing a kind of ladylike double-take, looking at Davis's uniform. "Oh. Excuse me, I thought—" She managed to stop before actually saying, "I thought you were a real policeman." It was there on her face, though.

Davis looked again at the pendant, turning it over in his hand, finding the little white price tag stuck on the back of the running dog: $34.95. A ripoff even in the present wildly-inflated money; but after a moment he reached for his wallet and said, "Ma'am, how about if I just pay you for it?"

The woman started to speak and then stopped, her eyes locking on the wallet in his hand. Not doing much business these days, he guessed; who had money to waste on junk like this?

While she hesitated, Davis pulled out two twenties and laid them on the nearby counter top. "With a little extra to pay for your trouble," he added.

That did it. She let go the girl's arm and scooped up the money with the speed of a professional gambler. "All right," she said, "but get her out of here!"

The girl stood still, staring at Davis. The woman said, "I mean it! Right now!"Davis tilted his head in the direction of the door. The girl nodded and started to move, not particularly fast. Davis followed her, hearing the woman's voice behind him: "And if you ever come back—"

Out on the sidewalk, Davis said, "I'm parked down this way."

She looked at him. "You arresting me?"

Her speaking voice—he realized suddenly that this was the first time he'd heard it—was surprisingly ordinary; soft and high, rather pleasant, but nothing to suggest what it could do in song. There was no fear in it, or in her face; she might have been asking what time it was.

Davis shook his head. "Like I told that woman, I don't have any authority here."

"So you can't make me go with you."

"No," he said. "But I'd say you need to get clear of this area pretty fast. She's liable to change her mind and call the law after all."

"Guess that's right. Okay." She fell in beside him, sticking her hands in the pockets of the blue dress. He noticed her feet were barely covered by a pair of old tennis shoes, so ragged they were practically sandals. "Never rode in a police car before."

As they came up to the parked cruiser he stopped and held out his hand. "Here. You might as well have this."

She took the pendant and held it up in front of her face, looking at it, swinging it from side to side. After a moment she slipped the chain over her head and tucked the pendant down the front of her dress. "Better hide it," she said. "Ricky sees it, he'll steal it for sure."

He said, "Not much of a thing to get arrested for."

She shrugged. "I like dogs. We had a dog, back home in Georgia, before we had to move. Daddy wouldn't let me take him along."

"Still," he said, "you could have gone to jail."

She shrugged, a slight movement of her small shoulders. "So? Wouldn't be no worse than how I got to live now."

"Yes it would," he told her. "You've got no idea what it's like in those forced-labor camps. How old are you?"

"Seventeen," she said. "Well, next month."

"Then you're an adult, as far's the law's concerned. Better watch it from now on." He opened the right door. "Get in."

She climbed into the car and he closed the door and went around. As he slid in under the wheel she said, "Okay, I know what comes next. Where do you want to go?"

"What?" Davis looked at her, momentarily baffled. "Well, I was just going to take you home. Wherever your family—"

"Oh, come on." Her voice held an edge of scorn now. "You didn't get me out of there for nothing. You want something, just like everybody always does, and I know what it is because there ain't nothing else I got. Well, all right," she said. "I don't guess I mind. So where do you want to go to do it?"

For a moment Davis was literally speechless. The idea simply hadn't occurred to him; he hadn't thought of her in that way at all. It surprised him, now he considered it. After all, she was a pretty young girl—you could have said beautiful, in a way—and he had been living alone for a long time. Yet so it was; he felt no stirrings of that kind toward this girl, not even now with her close up and practically offering herself.

When he could speak he said, "No, no. Not that. Believe me."

"Really?" She looked very skeptical. "Then what *do* you want?"

"Right now," he said, "I want to buy you a pair of shoes."

An hour or so later, coming out of the discount shoe store out by the highway, she said, "I know what this is all about. You feel bad because you run us off, back last week."

"No." Davis's voice held maybe a little bit more certainty than he felt, but he added, "Just doing my job. Anyway, you couldn't have stayed there. No water, nothing to eat, how would you live?"

"You still didn't have no right to run us off."

"Sure I did. It's our land," he said. "All we've got left."

She opened her mouth and he said, "Look, we're not going to talk about it, all right?"

They walked in silence the rest of the way across the parking lot. She kept looking down at her feet, admiring the new shoes. They weren't much, really, just basic white no-name sport shoes, but he supposed they looked pretty fine to her. At that they hadn't been all that cheap. In fact between the shoes and the pendant he'd managed to go through a couple days' pay. Not that he was likely to get paid any time soon; the tribe had been broke for a long time.

As he started the car she said, "You sure you don't want to, you know, do it?"

He looked at her and she turned sidewise in the seat, moving her thin pale legs slightly apart, shifting her narrow hips. "Hey," she said, "somebody's gotta be the first. Might as well be you."

Her mouth quirked. "If it ain't you it'll prob'ly be Ricky. He sure keeps trying."

With some difficulty Davis said, "Turn around, please, and do up your safety belt."

"All right." She giggled softly. "Just don't know what it is you want from me, that's all."

He didn't respond until they were out of the parking lot and rolling down the road, back into Waynesville. Then he said, "Would you sing for me?"

"What?" Her voice registered real surprise. "Sing? You mean right now, right here in the car?"

"Yes," Davis said. "Please."

"Well, I be damn." She brushed back her hair and studied him for a minute. "You mean it, don't you? All right...what you want me to sing? If I know it."

"That song you were singing that morning up on the reservation," he said. "Just before we arrived."

She thought about it. "Oh," she said. "You mean—"

She tilted her head back and out it came, like a flood of clear spring water:

> *"Oh, when this world is all on fire*
> *Where you gonna go?"*

"Yes," Davis said very softly. "That's it. Sing it. Please."

Her family was staying in a refugee camp on the other side of town; a great hideous sprawl of cars and trucks and buses and campers and trailers of all makes and ages and states of repair, bright nylon tents and crude plastic-tarp shelters and pathetic, soggy arrangements of cardboard boxes, spread out over a once-beautiful valley.

"You better just drop me off here," the girl said as he turned off the road.

"That's okay," Davis said. "Which way do I go?"

At her reluctant direction, he steered slowly down a narrow muddy lane between parked vehicles and outlandish shelters, stopping now and then as children darted across in front of the car. People came out and stared as the big police cruiser rolled past. Somebody threw something unidentifiable, that bounced off the windshield leaving a yellowish smear. By now Davis was pretty sure this hadn't been a good idea.

But the girl said, "Up there," and there it was, the old truck with the homemade camper bed and the blue plastic awning rigged out behind, just like before. He stopped the car and got out and went around to open the passenger door.

The air was thick with wood smoke and the exhausts of worn-out engines, and the pervasive reek of human waste. The ground underfoot was soggy with mud and spilled motor oil and God knew what else. Davis looked around at the squalid scene, remembering what this area used to look like, only a few years ago. Now, it looked like the sort of thing they used to show on the news, in countries you'd never heard of. The refugee camps in Kosovo, during his long-ago army days, hadn't been this bad.

Beyond, up on the mountainsides, sunlight glinted on the windows of expensive houses. A lot of locals had thought it was wonderful, back when the rich people first started buying up land and building homes up in the mountain country, getting away from the heat and the flooding. They hadn't been as happy about the second invasion, a year or so later, by people bringing nothing but their desperation....

Davis shook his head and opened the door. Even the depressing scene couldn't really get him down, right now. It had been an amazing experience, almost religious, driving along with that voice filling the dusty interior of the old cruiser; he felt light and loose, as if coming off a marijuana high. He found himself smiling—

A voice behind him said, "What the hell?" and then, "Eva May!"

He turned and saw the man standing there beside the truck, still wearing the red cap and the angry face. "Hello," he said, trying to look friendly or at least inoffensive. "Just giving your daughter a lift from town. Don't worry, she's not in any trouble—"

"Hell she's not," the man said, looking past Davis. "Eva May, git your ass out of that thing! What you doing riding around with this God-damn woods nigger?"

The girl swung her feet out of the car. Davis started to give her a hand but decided that might be a bad move right now. She got out and stepped past Davis. "It's all right, Daddy," she said. "He didn't do nothing bad. Look, he bought me some new shoes!"

"No shit." The man looked down at her feet, at the new shoes standing out white and clean against the muddy ground. "New shoes, huh? Git 'em off."

She stopped. "But Daddy—"

His hand came up fast; it made an audible crack against the side of her face. As she stumbled backward against the side of the truck he said, "God damn it, I *said* take them shoes off."

He spun about to face Davis. "You don't like that, Indian? Maybe you wanta do something about it?"

Davis did, in fact, want very much to beat this worthless *yoneg* within half an inch of his life. But he forced himself to stand still and keep his hands down at his sides. Start a punch-out in here, and almost certainly he'd wind up taking on half the men in the camp. Or using the gun on his belt, which would bring down a whole new kind of disaster.

Even then he might have gone for it, but he knew that anything he did to the man would later be taken out on Eva May. It was a pattern all too familiar to any cop.

She had one shoe off now and was jerking at the other, standing on one foot, leaning against the trailer, sobbing. She got it off and the man jerked it out of her hand. "Here." He half-turned and threw the shoe, hard, off somewhere beyond the old school bus that was parked across the lane. He bent down and picked up the other shoe and hurled it in the opposite direction.

"Ain't no damn Indian buying *nothing* for my kid," he said. "Or going anywhere *near* her. You understand that, Chief?"

From inside the camper came the sound of a baby crying. A woman's voice said, "Vernon? What's going on, Vernon?"

"Now," the man said, "you git out of here, woods nigger."

The blood was singing in Davis's ears and there was a taste in his mouth like old pennies. Still he managed to check himself, and to keep his voice steady as he said, "Sir, whatever you think of me, your daughter has a great gift. She should have the opportunity—"

"Listen close, Indian." The man's voice was low, now, and very intense. "You shut your mouth and you git back in that car and you drive outta here, right damn *now*, or else I'm on find out if you got the guts to use that gun. Plenty white men around here, be glad to help stomp your dirty red ass."

Davis glanced at Eva May, who was still leaning against the truck, weeping and holding the side of her face. Her bare white feet were already spotted with mud.

And then, because there was nothing else to do, he got back in the car and drove away. He didn't look back. There was nothing there he wanted to see; nothing he wouldn't already be seeing for a long time to come.

*   *   *

"Blackbear," Captain Ridge said, next morning. "I don't believe this."

He was seated at his desk in his office, looking up at Davis. His big dark face was not that of a happy man.

"I got a call just now," he said, "from the sheriff's office over in Waynesville. Seems a reservation officer, man about your size and wearing sergeant's stripes, picked up a teenage girl on the street. Made her get into a patrol car, tried to get her to have sex, even bought her presents to entice her. When she refused he took her back to the refugee camp and made threats against her family."

Davis said, "Captain—"

"No," Captain Ridge said, and slapped a hand down on his desk top. "No, Blackbear, I don't want to hear it. See, you're about to tell me it's a lot of bullshit, and I *know* it's a lot of bullshit, and it doesn't make a damn bit of difference. You listen to me, Blackbear. Whoever those people are, you stay away from them. You stay out of Waynesville, till I tell you different. On duty or off, I don't care."

He leaned back in his chair. "Because if you show up there again, you're going to be arrested—the sheriff just warned me— and there won't be a thing I can do about it. And you know what kind of chance you'll have in court over there. They like us even less than they do the squatters."

Davis said, "All right. I wasn't planning on it anyway."

But of course he went back. Later, he thought that the only surprising thing was that he waited as long as he did.

He went on Sunday morning. It was an off-duty day and he drove his own car; that, plus the nondescript civilian clothes he wore, ought to cut down the chances of his being recognized. He stopped at an all-hours one-stop in Maggie Valley and bought a pair of cheap sunglasses and a butt-ugly blue mesh-back cap with an emblem of a jumping fish on the front. Pulling the cap down low, checking himself out in the old Dodge's mirror, he decided he looked like a damn fool, but as camouflage it ought to help.

But when he got to the refugee camp he found it had all been for nothing. The truck was gone and so was Eva May's family; an elderly couple in a Buick were already setting up camp in the spot. No, they said, they didn't know anything; the place had been empty when they got here, just a little while ago.

Davis made a few cautious inquiries, without finding out much more. The woman in the school bus across the lane said she'd heard them leaving a little before daylight. She had no idea where they'd gone and doubted if anyone else did.

"People come and go," she said. "There's no keeping track. And they weren't what you'd call friendly neighbors."

Well, Davis thought as he drove back to the reservation, so much for that. He felt sad and empty inside, and disgusted with himself for feeling that way. Good thing the bars and liquor stores weren't open on Sunday; he could easily go on a serious drunk right now.

He was coming over the mountains east of Cherokee when he saw the smoke.

It was the worst fire of the decade. And could have been much worse; if the wind had shifted just right, it might have taken out the whole reservation. As it was, it was three days before the fire front crossed the reservation border and became somebody else's problem.

For Davis Blackbear it was a very long three days. Afterward, he estimated that he might have gotten three or four hours of sleep the whole time. None of the tribal police got any real time off, the whole time; it was one job after another, evacuating people from the fire's path, setting up roadblocks, keeping traffic unsnarled and, in the rare times there was nothing else to do, joining the brutally overworked firefighting crews. By now almost every able-bodied man in the tribe was helping fight the blaze; or else already out of action, being treated for burns or smoke inhalation or heat stroke.

At last the fire ate its way over the reservation boundary and into the national parkland beyond; and a few hours later, as Wednesday's sun slid down over the mountains, Davis Blackbear returned to his trailer and fell across the bed, without bothering to remove his sweaty uniform or even to kick off his ruined shoes. And lay like a dead man through the rest of the day and all through the night, until the next morning's light came in the trailer's windows; and then he got up and undressed and went back to bed and slept some more.

A little before noon he woke again, and knew before he opened his eyes what he was going to do.

Captain Ridge had told him to take the day off and rest up; but Ridge wasn't around when Davis came by the station, and nobody paid any attention when Davis left his car and drove off in one of the jeeps. Or stopped him when he drove past the road-blocks that were still in place around the fire zone; everybody was too exhausted to ask unnecessary questions.

It was a little disorienting, driving across the still-smoking land; the destruction had been so complete that nothing was rec-ognizable. He almost missed a couple of turns before he found the place he was looking for.

A big green pickup truck was parked beside the road, bear-ing the insignia of the U.S. Forest Service. A big stocky white man in a green uniform stood beside it, watching as Davis drove up and parked the jeep and got out. "Afternoon," he said.

He stuck out a hand as Davis walked across the road. "Bob Lindblad," he said as Davis shook his hand. "Fire inspector. They sent me down to have a look, seeing as it's on federal land now."

He looked around and shook his head. "Hell of a thing," he said, and wiped his forehead with the back of his hand.

It certainly was a strange-looking scene. On the northeast side of the road there was nothing but ruin, an ash-covered deso-lation studded with charred tree stumps, stretching up the hill-side and over the ridge and out of sight. The other side of the road, however, appeared untouched; except for a thin coating of powdery ash on the bushes and the kudzu vines, it looked exactly as it had when Davis had come this way a couple of weeks ago.

The Forest Service man said, "Anybody live around here?"

"Not close, no. Used to be a family named Birdshooter, lived up that way, but they moved out a long time ago."

Lindblad nodded. "I saw some house foundations."

Davis said, "This was where it started?"

"Where it *was* started," Lindblad said. "Yes."

"Somebody set it?"

"No question about it." Lindblad waved a big hand. "Sign all over the place. They set it at half a dozen points along this road. The wind was at their backs, out of the southwest—that's why the other side of the road didn't take—so they weren't in any dan-ger. Bastards," he added.

Davis said, "Find anything to show who did it?"

Lindblad shook his head. "Been too much traffic up and

down this road, last few days, to make any sense of the tracks. I'm still looking, though."

"All right if I look around too?" Davis asked.

"Sure. Just holler," Lindblad said, "if you find anything. I'll be somewhere close by."

He walked off up the hill, his shoes kicking up little white puffs of ash. Davis watched him a minute and then started to walk along the road, looking at the chewed-up surface. The Forest Service guy was right, he thought, no way in hell could anybody sort out all these tracks and ruts. Over on the unburned downhill side, somebody had almost gone into the ditch.

Davis almost missed it. A single step left or right, or the sun at a different angle, and he'd never have seen the tiny shininess at the bottom of the brush-choked ditch. He bent down and groped, pushing aside a clod of roadway dirt, and felt something tangle around his fingers. He tugged gently and it came free. He straightened up and held up his hand in front of his face.

The sun glinted off the little silver dog as it swung from side to side at the end of the broken chain.

Up on the hillside Lindblad called, "Find anything?"

Davis turned and looked. Lindblad was poking around near the ruins of the old house, nearly hidden by a couple of black tree stubs. His back was to the road.

"No," Davis yelled back, walking across the road. "Not a thing."

He drew back his arm and hurled the pendant high out over the black-and-gray waste. It flashed for an instant against the sky before vanishing, falling somewhere on the burned earth.

AUTHOR'S NOTE:

This story has a rather unfortunate history. I wrote it on request for an anthology of SF stories by Southern writers; but then there was a stupid and unnecessary misunderstanding (at least fifty percent my fault) over the payment arrangements, and I wound up withdrawing it. Gardner Dozois then picked it up for *Asimov's*, where it finally appeared.

I had been reading up on global warming, and getting seriously worried; it is indeed a frightening subject. This was intended as a cautionary tale, but as soon as I started work on it the human aspects took over and I got deeply involved with the characters—as always seems to happen—and in fact became badly depressed for several days until it was finished. Yes. The writer who cries and drinks because he's writing a sad story isn't just a TV-comedy gag; it actually happens, because real-life writers are such neurotic idiots. We kill me sometimes.

SMOKE

Standing on the bank of the little stream, facing the sun that was just beginning to rise over the nearest ridge, the old man named Smoke poured tobacco into his palm, cautiously shaking the little buckskin bag until it was empty and tucking it into a fold of his fringed hunting coat. He raised both hands to face level, so that the rays of the rising sun shone full on the small mound of dark Cherokee leaf.

Now he stuck the forefinger of his free hand into the little pile of tobacco and began stirring with a gentle circular motion. As he stirred, he raised his dry old voice in an *igawesdi* medicine song, chanting the secret words that were not Cherokee but a much older language, no longer spoken by any living people.

At the end of the song he paused and blew very lightly on the tobacco; then he raised it to the sun again and began the *igawesdi* once more. Four times in all he sang the song, always stirring, always keeping the tobacco in the sunlight; four times he blew on the acrid crumbled leaves.

Done, he got out the little bag and carefully refilled it, making sure not to spill so much as a flake of the tobacco. It was good strong tobacco; he had grown it himself, in a secret mountainside clearing, protected by a charm to keep hunters and others away, since of course serious tobacco had to be grown absolutely unseen by anyone but the one who would be using it.

Now, however, it was "doctored" tobacco, "remade" for a particular purpose, and needing only to be smoked in order to release its power. And so it was to be treated with respect; it would have been very bad to drop any.

Stowing the buckskin pouch in the bigger medicine bag that hung at his hip, he turned and started down the narrow trail that ran alongside the fast-running little creek. But he had taken only a few steps when he heard the high young voice from somewhere downstream: *"Ni, edutsi!"*

He stopped, his dark lined face registering anger. Then his expression cleared and he smiled very slightly. *"Ni,"* he called back.

A moment later the spring-green bushes parted and a half-grown boy appeared. *"Osiyo, Inoli,"* Smoke said. "What do you mean, coming up here and hollering when I'm making medicine?

You know better than that."

The boy called Badger said, "I heard you singing, Uncle. I waited till you were through."

"How did you know I was done?" Smoke asked, trying to sound angry but not doing it very well. Badger was his only sister's daughter's boy and his favorite of all his younger relations.

"You taught me that *igawesdi*," Badger said. "For finding lost things, right? Did you lose something?"

"Never mind that." In fact Smoke had lost a treasured ear ornament the other night at a stomp dance and was hoping to use the tobacco to help him find it, but he wasn't going to admit that to the boy. "Anyway," he added. "you shouldn't trail your elders and sneak up on them like that."

Badger tossed his shaggy black hair back. It was a warm day and he wore only a buckskin breechclout and pointed-toe moccasins.

He said, "Nine Killer wants you. Something bad has happened."

"*Doyu?* Then let's go." Nine Killer was the town headman. Not that that gave him any right to issue orders to Smoke or anyone else—a Cherokee headman's power was very limited, a matter of personal prestige rather than any vested authority. But Nine Killer was a good smart headman, and respectful of custom; he wouldn't have sent for the town's senior medicine man without good reason. "What's the matter?" Smoke asked as Badger led the way back down the trail.

"Otter's dead," the boy said over his shoulder. "Somebody killed him."

"*Eee,*" Smoke said, surprised. "Who did it?"

Badger stepped over a fallen log and looked back. "Nobody knows," he said. "That's why Nine Killer wants you."

"Big Head found him," Badger told Smoke. "He was going fishing this morning and when he went down to the river there was Otter, lying on that sandbar below the bluff, with a knife stuck in him."

By now they were passing through the town, which had come unusually alive this morning, though nobody much seemed to be doing any useful work; people talked excitedly in little groups, while others were walking in the direction of the river. News of

Otter's death must have spread like a brush fire in a dry summer.

The town was a fairly typical Overhill Cherokee community of the time: a loose collection of houses strung out along the river, between the high-water mark and the cultivated fields beyond. Most of the houses were solid log cabins, chinked with mud and roofed with pine bark, though a few families still lived in the old-style wattle-walled homes.

In Smoke's youth the town had been a closer place, the houses clustered tightly together around the big central council house, and surrounded by a high palisade for protection against attack. But the raiding days were all but over, now; most of the traditional enemy tribes—such as the distant but dreaded Iroquois Nations to the north—were paying a brutal price for having helped the English King in his recently-ended war with the white colonists, and were having all they could do just to survive, never mind bothering anybody else.

As was true for the Cherokees as well, of course; the final peace with the Americans had cost the Principal People much of their best lands, and yet still the pressure continued from the insatiable white settlers . . . but at least the days of blood were more or less at an end. Now the People could live in peace while they tried to adjust to the enormous changes in their world.

Only now something had happened that might destroy that peace. Smoke pulled his hunting coat closer about him; warm as the day was, he felt suddenly a little cold.

There was a considerable crowd down by the riverbank when Smoke and Badger arrived. They all stood well back, though, up in the shadow of the trees, above the still-fresh marks of the last spring flood.

The little sandbar lay white and clean in the sunlight, sloping gently down to the water's edge. It would have been quite a pretty little scene, if it hadn't been for the dead man lying on his back on the sand, a few bowstrings' length back from the water's edge. Even from the high-water line, Smoke could see the knife handle protruding from the body.

Nine Killer stood beside the corpse, along with the man named Big Head. Both of them were looking very serious. So was everybody in sight, come to that. Except for the dead man, who didn't look any particular way but dead.

"Stay back there," Nine Killer called as Badger pushed through the crowd. Then he recognized Smoke. *"Osiyo, Gog'sgi,"* he said then, relief in his voice. "Come see."

Smoke walked slowly down the bar, watching the ground, keeping well clear of the lines of tracks that already marked the sand. *"Osiyo,"* he greeted Nine Killer and Big Head, and looked down at the body. *"Osiyo,* Otter, you drunken fool," he muttered. "What did you get yourself into this time?"

"I found him," Big Head said. His voice was a little unsteady. "He was just lying here like this."

"Anybody else around?" Smoke asked.

"No," Big Head said. His head wasn't particularly big; the name came from a dream he had had. "Didn't see anybody at all, all the way to the river."

"I made everybody stay clear," Nine Killer said to Smoke, "until you could get here. Figured we didn't need a lot of people tracking around, messing up the sign."

Smoke gave a quick nod of approval, without looking at Nine Killer. He was studying the body at his feet. Otter lay with his arms flung out to either side, his eyes open, staring up blankly at the sky; a thin, long-limbed young man dressed in badly fitting trousers of dark blue broadcloth, such as the traders sold, but no shirt. His hair was chopped off at neck length, in the style some of the young men now favored.

The knife had gone in just below his breastbone; the angle of the handle showed that the killer had given an upward thrust, to be sure of getting the heart. The sand beneath and around the body was soaked with blood; the flies were already swarming, paying little attention to Big Head's attempts to shoo them away.

"This is bad," Nine Killer said in a low voice.

Smoke looked up sharply, switching his attention momentarily from Otter to the headman. Nine Killer was an imposing figure, tall and powerfully built; no longer the young warrior who had killed nine Catawbas in a single battle, he was still a man in the prime of life, and age had only added dignity to his bearing. Standing there now, wearing only a breechclout and a blanket thrown over his shoulders—Smoke guessed he had come quickly when he heard about Otter, not waiting to dress properly—he could not have been mistaken for anything but a leading man.

But just now he looked worried; there were lines about his eyes besides the ones the years had put there.

"A very bad thing," he said, and shook his head. "There could be big trouble."

Smoke knew exactly what Nine Killer meant; he had been thinking along the same lines, all the way down the hill with Badger. The situation had all sorts of ugly possibilities.

Murder was not unknown among the Cherokees, but it was far from common. Killing an enemy was an honored act—probably half the men in the town had names incorporating the verb "to kill"—but among themselves the Principal People were expected to keep their violent impulses firmly in check.

The penalty for transgression was simple and, except in very unusual cases, without appeal: the victim's clan kin would take blood vengeance, a life for a life. It was not merely their right but their absolute duty.

If possible, the avenging clan would kill the slayer; but if this proved impracticable, any member of the killer's clan could be taken instead. Either way, the execution would be a privileged act; no counter-retaliation would take place. There would be no long-running blood feud.

Still, as Nine Killer said, there could be much trouble before this affair was settled. Tensions always ran high in the wake of a killing, and the sacred harmony of the community would be endangered. Nine Killer was right to be worried.

"Otter was Wolf Clan," he said to Smoke. "They'll be demanding blood. And right now we don't even know who did it. Is there any way you can tell?"

Smoke looked at the headman for a moment. "A finding medicine for the truth?"

"Something like that."

"Huh. Maybe." Smoke kept his face straight. "Maybe we won't need it. Let's try using our own eyes, first, and our good sense. Sometimes that's all the medicine you need."

He studied the ground for a moment. "Look at the tracks," he said. "What do they tell you?"

The other two men glanced briefly at the lines of footprints in the crumbling sand. That was all it took; they were, after all, Cherokees.

"One set of tracks," Big Head said. "Came out here, walked back."

"A lot deeper coming out than going back," Nine Killer added. His forehead wrinkled itself up like a folded blanket.

"Somebody killed Otter and then carried him out here? That's crazy."

"Crazier than that. Look at all the blood," Smoke said. "All of it right here, not a drop anywhere else. Otter was carried here while he was still alive. Then the other man stabbed him."

Big Head and Nine Killer stared at him. "*Eee,*" Big Head said finally. "Why would anybody do that?"

"And *how?*" Nine Killer asked. "Otter wouldn't just let himself be carried around, like a baby, and then lie there and let somebody stick a knife in him." He looked down at the body again. "Maybe he was tied?" he said doubtfully.

"*Unh-tla,*" Smoke said, and pointed. "No marks on his arms or legs. Besides, tied or not, he'd have struggled. And the sand under him isn't disturbed at all."

A voice said, "I can tell you that part."

All three men turned, as a short, stocky young man came through the crowd and stepped out onto the sand. He was dressed in ragged, rather dirty white-style shirt and trousers. His face was a bad color and he moved slowly, as if in pain.

"Yellow Bird," Nine Killer said. "What can you tell us?"

Yellow Bird started toward them, stumbling a little, walking right across the line of footprints. Nine Killer started to speak but Smoke said quietly, "It's all right. The tracks have told us all they're going to."

"Otter was drunk," Yellow Bird said as he came near. His voice was thick and dry. "We got drunk last night, Otter and me, out at Fenn's place."

The three older men looked at one another. Jack Fenn was a half-breed, the son of a white trader—killed, some years ago, by a Creek raiding party—and a Deer Clan woman. He lived just outside of town, in a big house his father had built, like a white man's home; there he sold the usual trade goods—powder, beads, cloth, metal pots, knives, whatever the People wanted—in exchange for furs and deerskins.

All of which was fine, but he also sold whiskey and rum; he even kept a room where people could buy the stuff by the drink. Fenn's place had been the scene of many fights and other troubles, and the liquor he sold had caused endless problems among the people of the town. There had been talk of running him off; but he was still one of the People—even if he didn't act like it—and under the protection of the powerful Deer Clan.

"We got drunk," Yellow Bird repeated. His eyes were red and his face looked swollen. "We got a jug and we came back this way and we sat down under a tree, up by the river trail, and drank some more, and finally we went to sleep on the ground. Anybody could have picked Otter up and carried him off," Yellow Bird said. "The shape he was in, he wouldn't have known it."

Nine Killer was looking disgusted. "And you didn't see or hear anything?"

"I was as drunk as he was," Yellow Bird confessed. "Whoever did it, they could have done the same to me if they wanted."

He looked down at the body. "Can I see that knife?"

Smoke said, "Sure," and bent down and pulled the knife from Otter's body, feeling the back edge of the blade grate slightly on bone. The handle was covered with sticky drying blood and he didn't like the thought that he was getting it on his hand, but then he'd have to smoke himself clean after this anyway.

The knife was an ordinary butcher knife, of the kind sold by traders throughout the First Nations, with a wide curving blade and a plain wooden handle. The edge had been resharpened in the usual way, so that the bevel was all on one side, for skinning—or for scalping, which after all was basically a skinning job.

There was nothing unusual about it except the rawhide wrapping around the handle. But Yellow Bird said, "That's Otter's own knife. I remember when he put that rawhide on, after he dropped it on some rocks and broke a piece off the handle."

"Huh." Smoke looked at the knife a moment longer and then turned and spun the bloody weapon out across the river, where it skipped a couple of times before disappearing beneath the cool green water. Nobody objected.

"Could it have been an enemy raid?" Big Head mused. "No, they'd have scalped him. White men, maybe?"

"No white men could have come through here without our knowing it," Smoke told him. "Anyway, those tracks were made by pointed-toe moccasins. No, it wasn't an outsider. Whoever did it is right here in this town."

Turning back to Yellow Bird, he said, "Did anything happen out at Fenn's place? A fight, maybe?"

Yellow Bird rubbed his eyes with both hands, like a sleepy child. "There was something," he mumbled. "Some trouble between Otter and Fenn. I don't remember much, though. It's all like a fog inside my head."

"What's inside your head," Nine Killer said angrily, "is that buzzard piss you got from Jack Fenn. If you—"

He stopped suddenly, looking back up the sandbar. "Panther Shooter," he said in a different voice. "I was wondering when he would show up."

A big, heavyset man was walking down the bar toward them with slow deliberate steps. His upper body was wrapped in a red trade blanket, though his muscular legs were bare. His head was down as he studied the footprints in the sand. There would be no need to explain their meaning to him; as the town's most successful hunter, Panther Shooter could read sign as well as any man alive.

He was also Otter's mother's eldest brother, and the leading warrior of the Wolf Clan. Now, Smoke thought, the trouble begins.

Sure enough, Panther Shooter's first words to Nine Killer were, "Who did this?"

"We don't know yet," the headman said.

"He was drunk," Yellow Bird put in stupidly.

Panther Shooter gave the younger man a look that would have withered a whole cornfield. "With you, I guess? Drinking Fenn's whiskey again?" He spat on the sand. "No matter," he said, speaking to Nine Killer again. "He was a worthless fool, but he was the Wolf Clan' worthless fool. We will do the right thing. We will cover Otter's bones with blood."

"Yes," Smoke told him, "but whose blood? That's what we're trying to find out."

Nine Killer began walking back up the sandbar, toward the still-growing crowd of onlookers. The other men followed close behind.

"Listen," he cried. "We want to know what happened here. Does anybody know anything about it?"

From the back of the crowd a strong deep voice said, "I can tell you a little."

The crowd parted, with a certain amount of jostling, and a lean, handsome-faced young man came striding through. He wore the old-fashioned buckskin breechclout and leggings. That was no surprise; Little Dog was one of the conservative faction among the People, opposed to the growing tendency to adopt white ways, and he made a point of dressing in traditional style.

"I was at Fenn's place last night," he said. "I saw what happened there."

"You?" Nine Killer said. "At Fenn's? Why?"

Little Dog looked away. "My sister," he said, and everyone sighed in understanding. Little Dog's sister Walela had been Otter's wife; still was, strictly speaking, but just barely, because a couple of moons ago she had taken up with Jack Fenn.

Cherokee marriages tended to be pretty loose and short-lived; there was no penalty for adultery, and either spouse could call it quits at any time, for any reason or none. Walela, however, had been particularly shameless, ever since she first tasted whiskey, first lying with any man who would get her a drink, then going right to the source. Nowadays it was common knowledge she spent more nights at Fenn's than at home.

"I went to Fenn's to see if she was all right," Little Dog said, "and to try to get her to stop shaming the family. She wouldn't listen. She was already pretty drunk herself."

"And Otter was there?" Smoke asked.

"No. He came in just as I was about to leave. Yellow Bird was with him," Little Dog said. "They were drunk too. Otter wanted Walela to come home with him. She said no and he grabbed her arm and started to pull her toward the door. Fenn told him to stop it and he let go Walela's arm and pulled out his knife."

Several people sucked in their breaths and exchanged looks. Nine Killer said, "He went after Fenn with a knife?"

"Not really. He just waved it around, made a lot of talk, said he was going to kill Fenn, you know how he was when he was drinking." Little Dog's voice was level and without expression but his face showed profound contempt. "Then he picked up a jug of whiskey and said he was taking that in payment for Walela lying with Fenn." His voice did waver a little, now. "He said," Little Dog added with obvious difficulty, "that Fenn had to pay for riding his mare."

Little Dog paused; you could see him pulling himself together. "And then," he went on, "when Otter and Yellow Bird were going out the door, Fenn said, 'Some day somebody's going to take that knife away from you and kill you with it.'" He looked past Nine Killer and Smoke, at the body lying on the sandbar. "And it looks like somebody did."

"Fenn." Panther Shooter's voice was low and harsh, like the growl of an angry bear. "That's who did it. Good. I was afraid it would be somebody I wouldn't enjoy killing.

"Wait, wait," Smoke protested. "We don't know that yet."

"Good enough for me," Panther Shooter said impatiently. "Otter threatened Fenn. Fenn followed him and killed him when he was too drunk to fight back. Everybody knows what a coward Fenn is."

A murmur ran through the crowd, getting louder. But Smoke said again, "Wait," and held up both hands. "This is wrong. It's not fitting to be arguing like this in the presence of the dead."

"Smoke is right," Nine Killer said decisively. "We'll talk this out in the proper way, tonight in the council house."

He looked at Panther Shooter. "You will wait until then before you do anything?"

Panther Shooter didn't look happy about it, but after a moment he took a deep breath and let it out. "All right. Tonight."

"I didn't do it," Jack Fenn insisted. "I didn't kill him."

Evening, now, and everybody was gathered in the council house, each clan sitting together in its section around the big seven-sided building: elders in front, everyone else to the rear. Nine Killer sat on his bench in the center and, for this occasion, Smoke sat to his right.

Jack Fenn stood in front of the Deer Clan's section, facing Nine Killer and Smoke. "Why would I kill him?" he asked. "To get his wife? I already had her. Because he insulted me? I pay no attention to the barking of a scabby dog."

He was a short, wiry man, about thirty summers of age, dressed in white-style clothing—ruffled white shirt and dark trousers—though his feet were shod in center-seam Cherokee moccasins, and copper ornaments dangled from his earlobes. His hair was a dark reddish-brown rather than the glossy black of a fullblood; his skin was on the light side, too, and his features were small like those of a white man. But his eyes were the dark brown eyes of the People, and just now they showed desperation and fear. As well they might; here and now, he was safe—it was absolutely forbidden to bring weapons into the council house, or to commit any sort of violence in its sacred space—but if the decision went against him, he was a dead man as soon as he walked out the door.

Panther Shooter said, "Otter told you he was going to kill you. You saw a chance and killed him first."

Sitting to the rear, among the women of the Paint Clan, Otter's wife Walela spoke up. "He didn't do it," she said. She had once been a pretty woman but drink had aged her badly. "He was with me all night."

Panther Shooter snorted loudly. "You would say black was white for this half-*yoneg*," he said scornfully. "Besides, you were probably too drunk yourself to know anything."

Nine Killer said sharply, "None of that kind of talk inside the council house. Panther Shooter, you know better than that."

He looked at Jack Fenn. "Little Dog says you talked about killing Otter with his own knife."

"That's right," Yellow Bird put in. He looked a little better than he had that morning but not much. "I remember now," he said.

Fenn swung around to face Yellow Bird. "And how do we know *you* didn't kill him?"

"Me?" Yellow Bird looked shocked. "He was my friend."

Smoke cleared his throat. "Whiskey has led more than one man to kill a friend," he said pointedly. "But Yellow Bird was very drunk. And those footprints were not made by a staggering man."

"Locust, then," Fenn said, and gestured toward a broad-shouldered young man who sat in the middle of the Blue Clan's section. "He could have done it. He and Otter were enemies, ever since that business with the horse."

Everyone fell silent for a moment, considering this. It was true that there was bad blood between Otter and the man named Locust. A favorite horse of Locust's had disappeared one night, and had later turned up in the possession of a white settler, who refused to give the horse up. The white man hadn't known the name of the Cherokee who had sold the horse to him, but his description had sounded a lot like Otter; and Otter had vanished the same night as the horse, and had returned to town many days later, dressed in fancy new clothes—somewhat the worse for wear—and showing signs of having been on a long drunk.

Locust had accused Otter to his face of stealing the horse and selling it to the white man; and Otter had laughed, and told Locust a man shouldn't have a horse if he couldn't hold onto it. And Locust had said that the same thing ought to apply to wives, and the two men had scuffled in the town street before being separated by Nine Killer and others.

Locust rose to his feet in the middle of the Blue Clan's section. "It's true I hated Otter," he said calmly. "And I say right now that his death is no loss. But," he raised his voice over the general muttering, "I didn't kill him last night. If I had wanted to kill him I would have done it in the open, for everybody to see, and then admitted it like a man."

He sat back down. There was an uncertain pause. Fenn's eyes were those of a trapped animal, flickering now here, now there. He seemed about to speak.

But then Black Fox stood up beside Jack Fenn. A husky middle-aged fullblood, he was the brother of Fenn's dead mother and therefore Fenn's closest clan kin.

"I speak for the Deer Clan," he said. "We are not satisfied that our brother, here, is guilty of killing Otter. We have heard no one say they saw him do it. We have heard only a lot of guessing, like the gossip of old women."

He looked straight at Panther Shooter. "We do not accept our brother's guilt. If his life is taken, or that of any other of the *Aniawi*, we will take a life in turn."

Before Panther Shooter could reply, old Drowning Bear, of the Blue Clan, said, "We say the same, with regard to our brother Locust."

It was a bad moment. All about the big council house people were looking this way and that, and their faces, in the flickering light of the torches and the central fire, were not good to see. Violence and blood were in the air, held in check only by the sanctity of the council house.

But Nine Killer had risen from his split-log seat. *"Hesdi!"* he shouted. "Stop this!"

And, when quiet had been more or less restored, "People, this will not do. This is not right."

He turned slowly, looking at all of them in turn. "In all my life," he said, "I have never heard of such a thing, that one of the Principal People should kill another in secret. Or that any man should fail to step forward and accept the consequences of his acts. I think it must always have been unknown among us, because there is no tradition to guide us in this matter."

He reached out a hand and touched Smoke on the shoulder. "And so I am asking my old friend Smoke to help us. Perhaps his medicine can reveal the truth."

Smoke remained seated—enough people, he thought irritably, were popping up and down tonight, like so many ground squirrels—but he inclined his head. "I will try," he said.

Panther Shooter was talking in low tones with some of the other Wolf Clan men. After a moment he turned back to face Nine Killer. "All right," he said. "We can't do anything for the next three days and nights anyway. We have to bury our brother."

He folded his arms and looked at Smoke. "You have that long, then. In three days, if you can tell us the name of the killer, we will be in your debt. If not—" He glanced at Jack Fenn, then at Locust. "Then we will do as we see fit. *Nasgi nusdi*," he finished. "That's how it is."

Walking away from the council house, Nine Killer said, "Can you do it?"

"I'll try," Smoke said again.

"Good. I hope you succeed." Nine Killer's voice was heavy with worry. "Otherwise something very bad is going to happen . . . Fenn!" He fairly spat the name. "I could kill him myself."

"You think he did it?" Smoke asked mildly.

"Probably. I don't care," Nine Killer admitted. "Whoever actually did it, it was caused by that evil stuff he sells. I'd be glad to see the Wolf Clan rid us of Fenn," he added. "But then the Deer Clan will take a life in return, and then we'll have a blood feud that will destroy this town. Unless Black Fox and his brothers can be convinced that Fenn is really blood-guilty."

He gave Smoke a sidelong look. "So if you should find some way . . . you know what I'm saying."

"You want me to make false medicine?"

"Did I say that?"

The two men grinned at each other in the darkness. Smoke laid a hand on Nine Killer's arm. "Don't worry," he said gently. "Truth is a funny thing. It comes out in the strangest ways. I have some ideas."

Three nights later, Smoke stood in the center of the council house and said, "I guess you're all wondering why I called you all together here."

There was a chorus of chuckles, especially from the older men. Everybody in the council house—and it was packed tonight; people were standing up or sitting on the floor and a few young boys even sat in the rafters overhead—knew exactly why they were there. The old medicine man's sarcasm was what was needed, though, to ease the tension in the air.

Everybody was dressed in their best tonight, as befitted such a serious occasion. Most of the elders wore trade-blanket robes and fancy turbans with egret or eagle feathers. Shiny silver gorgets swung at the men's throats, and elaborate ornaments dangled from their stretched earlobes. The women too were decked out in their best dresses and even the children had been cleaned up a bit.

Smoke still wore his old fringed hunting coat, but he had put on his best turban and a couple of white egret feathers, and his good moccasins. He thought he looked pretty good.

He gestured to the boy named Badger, who stood behind him, next to a big honeysuckle-vine basket with a tight-fitting lid. Badger picked up the basket, looking a little nervous, and held it up at waist level.

Smoke said, "Jack Fenn, come here. Locust too. *Ehena*."

Jack Fenn rose from his seat and came forward. His face was almost green, but he held himself straight and he moved with a steady pace. Locust joined him with an air of almost bored calm; he might have been on a visit to an unusually dull bunch of relatives.

"Now," Smoke said, "we're going to settle this—"

With his left hand he removed the lid from the basket. Reaching inside with his right, moving very fast for an old man, he pulled out the biggest rattlesnake anyone there had ever seen.

"*Inada*, here," he said, over the sudden chorus of gasps and exclamations and the buzz of the snake's rattles, "is going to help us. I doctored him with a special medicine I learned from my grandfather."

Nobody was listening all that closely; they were all looking at the snake. It lay lazily across Smoke's hands—which were not gripping it, only supporting it—its big flat head slightly raised, seeming to look this way and that. Its tongue flicked in and out, in and out, almost too fast to see. Its dangling tail vibrated gently, sending out a low-pitched whir. It didn't give the impression of being angry, but how could you tell with a snake?

"Locust," Snake said, "come lay your hand on this snake, and tell us whether you are guilty of Otter's death. Tell the truth, and you have nothing to fear. But if you lie," he warned as Locust stepped forward, "he'll bite you. The medicine will tell him."

Locust shrugged. "And should I be afraid?" He reached out and laid a hand on the rattlesnake's body, midway between Smoke's hands. "I tell you, I did not kill Otter."

"Good," Smoke said approvingly. "Spoken like an honorable man. Go sit down."

He turned to Fenn. "And now—?"

Jack Fenn was staring at the snake. His face had gone whiter than ever, like the belly of a fish; his eyes were huge. "No," he said. "No." He said it first in English, then in Cherokee.

Behind Smoke, sitting on his bench, Nine Killer said, "You have to do it, Fenn. Or else we'll know why."

Fenn licked his lips with a long tongue. "No," he said once more, his voice gone hoarse.

His hand dived suddenly into the front of his broadcloth jacket and came out clutching a pistol. "Nobody touches me," he said, swinging the weapon from side to side, while everybody sat stunned by the incredible sacrilege. "Stay away."

He began backing toward the doorway. Behind him, a couple of men got to their feet, ready to jump him, but Smoke waved to them to sit down. "Let him go," he commanded. "No violence in the council house."

At the door Fenn called, "Don't come after me. I'll kill anybody who gets on my trail."

A moment later he was gone. Immediately the Wolf Clan men began getting to their feet, their faces furious; but Smoke cried, *"Hesdi!"* and they all stopped moving.

"You can go after him later, if you want," he told them. "Right now, we are not finished with this medicine. Sit down."

And, as they reluctantly re-seated themselves, he said, "Little Dog, come here."

"What?" Little Dog stood up, but he looked confused, and he made no move to come forward. "Why?"

"Yes," Panther Shooter said, "what does Little Dog have to do with this? We know now that Fenn killed Otter."

"Do we? Or do we only know," Smoke said, his voice rising,

"what everyone here already knew—that Jack Fenn is afraid of snakes?"

That got a moment's quiet. "It's so," a man said, somewhere over among the Hair Clan. "When he was a boy even the girls used to scare him with little green grass snakes."

"Little Dog," Smoke said, "you said something, that morning when we were looking at Otter's body. You told us Fenn had said somebody was going to kill Otter with his own knife, and then you said somebody had done it."

"I said that," Little Dog assented. "What of it?"

"But," Smoke said, "the knife was already gone. I threw it in the river myself. So *how* did you know it was Otter's knife?"

Everybody was staring at Little Dog now. They had even forgotten the rattlesnake.

"I," Little Dog said, and stopped. "I must have seen it—"

"You couldn't have seen it from where you were," Nine Killer spoke up. "Not well enough to recognize it. And you were too far away to hear Yellow Bird telling us whose knife it was. So how *did* you know?"

Little Dog's eyes were very strange. His mouth opened and then closed without any sound coming out.

"But you can settle these questions," Smoke said in a reassuring voice. "Just come up here and lay your hand on *inada*, same way Locust did. If you didn't do it . . . . "

Little Dog looked at the snake, which looked back at him. He started to take a step forward. Then he stopped.

"No," he said. His voice was almost steady. "No, I'd rather have a clean death. Put the snake away, old man. It's true. I killed Otter."

He turned to face the Wolf Clan men. "I stayed at Fenn's place a little while, after Otter and Yellow Bird left, trying to talk Walela into coming with me. When I left, I took the trail by the river."

He glanced over at Yellow Bird. "I saw those two drunken fools lying asleep under a tree, and I thought of what Otter had done to my sister, how he had been the first one to give her the whiskey that ruined her. And I picked him up and carried him down to the river and stabbed him with his own knife."

The council house was absolutely silent now. Even the rattlesnake had quit buzzing.

"I was going to throw him into the river," Little Dog added, "but then I remembered the fight, and I thought maybe Fenn would be blamed. Then he would be killed too, and then maybe Walela would become an honorable woman again."

He came forward, then, but not toward Smoke; he walked over and stood facing Panther Shooter. "I have some things I need to do," he said, "to make sure my family is all right. Will you give me until the next full moon?"

Panther Shooter didn't hesitate. "Yes."

"Then I'll be waiting for you. Down by the river, on the same sandbar. I think that's the best place, don't you?"

He turned and walked toward the door, not looking to either side. There was no need for further assurances. In all the long history of the Principal People, no man had ever failed to keep an appointment of that kind.

"Uncle," Badger said on the way home, "will you teach me that medicine some time? What you did with the snake?"

Smoke laughed softly. "Oh, yes, the snake. Hold on."

He stopped, looked both ways up and down the trail, and took the basket from Badger's hands. He took off the lid and tipped the rattlesnake gently out onto the ground. It made no move to coil or strike; it only lay there a moment and then slithered off into the brush, without so much as a rattle.

"I can teach you," Smoke said, "how to make a snake stupid with tobacco and some other herbs, till you can handle him without getting bit. And I can teach you how to milk his poison, so even if he does bite you it won't hurt. That's all the medicine I did tonight."

Badger said, "But you knew already that Little Dog was the one. So why did you go through all the rest of it?"

"It was a chance to get rid of Jack Fenn," Smoke said. "A worthless fellow, and a danger to the People with that whiskey of his. I remembered he was afraid of snakes. I figured he'd run, and he did. He won't be back."

He sighed. "And as for Little Dog, the snakes are in his own head. I think he's got some wrong feelings for his sister. That always makes a man crazy."

He reached out a hand and ruffled the boy's hair. "Come on. Let's see what your mama can give us to eat."

AUTHOR'S NOTE:

"Smoke" is, I suppose, the odd story in this collection, not being fantasy or science fiction. But somehow it seemed to me to fit, so I threw it in.

This was another anthology-invitation story. Sharan Newman asked me to contribute something to *Crime Through Time III:* the third (oddly enough) in a popular series of collections of historical mystery stories. I'd never done a mystery in the short form before. Never have since, come to think of it; "Smoke" was something of a one-off.

ABOUT THE AUTHOR

WILLIAM SANDERS was born in 1942. A graduate of Arkansas A&M College, he served in the US Army Security Agency from 1963 through 1966. Besides soldiering, he has at various times worked as a musician, shipping clerk, construction laborer, encyclopedia salesman, traveling preacher, and dishwasher at the New York Stock Exchange cafeteria. In 1973 he began writing for publication, first in nonfiction—eventually publishing four books on sports and outdoor subjects, as well as articles and columns in sports magazines—and then, in 1988, turning to speculative fiction.

His first published novel, the alternate-history comedy *Journey to Fusang*, was critically praised and got a nomination for the John Campbell Award. Since that time he has published several other SF novels, as well as mysteries and suspense thrillers. His short fiction has appeared in major magazines and anthologies and been nominated for various awards, including the Hugo and the Nebula; in 1998 his short story "The Undiscovered" received the Sidewise Award for Alternate History.

He lives in Tahlequah, Oklahoma, with his wife and his cat and his old motorcycle. Visit his website at:

http://www.sff.net/people/sanders/index.htp.

Printed in the United States
733800003B